■ □ ■ □ ■

VITA NUOVA

T0344641

■ □ ■ □ ■

WRITINGS FROM AN UNBOUND EUROPE

Vita Nuova

A Novel

BOHUMIL HRABAL

Translated from the Czech
by Tony Liman

NORTHWESTERN UNIVERSITY PRESS
EVANSTON, ILLINOIS

Northwestern University Press
www.nupress.northwestern.edu

This book is published with the support of the Ministry of Culture of the Czech Republic.

Printed in the United States of America

10   9   8   7   6   5   4   3   2   1

Library of Congress Cataloging-in-Publication Data
Hrabal, Bohumil, 1914–1997.
  [Vita nuova. English]
  Vita nuova : a novel / Bohumil Hrabal ; translated from the Czech by Tony Liman.
    p. cm.—(Writings from an unbound Europe)
  ISBN 978-0-8101-2546-9 (pbk. : alk. paper)
    1. Hrabal, Bohumil, 1914–1997. 2. Authors, Czech—20th century—Biography.
  I. Liman, Tony, 1966– II. Title. III. Series: Writings from an unbound Europe.
  PG5039.18.R2V5813 2010
  891.8635—dc22
                                                                        2010000273

Dedicated to my friend Karel Marysko
who for more than forty years has published
one samizdat a year and sent it to all
his friends and therefore he is king of the
covered courts number one and champion of the world

What is meant to hang will not drown
even if water should overrun the gallows

Folk saying

Poetry is an aspect of thought
beauty is an aspect of truth

Martin Heidegger

■ □ ■ □ ■

VITA NUOVA

■ □ ■ □ ■

Not far from Innsbruck lies Ambras Castle filled with curiosities collected from all over the world by the Hapsburgs and here in one of the
rooms I saw dozens of flagpoles streaming with peasant rights written
on strips of parchment and those strips were like the fluttering ribbons of a folk costume like the long hair of a horse's tail With every
movement and every quiver they commingled to form millions of
sentence combinations millions of word variations based on nothing
more than an alphabet of a few dozen letters As I stood staring at that
roomful of letteristic combinations I understood the excitement of
Dadaists when they cut apart newspapers and put the clippings into
a hat and pull out words at random to discover exciting new texts . . .

Now as I finish *Vita Nuova* a text I wrote in one long inhalation
and exhalation I realize the fundamentals of diagonal reading I realize that for a crosswise probe of the pages the eyes and mind do not
require punctuation I realize that not just I but millions of readers are
able to skim the pages of a long novel or a newspaper slowing only
when the brain signals there is something worthy of attention and
there they stop for a while to read horizontally . . . Before resuming
the diagonal reading . . . I allowed myself the luxury for different
reasons than Joyce whose morning monologue of Mrs. Molly Bloom
was written without punctuation a sort of *Schlummerlied* an inner
monologue that like Earth Gaia neither knows nor needs to know
punctuation or grammar . . . I allowed myself the luxury of diagonal
reading a priori because I used the same method to read my past to

draw on the deep-seated memories of my life which I then transferred to the page . . . I think I can liken this crosswise probe into my sub-conscious and beyond to the unexpected discoveries made by Mr. Barrande when he built the Prague railroad to his find of trilobites in the diagonal layers of rock . . . and so too in the diagonal reading one finds an impression of oneself . . .

■ □ ■ □ ■

CHAPTER ONE

This spring was most beautiful because my husband's friend Vladimir paid us a visit I'd heard so much about this tall young man who looked like he might play basketball or volleyball who when he saw me grew shy and called me madame and straightaway asked my husband Doctor are we going for a walk? And will we grab a couple of beers after? And will your missus let you go? And my husband said Why wouldn't she let me go Vladimir we'll bring her along have a nice dish to keep us company And I saw at once that Vladimir wasn't too taken with the idea he'd rather go out with my husband alone but I fetched my outfit and my parasol and those little high-heeled shoes of mine and got dressed behind the wardrobe door and my husband and Vladimir stood outside in the yard Vladimir carefully peeling the battered plaster off the wall examining it in the palm of his hand and speaking seriously to my husband So there they stood in the yard gazing up at the tall wall the wall that kept me up at night because behind it was a machine shop that thrummed with some kind of heavy machinery like a giant dental shop drilling a giant molar those machines made such a racket they rattled the cups and glasses on the shelf over the stove and sometimes the noise rose up so bad it was deafening and our brass bed aboard its tiny casters rolled away from the wall and I simply could not get used to the noise while my husband on the other hand was so enchanted by the rattling glasses he would even get up at night to stand next to the wall ear cocked trying to guess what was going on and when I wanted to send him over to have a look and raise a stink he wouldn't hear of it As soon as I see it the mystery is lost as soon as I find out what's going on over there that's all she wrote And when I stepped into the courtyard they were still there looking at the gigantic wall the wall that was at least ten meters wide by six meters high and the men were solemn and wide-eyed before that wall of brick laid bare and my husband put a finger to those arrogant lips of his and sure enough another chunk of plaster tore away and fell on the old shed kicked up a chalky cloud and we beat a retreat to the open laundry crumbling plaster flowing up to the doorsill and Vladimir was moved to tears and said Doctor this entire wall is active graphics made kinetic for six months I lived here passed right by it never noting the beauty of the thing Doctor only now do I realize that through my graphics I can unlock the metaphysical from the banal And I already had one foot on the stairs when I suddenly saw that huge wall for the first time exactly as Vladimir described it and I saw my husband standing there like some bumpkin like some rube next to this handsome young man who was all aglow and still holding that piece of plaster in the palm of his hand no bigger than the host we would receive at Communion the host I once spit into the palm of my hand and carried home in my prayer book And then we stepped into the hallway of that awful building of ours and once again Vladimir and my husband stood with their heads thrown back gazing at the rotten ceiling which peeled blue paint mixed with plaster the entire ceiling pockmarked and blistered and that blue plaster rained down quietly crumbled like puff pastry into the upturned faces of those two men who'd asked me out for a stroll and who could not tear themselves away from that ceiling which was damp as well and the bare bulb dripped water droplets to the damp checkered floor A sta-lactite cave is what that hallway of ours was like and anyone passing through would shiver with cold and hurry into the street for warmth or hurry into our little courtyard while brushing away flakes of wet blue plaster which fell from the ceiling like petals from the acacia tree growing in the courtyard of the Jewish synagogue And when we fi-nally emerged from that building of ours into the warm sunshine of the street Vladimir was still moved by that wall and by that blue ceil-ing in the hallway and just then I noticed he'd brought a little brief-case along and now he held it with both hands and I realized that Vladimir was self-conscious about those long arms of his that he toted that little briefcase around solely because he didn't know what to do with his hands I smiled at him and looked at that briefcase again and said Why I know all about it the only reason I like to carry my purse around is because I haven't the faintest idea what to do with my hands and do you know what's more? It's the same with my little parasol And Vladimir gave me a guilty smile the smile of a guilty little boy and now it seemed he didn't know what to do with that smile of his either and I was glad I had seen a bit of what made him tick glad I had the wherewithal to read between the lines And suddenly thanks to Vladimir I saw that dreadful hallway of ours in a whole new light a little chapel in the woods ceiling seeping rainwater and melting snow droplets of water and flakes of colored fresco raining to the ground And as we strode alongside the Rokytka River I noticed my sleeves glittered with flecks of paint from the ceiling of that hallway of ours flecks no bigger than the nail of my pinkie and I felt someone's eyes on me and when I looked up there was Vladimir and he nodded and smiled that guilty smile again because momentarily we had seen eye to eye and my husband as was his wont scampered back and forth like some kind of hound dog and we kept running into each other and it was like Vladimir and my husband were two little boys and I was their nanny like Vladimir and my husband were a couple of inmates out on Sunday loan from the asylum whom I had to get back to the ward by eight o'clock I felt like that children's book character Chubby Celia out for a stroll with her two little puppy dogs And as we walked along the Rokytka those two overgrown brats bolted down to the river and everything there fascinated them everything they found they dragged ashore and dropped at my feet A broken-down baby carriage gushing water they dropped at my feet along with pots and shards of glass plucked from the filthy creek muck and both men were driven to distraction it was wonderful for them the inside-out umbrella the mud-laden trench coat the drenched straw mattress The only thing they left was an old armchair so swamped with mud and water it sat mired like a stone And there aslant the Rokytka River grew a poplar that appeared to have been struck by lightning and when I caught up to Vladimir I gave him a look and planted my little parasol and turned out my little red high heel in the first position of dance and Vladimir stretched his arms out wide and up that slanted tree trunk he went up over the Rokytka River and from on high he turned around and my husband stood onshore on those fine bowlegs of his shielding his eyes and gazing at Vladimir and our admiration spurred him on And Vladimir ascended like a tightrope walker and there found his moment of glory the tipping point of the poplar trunk which now began to tilt slowly toward the other bank with the weight of Vladimir's body and just before it thumped to the ground mangled branches and all Vladimir hopped off and shot us a wan smile and then dashed back across the tree trunk like it was a footbridge only to pick up his little briefcase and stride alongside us while my husband stayed quiet for I knew he was dying of shame not because he couldn't run across that tree trunk he could if he wanted it's just that maybe he didn't quite have it in him anymore and so he walked along knees buckling while Vladimir strutted proud and nimble curly head held high in victory And then we walked for a while until we came to Okrouhlík Park where Vladimir scraped some moldy bark off an old felled log and I said This is the trunk of a pear tree I should know because my papa used to purchase not just the finest Finnish birch and Lebanese cedar but Papa's employees bought the loveliest pear and walnut straight from the village orchards and Papa always knew in advance where the best lumber was in all of Moravia and placed deposits on pear and walnut trees while they were still standing because my papa was counsel to Brno and Vienna and an authority on all the lumber used to make the finest furniture And my husband lifted his head proud of me at that moment and Vladimir knelt down and pulled a little card from his briefcase and a tube of glue and then he glued that fragment of pear tree bark to the cardboard held it up to my eyes like an open book and said that his active graphics work exactly the same way nature does to create this bark and this mold and my husband began to jump up and down and shout comically Organon Organon second nature! And Vladimir exulted saying Yes Yes Organon? Doctor if our young lady here allows you to come along I'm going to create a matrix and then a series of graphic prints to commemorate our walk but will you let him go madame? But you won't let him go with me or will you? And I said I will if he behaves himself I'll let him go why should I not let him go? And with great care Vladimir placed the card with the pear tree bark inside his briefcase and then he walked beside me and said You know madame when I get married I won't move an inch from my wife I won't let her out of my sight she must never abandon me not even in her thoughts for if she shows a sliver of reserve I'll run off and hang myself tie a noose and simply hang myself Vladimir was quite serious and my husband waved his arms as if to chase those images away and there the hillside was arrayed with little gardens and my husband was in his element now he pointed out the different kinds of fruit trees and named the types of fruit they would bear and he thrust his hand through a fence to scoop up some freshly turned earth and brought us a handful that looked like ground coffee and not only did we have to savor the aroma but we had to mince it between our fingers like salt or like we were appraising a swatch of fine cloth And in return Vladimir carefully scraped some lichen off the north face of a nearby pine tree and then pulled a sketchpad from his briefcase and dabbed some glue onto the page along with shavings of bark and colored lichen and then he picked a little flower and then caught a yellow butterfly and he set that butterfly onto the page next to the flower and gently pressed the pages of the sketchpad together and when he opened it again and offered me a look at what was inside I shouted Wow! and my husband came running to have a look and Vladimir smiled and my husband said But Vladimir that's you in a nutshell! You've created a painting a little painting which requires nothing more not a brushstroke not a human face there's no need for you to paint trees and babbling brooks flowing through fields of wildflowers no need for anecdotal narrative or allegory this thing you've made here is simply a continuation another link in the chain of your great lyricism And now Vladimir the moment has come for me to tell you for God's sake quit those miniatures! Work in large format get yourself a bigger rolling press! my husband shouted and backed away beating his chest and I held my little blue parasol open to the sun and the path wound through the birch trees and I could see Vladimir draw back his ears like a mean horse but my husband was oblivious and kept hammering away at Vladimir to start a new life to make his graphics bigger his plates bigger his rolling press bigger and while I hadn't the foggiest what a rolling press was I did know that Vladimir was doing his best to keep from shoving my husband into the ravine from knocking his teeth down his throat But my husband probably figured there's no time like the present to say what he wanted to say to Vladimir to blaze him a new trail a new system whereby Vladimir could one-up himself become an even bigger numero uno advance to champion of the world so long as he heeded my husband's advice to start work in larger format and my husband fancied the same grand ideas for himself a few years more and the skies would suddenly part and a voice from above would anoint him champion of the world too And Prague down below glittered through the birch trees and I strolled along spinning my little blue parasol and smiling to myself and there beneath the giant oaks I felt like I was walking through an impressionist painting like I could see myself as a component of an impressionist painting bathed in blue under my little blue parasol and I had the feeling those two screaming lunatics of mine belonged to the impressionist painting as well and that the whole picture was moving with us up the hillside I smiled even though Vladimir was shouting at my husband Doctor you should have stayed a dispatcher by now you and those opinions of yours would have made station-master at some puny train station somewhere and come summer you'd wear white pants and a shiny polyester jacket and afternoons go bowling at the garden restaurant and your wife would be the wife of a stationmaster and she'd certainly bear you a couple of healthy brats and doubtless you'd weigh a ton! And my husband stood there speechless choked with anger but I just kept walking until the path opened onto a meadow and a small lake and the looming cupola of a plane-tarium and there stood an abandoned old postal wagon and I stepped onto the footboard swung myself up to the driver's seat of that old blue postal wagon which once upon a time delivered parcels and love letters and death notices and registered mail and I watched those two men those two future number ones those champions of the covered courts and they struck me as ridiculous for I too had wanted to be a number one I too had taken dance lessons I too had wanted to be a ballerina and if not a prima ballerina then at least a dancer like La Jana and now I was a cashier at the Hotel Paris I'd ended up just like these two men would probably end up and they went on shouting at each other in fact now they stood eyeball to eyeball fists at the ready threatening to knock each other down but I knew even if it came to blows these two would never abandon each other they loved each other couldn't exist without each other and even if they were at op-posite ends of Prague they'd still be joined at the hip by the idea they were number ones And they stood there so engrossed in their spat about who'd be champion of the world they didn't even notice the group of schoolchildren gathered around the large circular slab next to the planetarium The slab was mounted on a pedestal and the children pointed at something there so I hopped down off the abandoned postal wagon and with my little parasol open wide approached the children and peered over their shoulders and for the umpteenth time that day was surprised for etched into that giant mill wheel of a slab were lines and arrows and arrayed like the hours on the face of an astronomical clock were the names of European cities and distances in kilometers to those cities from the very heart of this stone slab And the teacher helped a little girl up onto the stone and the girl shielded her eyes with her hands and called out . . . I spy with my little eye Warsaw! and she glanced down and read another name off the stone and shielded her eyes with her hands and called out . . . I spy with my little eye I spy Berlin and I spy Moscow! And then the girl jumped down and a boy took her place and he read off the stone and shielded his eyes and cried . . . I spy with my little eye Vienna and I spy Rome! And now my husband and Vladimir wandered up and they stopped arguing and looked at me and I put a finger to my lips and those two men were moved as they watched one child after another hop onto that stone slab and shield their eyes and call into the distance out past the borders out to where the arrows carved into the circular stone slab pointed hundreds and thousands of kilometers away and each child really could see their capital city across that vast distance from right here in Ládví . . . And when they'd all had a turn the teacher nodded it was time to go and set off along the little path that led down there to Ďáblice while Prague glittered in the distance like an impressionistic backdrop And Vladimir and my husband ran their fingers over that stone slab high atop Ládví and read off the names of the cities and distances in kilometers carved into stone and I hopped up and stood in the middle of the slab and pointed my parasol off in the direction of Vienna and called out I spy with my little eye I spy my Auntie Pišinka strolling along Mariahilferstrasse and there she goes into the Café Deml . . . and I turned and pointed my parasol in the direction of Heidelberg and called out I spy! There in Schwetzingen my mama taking our little doggy out for a walk in the Schlossgarten and I spy my little sister Wutzi returning from the shops and now I see everything! My three nieces running out of the house at number two Siecherstrasse and pouncing on the shopping bags to get at the goodies! And I hopped off and my little blue parasol slowed my way as my red stilettos hit the grass and then Vladimir dropped his briefcase and hopped onto the stone slab and shielded his eyes and called out I spy with my little eye! Over there is Warsaw and I spy the Crooked Wheel and the director Mr. Boguš who arranged my first famous exhibit! And I spy all the way across the ocean Mr. Davis in Miami who put together my second exhibit in America! And now I spy Paris and Mr. Mathieu brush in hand attacking those giant canvases of his the same way I go at my tiny duralumin plates with my active graphics! Greetings Mr. Mathieu! You're number one in Paris just like I'm number one here in Prague do you hear me Mr. Mathieu! And over there in Paris I even spy Mr. Scufaur who wrote that abstract lyrical graphics are my invention my active graphics my explosionalism! And I even see all the way to America where Jackson Pollock is raising those dark cathedrals with his action painting Greetings Mr. Pollock all the way from Prague . . . In all the world only two number ones remain you Mr. Pollock and I two focal points of the one ellipse . . . And Vladimir jumped down and gave my husband a look of victory and my husband brightened and glanced at me and I saw how beautiful his eyes were now the eyes of a child that has ceased to cry and instead of jumping up onto that stone slab he had to hoist himself up on one knee support himself with both hands and Vladimir looked at me and smiled and shook his head amused I'd married a man who was starting to go downhill a bit but now my husband stood erect and dead center of those numbers and arrows pointing off hither and yon and he shielded his eyes and instead of calling into the distance called down into Vladimir's upturned face Vladimir I spy with my little eye that Jackson Pollock is no longer with us that Jackson Pollock drank his last glass of whiskey at the Cedar Bar though doubtless he managed a few casks over the course of his short life and when he finished smoking his last Pall Mall he got into that Ford of his and slammed it into a wall somewhere and killed himself and listen up Vladimir! He was only forty-four years old and not even his wife Lee Krasner could help him not even his energy made visible drip painting could help him not even his loyal doggy could help him Vladimir Mr. Jackson Pollock is dead . . . My husband squatted down in the center of the stone slab and spoke to Vladimir eye to eye and Vladimir stopped laughing the smile frozen to his face and I stood there and folded up my little parasol and watched the two men and I felt a slight chill pass over me and my husband said I spy with my little eye over there in Paris Antonin Artaud who is also no longer with us I spy that sentence of his he wrote and Vladimir listen up because the sentence applies to you as well . . . The day will come when we must answer even for our premature death . . .

■ □ ■ □ ■

CHAPTER TWO

It was the first of May it was a time for love and my husband and I were all dressed up in our Sunday best I had never been to a May Day parade it had never even occurred to me to go nor to my husband in fact Mother told me that back in Nymburk my husband liked to empty out the crap from the septic tank on the first of May which explains why folks in Nymburk weren't too fond of him and it's no wonder said Mother that my husband penned his own indictment with that crap But today he was in a festive mood a little kid looking forward to a parade and so we stepped out of that building of ours on Na Hrázi Street and my husband took me by the elbow and droned into my ear Look here sweetheart that which you forswear becomes your greatest temptation why even you could be a writer so look here I can only tell you what rings true to me so look here . . . At first there's astonishment but then you begin to analyze which in turn leads to a remoteness a certain passivity but not to worry that's nothing but humility a spark of anticipation a moment prior to the holy announcement when your eyes are wide open and your soul is wide open and suddenly the passivity is turned on its head and it's not just that you *want* to take it all down you *must* take it all down and a writer is one who transcribes what he has seen what has been revealed and the whole thing is a huge kick in the pants knowing there's something out there other than yourself . . . So my husband blathered on and I was grateful he wasn't scampering ahead of me as was his wont he stuck beside me like a gentleman and even held my hand probably for the first time since we were together and thus we strode along the main street through the flying snow my husband droning on . . . The thing is sweetheart you must have the capacity to ask yourself the dumb questions . . . Like how much longer till I bubble up from the fermenting pipes a clean draft of wine . . . You've got to know how to ask yourself these things . . . Look sweetheart how long you think it's going to take walking the forward path before you're right back where you started? Aha! How much longer until you start traveling in the opposite direction and your future becomes your past? Where the ebb and flow of all things and all creatures returns you to that beautiful nothingness? Where there is no beginning and no end Where the cord and tangent meet Where fire water air and sun are one The terminal station of all those underground rivers Where all must disembark and attain the ultimate void? My husband's questions were more to himself than to me and the wind blew through Palmovka and the snow beat at us and from the direction of Vysočany marched a column of flags followed by Pioneers shaking like dachshunds and then the people's militia which still sent a shiver up my spine and then music and marching portraits of statesmen and politicians alive and dead and the wind blew in from Karlín and from the station and from over the Jewish cemetery walls and whipped up the people bearing the banners and that whole parade seemed almost intoxicated there in Palmovka a mishmash of standards and flagpoles but the parade marched along easily a sort of drunken procession was this first of May parade and somewhere off in Štrasburk a brass band faded and another made its approach from Balabenka and took up the cause and people stood on the sidewalks and watched the parade tried to pick out people they knew but the wind blew and the snow swirled and my husband took me by the elbow craned his neck and squinted to get a better look at the advancing ranks of factory workers coming from the direction of Merkur emerging from the blowing snow and he rubbed his hands together and greeted people on the sidewalk they were all from those pubs and bistros of his just out for a look they didn't have the wherewithal to march all the way into Prague center in a parade and so they stood there in Palmovka and waved at the procession Some doffed their caps and hats when the state flag and portraits and party flags went by And here and there a strong gust of wind carried off a hat or blew in some beer cups and paper napkins from the direction of the station and mustard-stained trays flew in from the sausage stands that cracked their tarps like whips in the wind And then my husband cried happily Here he comes! And as one column vanished into the snowstorm past Mrklas Hardware an even larger one appeared and in the lead was Vladimir carrying the state flag and marching as if there was no wind marching proudly head held high flagpole set in his belt the giant flag snapping and jerking in fits and starts but Vladimir held on tight and my husband watched him with a keen eye and it really was something to watch because Vladimir marched bareheaded and freshly coiffed curls barely ruffled by the wind and he wore his turtleneck and his blue jacket and he marched like a bona fide flag bearer and everyone on the sidewalks in Palmovka noticed him couldn't help but notice him the way he marched in time to the approaching music and while the banners and portraits and heads of state swayed to and fro at the mercy of the wind only Vladimir marched impervious to the falling snow and blowing wind his legs moved rhythmically in their finely creased gray pants and now he saw my husband and me and he gave us a look and now he knew we were watching him and so he marched for our benefit even more distinguished than before . . . That May Day parade in fact was Vladimir's parade a parade he had prepared for maybe even rehearsed for somewhere down by the Vinohrady Cemetery wall where my husband said Vladimir liked to go at night to sing and play fiddle for the dead But sweetheart my husband said so far the parade's only in Libeň think what it'll be like for Vladimir when he leads the ČKD vanguard through Poříčí and then carries the flag through Wenceslas Square and then the final march past the ceremonial tribune I shudder to even think about it my husband said and Vladimir's figure a full head taller than everyone else in the parade descended the little hill by Mrklas Hardware his curly hair flashing through the swaying banners and portraits marching toward Prague center You witnessed an extraordinary event my husband said solemnly Vladimir's going to live off this parade for the next six months but see here darling that passivity and anticipation and wonder at writing that's not the whole story Look sweetheart once you start writing you have to pay particular attention to when all of a sudden the writing starts to give you something different something you never anticipated that's when the hundred-proof starts to flow when you learn something about yourself something that never even occurred to you and then there it is something yours alone yours exclusively . . . it's akin to a machine on a factory floor suddenly churning out rejects it must be shut down right away because of those rejects but when it comes to writing it's the rejects that are the genuine article and real writing is all about waiting for the moment when you start to produce those rejects . . . that's the young wine the stuff generations of winemakers wait for wine that when it's not much more than crushed grapes starts to agitate to ferment to climb in temperature and then the juice starts going bad turns into this café au lait–colored reject that's the time whole families of winemakers guzzle their young wine that's like penicillin it's got all the right medicine and that medicine is basically organized rejects just like penicillin is basically mold . . . And look here little girl over in Moravia every wine cellar has its own little garret decked out with its own little room and back in the day when the season for young wine came around Jews would come from Vienna and drink that reject that penicillin that young wine for a whole week and that's how they detoxified and because Jews suffered from kidney and liver ailments the young wine put them back together again so they could go back to Vienna and their duck and their cholent and foie gras and to indulging themselves after Sabbath and the like until it was time for next year's young wine and the winemaker's cure there in the little garret room atop the Moravian cellar . . . I walked beside my husband but even while he spoke to me my thoughts were on Vladimir it scared me the way he carried the flag in the parade how he didn't notice or register the weather the wind and the snow how he marched as if in a dream not as if leading a May Day parade but as if he were Christ Himself at the head of all the resurrected mad zealots As if Vladimir was the chosen one the firstborn son of all those long-deceased fathers of communism I could see how proud Vladimir was to represent his factory with his banner how honored he was by that banner how dazzled at the luck that his factory had chosen him to lead it past the ceremonial tribune in the heart of Prague I wanted very much to get down there to the tribune in Wenceslas Square to see if Vladimir would march with the same impregnable face the chosen one . . . In Palmovka Vladimir had revealed himself to me as the ideal communist one who loves going to work and doing his work and who does his art just like he's one of the crowd and asks nothing in return and is simple and modest and at the same time proud of who and what he is honored to be a worker and at the same time an artist who needs no studio and as my husband says nothing more than a few cigarettes in the evening and a bit of change for the tram to get him home to Žižkov In fact the only reason Vladimir had invited my husband and me to Palmovka for May Day was so we could see for ourselves whose side Vladimir was on where he stood who he sympathized with and who meant more to him than my husband and me Thus the cold and at the same time victorious expression thus the look in the eye and the look he gave me that said my husband belongs to a society whose time is up And my husband walked beside me and I knew he was thinking the same thing and he looked at me and smiled and shrugged and raised a finger in the air and said emphatically I'm a small towner I'll always be a small towner but I'll never be petit bourgeois . . . And my husband opened a door flung back a red portière and invited me in to Ženiška's for a drink and I sat down and had a look around at this pub I'd never been to and my husband ordered a beer for himself and a grog for me and whispered At one time this pub was frequented by church VIPs as well as by the mayor and his advisors and their lady friends This little enterprise catered exclusively to Libeň high snobiety but now that's been turned on its ear just like everything else Now it's a dump that opens at six in the morning to serve the guys who get the shakes at work if they don't get a shot of rum in them first thing in the morning . . . Who else opens at six in the morning? my husband asked himself furrowing his brow trying to remember Well there's Linhart and then there's the King of the Railroad and then Kalenda's but not the one by the academy but across from the harbor on the riverside and then there's By the Smithy and what's the name of that place in Podolí? my husband said trying to remember . . . There's a butcher shop right next door . . . I got it it's By the Brewery and then of course there's By the Picture of the Virgin Mary across from Masaryk Station and Pasovský's over the other side of Havlíček Square But my favorite is the Bistro La Paloma that's where soldiers go to . . . I know I interrupted my husband I've heard this one before . . . the Bistro La Paloma . . . where soldiers go to screw . . . And as soon as I said it it was like a deadweight lifted off my shoulders and I laughed and laughed until all of Ženiška's high snobiety was staring at me and now someone tried to open the door from the outside a long arm tried to brush back the portière but failed and withdrew and that glass door with the well-worn red velvet portière slammed to . . .

■ □ ■ □ ■

CHAPTER THREE

The sole reason I did needlepoint was because I knew it sent my husband around the bend But certainly what gave me the greatest pleasure was to practice my multicolored needlepoint patterns when my husband's friends were around those future number ones who viewed my work with disgust and my husband with pity . . . And I showed them my unfinished creations and begged for their advice begged them to please help me select what color of wool I should use . . . But those future champions of the world hunched their shoulders and backed away and went on with their discussions of what particular movement was shaking up New York and Paris at that very moment . . . they talked of abstract expressionism and *art brut* and lyrical abstraction and of Camus and Sartre and the beatniks and Sandburg and Ferlinghetti and Kerouac and of how Ezra Pound at his age still had the juice . . . And I listened in and tried to decide what color wool I was going to use to stitch my Prague Castle pattern . . . and my husband's friends circulated behind my back and with feigned interest and concentration I worked the stretched canvas which already showed a stitched blue outline of Prague Castle . . . and around me my husband's friends shouted And what about Picasso? And what about Salvador Dalí? And what about Rauschenberg and what about Allan Kaprow? And I continued my color selection I held the wool up and compared it to the color on the pattern and then I threaded the eye of the large needle and slowly but surely the picture took shape and I learned to work in from the edges toward the center I enjoyed when the picture was still just random bits and pieces it was most beautiful when the colorful picture didn't quite yet make sense . . . and my husband and his friends went on with their soulful conversations and my husband took that picture of mine and displayed it theatrically for those number ones of his to see he was under the impression that he could humiliate me and put me down and those champions circled my picture ignored my contempt for them discussed at my expense how I should rip that picture to shreds and make a collage of it work in a battered alarm clock throw in a watch face from a pocket watch . . . And just to show them I brought in my completed picture of the Lüneburg Heath and as one they plugged their ears and covered their eyes and stomped about and made a production of how it pained them to their very souls how one after the other they were going to leap from the window if only we lived on the third floor . . . And I shook my head and tapped my temple I had their number those jokers and my needlepoint was my payback to my husband's friends for never letting me get a word in edgewise in fact whenever I wanted to add something to a debate my husband just waved his hand and the rest of them cut off the few words I did manage to get in cut me off at the knees because they didn't consider me a worthy participant in those conversations of theirs where no one listened to what anyone else was saying anyway since it was all about the chance to butt back into the conversation and propagate opinions defend individual hang-ups . . . and I realized I was no worse off than those guests of ours and so I displayed my works-in-progress on the mirror in the windowsill the mirror reflecting the hanging tendrils of the wild asparagus . . . I examined that artifact of mine hands cupped around my eyes as if through an opera glass satisfied with myself for I was the only one who actually managed to create something real as opposed to my husband's friends who merely spouted off about how their time was coming how they'd be number ones . . . Occasionally I'd acquaint this crowd with *Golden Prague* magazine copies of which my husband brought me from the paper salvage on Spálená Street I'd thumb through the illustrations and just to raise their hackles open the magazine and pass it around like the missal for my husband's friends to gawk at but even my husband stared right through me like I wasn't even there . . . I was having none of it however and I laid *Golden Prague* magazine open on the table and in a raised voice recited the poetry of Bogdan Kaminsky . . . They couldn't believe their eyes or their ears they listened briefly and then two of them rushed outside straight to the WC in the courtyard and pretended to vomit . . . and while the others offered my husband their sincerest condolences I finished reciting Bogdan Kaminsky's poetry . . . When I sent my mother in Germany my wedding photos she jokingly replied . . . she was happy I'd wed a Russkie judging by the photographs by the high cheekbones he hailed from somewhere in the Urals . . . and she was right because even my husband liked to say that he and his ancestors all had the high cheekbones that the Moravian race was in fact shot through with Avars and Tatars and Hungarians . . . I noticed my husband's cousin Milada also had the high cheekbones and angular lines to her face Milada often brought out a large album and leafed through it reverently pointed out her parents and their brothers and sisters and groups of country folk with the stern countenance of old Austria and even my husband had trouble figuring out who was who only the high cheekbones helped him recognize his own relatives . . . but because of the great number of great-uncles and -aunts my husband simply gave up trying to tell me all their names and what had become of them Though Milada tried I too had trouble connecting the names with the faces But regardless every person in those photographs wore an expression as proud as a king or a queen Every face showed that life in old Austria was no easy thing every figure was marked with the endless toil hands worked to the bone every man was prematurely old with a quirk in his eye like one eye was off kilter like he was looking off to infinity like he'd glimpsed the great beyond . . . and even the women with their prayer books clutched in their hands had the look . . . as if the Catholic hymnal the Marian chants flowed through their eyes through their very souls . . . Sometimes when my husband and I were in Nymburk and outside it was raining or when the mood caught him he'd bring out an album similar to Milada's bound in plush red and trimmed in gold And like Milada Mother would try to connect the names and faces of the aunts and uncles and extended family but as she listed through the album as she turned the pages the names and the individual faces disappeared . . . so closely did people resemble one another back then . . . And my husband said he'd been working on these names and faces from when he was ten years old . . . he used to love going through this album because it sat on a little table between the front windows at his grandmother's house . . . And when Grandmother passed away at the brewery when as my husband liked to say the Virgin Mary leaned down from the heavens above the brewery to take Grandmother by the hand and help her up to heaven . . . my husband leafed through that album hundreds of times more and the only faces he recognized were those of his grandmother and grandfather and a handful of relatives on Milada's side . . . I know my husband was scared of that old world he said just one look from one of those men of old Austria would send him flying out the window or under the wheels of a train because back then life had rules and suffering but it had joy and purpose as well He pointed to a picture in the album and said Milada's father was a foreman in a textile mill and her mother and his own grandma and grandpa were just regular folks who went to work every day but when goose season came around in Brno they roasted that first goose on a Sunday and the workers at the Jewish mills got their Saturdays off by working double shifts and come Saturday they headed out to the country those distant relatives of my husband's to visit their brothers and sisters . . . At Milada's we liked to discuss what those folks had on the menu for the week there were always pickles and smoked meat and lentils and beans too and Fridays had sweet rolls and egg-drop caraway soup and Sundays sauerkraut and beef cabbage and boiled beef was a must and in the evenings bread and butter and Olomouc cheese and a pitcher of beer and bread with cottage cheese sprinkled with chives and sausages with onions and golden beef soup made from half a kilo of beef the kind of soup you can't get anymore because you just can't get that kind of beef anymore and boiled beef short ribs the kind that bubble up and make the golden suet and pork roast wafting through the whole house and out the windows into the street . . . My husband fondly remembered his uncle Hudec an excellent laborer at the munitions plant but a man who prized his friends and whiled away his Saturdays and Sundays with them at the pub drinking beer and singing and shooting the breeze and my husband identified with this Hudec loved to reminisce and tell the same story month in and month out of the time his grandmother and her sister were on their way to church in Ořechovičky after a rain shower all gussied up prayer books in hand and as they and their group approached the church who should tumble out of the pub drunk and jubilant but Mr. Hudec and his friends but when Mr. Hudec saw his wife in those clothes resembling a hussar uniform the tight-fitting tunic the silk scarf tied into a ribbon around the chin when he saw the look of malicious glee on the faces of the other churchgoers and the damage he had done why he dropped to his knees right then and there in the mud knelt in a puddle of water before his wife and his sister-in-law and her boy with his arms outstretched and cried . . . Mother forgive me! But Auntie strode right by clutching her prayer book while Uncle Hudec knelt in the mud arms open to the heavens and wept . . . It was a good thing that I worked the needlepoint of the Lüneburg Heath that I recited the poetry from *Golden Prague* magazine to my husband's friends because not only did they begin to avoid me but they stopped coming around altogether and if they did happen to find me there they dredged up any excuse to be on their way as quickly as possible and just to be on the safe side I took my canvas and basket of colorful wool outside to the veranda in the afternoons and Liza and I sat there and across the courtyard the door to our flat was open and the windows were open because my husband didn't believe in locking up not even at night that was his thing leaving everything open . . . And I began work on a new picture *The Angelus* while Liza knitted her mittens and continued her endless monologue about how incomprehensible it was the Germans had lost the war and she went on about how it was all Hitler's fault not of course the killing of six million Jews in the gas chambers . . . that was as it should be but it was Hitler who'd launched a war against the Soviet Union . . . after victories over Poland and France and Belgium and the Netherlands and after occupying Austria and Czechoslovakia . . . he should have focused strictly on reinforcing and holding what he had . . . so that when he died one day he could be declared Father of the Country . . . because national socialism was something beautiful something that had woken all Germans up right across Europe . . . except that by engaging in war with the Soviets he'd made the Germans pay a horrible price . . . And I picked out some blue wool and followed the pattern and stitched the stretched canvas and suddenly I heard footsteps in the downstairs hall and by the sound I knew it was Vladimir who took the stairs in three huge leaps same as my husband . . . and Vladimir's tall frame and curly head strode toward our door and then I heard . . . Doctor are you there?

And I put down my work and leaned out the open veranda window and said . . . No he's not at home Vladimir he went to Košíře . . . And Vladimir walked under the veranda window and looked up . . . And when madame does the little husband plan to make his return? And I frowned and said . . . That I can't tell you the neighbor's rabbit is in heat so he carted her off to Košíře to see the buck . . . Vladimir was horrified . . . What? And I said . . . Yes Mr. Maňas has a rabbit in heat . . .Vladimir just waved his hand and crooked his leg up on the wall and put his briefcase on his knee and a pad of white paper on his briefcase and his eyeglasses on his face and then he began to write and recite aloud what he wrote . . . Dear Doctor . . . I have begun a new type of active graphics . . . Mr. Kolář showed me how Lucio Fontana sliced through a canvas and simply signed it and that was that . . . and now I'm going to cause injury to that matrix of mine punch a hole in it . . . the dawn of a new era for my art . . . heart and soul I now know those prints of mine were too passive . . . could be explained by association . . . were worthy of psychoanalysis . . . but now I leave literary device behind now my graphics will be governed by a new law . . . everything without association . . . hurt the copper matrix like Lucio Fontana hurt his canvas . . . I will begin a brand-new action in the streets I'm going to open people's eyes and if they refuse to see I'm going to open them by force . . . Chachachachaaa! And Vladimir finished writing and I looked down on his beautiful egg-shaped skull and then Vladimir glanced up at me and I picked up my half-finished *Angelus* needlepoint and showed it to him and said . . . Mr. Vladimir I'm doing the same thing myself at this very moment leaving out colors and disturbing shapes and leaving empty spaces . . . getting some air into my pictures like Cezanne . . . that's what my husband recommends . . . Vladimir hopped up onto the little wall and handed me the letter and I leaned out and took it from him and he hopped back down and cried . . . Tell your husband madame I'm launching into the streets again tell him just to keep waiting for the fame to come to him to keep taking those rabbits out to Košíře . . . tell him to buy a little carpet and a bookcase to spiff up that flat of his to go on ad nauseam about those damned poets and van Gogh and Munch . . . but also tell him I've rid myself of that studio of mine that cellar flat in Charnel Square . . . I gave it to a friend who's got nowhere to live and I'm going back to the streets I'm going to continue making my active graphics at the factory tell him that my studio is wherever I happen to be . . . and my rolling press I shoved under the bed in the garret . . . But madame what you said about disturbing the structure of those colorful stitched paintings of yours delights me to no end . . . madame you might just make it further than that husband of yours . . . And Vladimir laughed and raised his hand and mumbled something and I saw he had a toothache again that his cheek was swollen . . . and he descended the stairs and then he disappeared and I heard his footsteps in the hallway and then the door slam closed . . . Liza couldn't wait for me to sit back down to work but first I read Vladimir's letter to my husband and I saw that his handwriting portrayed him even more accurately than those graphic prints of his . . . right down to his Chachachachaaa! reproduced exactly as it had come out . . . And Liza couldn't wait to get back to her running monologue about how if Hitler hadn't gone to war with the Soviets today he'd be honored as Father of the Country . . . but what good was the bravery of those German soldiers what good the sacrifice and patience of citizens of the Reich what good the Germans winning nearly every battle when in the end they lost the whole war . . .

Tonight my husband was so dog-tired from work it's like he fell off a cliff he lay moaning with his arms splayed and it worried me because it was at odds with his cheerful mood earlier And around midnight he fell into such a deep sleep I thought he died on me I got up and turned on the light and shook him awake I was so worried . . . You scared me I said And he said Darling this life of mine it's a hospital it's a prison I've got the same stubby fingers I had back when I pursued gardening and piano playing with equal passion and back then it didn't work just like it didn't work today when I wanted to type and my fingers wouldn't listen to what I wanted to get down on the typewriter . . . And my husband that future number one of mine lay there and rolled over and groaned . . . and then he got up heavily and made his way over to see what time it was and I already knew that whenever he got up to check the time he was hoping it was five o'clock already when in fact it was still only three . . . and dejected he shuffled back to bed and rolled onto his side and though it was dark I knew his eyes were open because he just couldn't wait for morning to come and eventually he got up again to check the time and then to make himself some coffee to sip it like a drug and with his coffee he smoked his two strong American cigarettes and only then did he come around and since it was my day off I stayed in bed while he prepared for work and he came and went and leaned over me and I pretended to be asleep and even with my eyes closed I knew as he leaned over me he loved me and gazed at me as my mother had when I was a child . . . And when he left I fell into a deep sleep and waking up again my thoughts were on my husband I was stubbornly set on his not going back to work he had to start writing had to prove not just to himself and to his friends he had what it took but to his mother as well who was convinced her little boy would make it not that she cared all that much but it just had to happen because she had her own dreams of becoming a number one on the world stage . . . Lying in bed I figured it would be worth the effort . . . I'd bring in enough money for the both of us and register my husband as stay-at-home and then he'd be forced to face the music then we'd see he didn't have what it took to be a writer that he was only playing at it . . . and quitting work on Spálená Street would be justified if for no other reason than the stress and the drudgery and the cold were taking their toll on him as was the awful consumption of pitchers and pitchers of beer and then the hard liquor at the King of Brabant with Venca and Tonča after work and always the talk and more talk and the putting off of the simplest thing of all . . . sitting at home at the typewriter and writing that single great book that was the be all and end all . . .

That husband of yours . . . my Nymburk mother told me proudly . . . if he was going to grade school today he'd have to transfer to a school for the challenged because from the time he was in third grade that sonny of mine had to be home tutored on account of all the D's he had on his report cards . . . So Mr. Krajský the retired headmaster visited the brewery he was a giant whose full mustaches made him look like a walrus and he suffered from rheumatism and though he lived just a fifteen-minute walk away in Zálabí it took him over an hour to get to the brewery And when he finally made it he'd collapse onto the little bench under the brewery office window . . . And my sonny was there waiting on him and one time he was playing with his doggy Mucek and the minute Mr. Krajský collapsed on the bench my sonny patted the headmaster on the knee and called Mucek Here Boy! and the doggy jumped up and wrapped his front paws around the headmaster's knee and with his head cocked to one side proceeded to have his way with the headmaster's knee like it was a little bitch . . . and the headmaster was red with shame for he was a product of an Austrian upbringing and my sonny howled with laughter and no one came to the headmaster's rescue and so Mucek and the knee were a source of great entertainment to my sonny who often gave Mucek his own knee and Mucek had his way with that too . . . He was punished . . . my sonny and Mucek got their comeuppance and even though he got D's in most of his subjects my sonny did have his fair share of bright ideas . . . But on to something more pleasant sweetheart the reason I'm telling you all this is so you're aware of who it is I handed over to you . . . When my father passed away in Židenice my sonny transferred to high school there for a year so Grandma wouldn't feel lonely . . . And right off the bat he got a C for conduct on his midterm report card and six F's he failed six courses . . . the C for conduct he got from his professor of German a fellow named Knourek who looked like the emperor's consul . . . my sonny had to sit in the front row of Knourek's class and back then the desks had sliding tops with inkwells inside and as Professor Knourek went about the room teaching the students their *der die das* my sonny noticed a white string hanging from the professor's half-open fly . . . And the professor happened to stop at my sonny's desk and just then my sonny got an idea . . . it was now or never . . . he slid open the desktop and allowed that white string to descend and then he slid the desktop closed and held it fast with his knee and waited for Professor Knourek with his open German textbook to walk back to the window . . . but Knourek was tethered so he gave a mighty jerk and his fly ripped open and a button plinked off the window and the professor stood there looking at my sonny's knee and at that string held firmly in place by the sliding desktop . . . And that's how my sonny got a C for conduct . . . although I find it hilarious today sweetheart back then I cried when my brother Bob broke the news . . . back then I was mortified but as you can see today it tops my list of anecdotes when company comes over . . . So sweetheart that sonny of mine studied in Brno for a year and his granny was happier left to her loneliness than with that grandson of hers who was friendly with the kids on the street but who once locked them up in a house under construction and threw away the key and the kids went into fits . . . and another time he brought Grandma a load of corn . . . filled the hallway with stolen corn . . . and the farmer wanted to sue Grandma . . . and on All Souls' Day to honor the dead he stood at the open window with a flaming torch and set Grandma's curtains on fire and got a big kick out of it . . . and when he came back from school with no report card he claimed it wasn't ready yet and that it would arrive COD . . . after which he said his report card along with all the others burned up in a chemistry lab explosion . . . so Francin wrote a letter to the high school principal explaining his son had lost his report card and requesting a duplicate so his son could go on flunking high school in Nymburk . . . And the duplicate arrived just before the new school year and there were my sonny's six F's and his C for conduct . . . and lo and behold at that very moment that jewel of mine recalled he in fact did have the original report card in his schoolbag and as a result we've got two of the same report card at home . . . So said my Nymburk mother as if her sonny my husband had won an award for something . . . And when my husband regaled me with stories about himself he did so in very much the same way He always described some horribly unpleasant event some person who'd done terrible things . . . but both my husband and his mother were always jubilant in the telling . . . but that was probably because back there in Brno in Židenice the boys heaped praise on my husband and spoke of him in superlatives . . . Yessir Boho you dirty swine! And when my husband told me this his eyes welled up with tears he was so very proud of that praise from his friends . . .

■ □ ■ □ ■

CHAPTER FOUR

I finally decided to bite the bullet and do a huge load of laundry at home for the first time in my life My husband requested a day off like I was ill or like we were having another wedding or a divorce or a death in the family and in the end I was glad he helped me soak the laundry and draw a clothesline across the courtyard and light a fire under the cauldron in the laundry room first thing in the morning that was his thing he just couldn't get enough of the fire roaring under the cauldron and it was my stuff that went into the Swedish washing machine first and my husband went from the courtyard to the flat and got the stove in there going as well . . . I was glad he worked as my fireman and he smiled and launched into a lecture that he should have saved for himself he tried to tell me that writing wasn't all that hard that it didn't take much more than a healthy dose of arrogance to get down those first few lines and then it just ran on its own like a thread from an old sweater coming apart at the seams Well my dear he said standing over me and disappearing into the steam that rose from the cauldron I don't have a studio and Vladimir doesn't have a studio but what we do have is the nerve to figure our studio is wherever we happen to be at that moment . . . if I had the wherewithal I'd even take that typewriter of mine to the pub with me and write there I might even write on the tram but just like Vladimir I'm certain in the knowledge that my idea won't run away from me that it'll be my constant companion . . . I write wherever I go I write everything down in my head first and then I tell it to people to see if I've hit the right note to see if it grabs them and the minute someone at the table loses interest I say to myself Look out buddy! you're probably off the mark . . . So said my husband and I fished my negligees and panties out of the tub with a huge wooden spoon and my husband ran his hand through the cooling water agitated those under-things with great interest and smiled pornographically and rambled on in those clouds of steam and the steam rolled through the open door and rose quickly to the heavens and my husband stoked the fire below the cauldron and wrung the water from my under-things and tossed them one at a time into the basket and I carried my under-things out to the courtyard and hung them up on the clothesline lost in my own thoughts . . . I'd always been under the impression that a writer or a painter must have their own studio their own workspace that they required peace and quiet for their work that inspiration came in the moment just like making love and that someone like Vladimir had to have an easel a white smock and certainly going to work was out of the question because I'd never seen a painter who worked in a factory and who painted on weekends sure people like that existed but they were strictly amateurs akin to stamp collectors or insect collectors or butterfly collectors and after all a writer couldn't sit around shooting the breeze in some tavern and what exactly did he propose to write while going for a stroll a writer had to write every single day to make something of himself but I guess my husband probably never would be a writer because the only time he was a writer was first thing in the morning when he was someplace else entirely when he sipped his coffee and smoked his cigarette and gazed out the window at the sliver of sky over the slanted roof and I dared not speak to him because he probably would have dumped his coffee on me scorched my hand with his burning cigarette knocked my teeth down my throat simply for interrupting him while he was lost in thought completely estranged in the depths of his writing And finally I grew accustomed to this ritual and sipped my coffee and kept to myself and we got used to this morning siesta and came to respect each other indulge each other this quiet time this quarter of an hour during which perhaps more passed between us on some deeper level than would have otherwise Early on in our marriage I was under the impression it was my duty to entertain that little husband of mine even while we were at breakfast but all it took to provoke a terrible reaction was a question or a word and now I realize that by interrupting him I blurred those images flowing through his mind's eye I offended him by daring to say something and when it happened he'd angrily stub out his cigarette in the ashtray and push his coffee away and mumble something to himself and give me a terribly cold look like I was a complete stranger like I was his landlord busting in on him without knocking . . . And I went back to the laundry room empty basket in tow completely drenched my high heels soaked and my husband's trousers were drenched and his sneakers soaked too but we pushed on with the laundry escapade my husband and I fished out the monstrous bedsheets like they were giant cow skins at the abattoir and the water gushed and fell back into the washtubs and we hoisted one end of the sheet into the washing machine while the other lay in the tub of cold water and eventually we managed to cram everything into the washing machine and get the lid closed and we stood there in the clouds of steam rising off the boiling cauldron and then we noticed the wringer machine in the corner it was a Swedish make too and my husband turned the machine on and the racket it made was worse than the washing machine and we stood there side by side soaked to the bone like we'd just come in from a rainstorm and we looked at each other and I knew he was thinking why'd we bother with this at all we just as soon could have gone for a walk or taken a trip to Nymburk . . . in fact we would have been better off at work than here with this giant laundry stretching into the afternoon and doubtless we'd take everything to the Laundromat next time except for a few of my under-things and the like . . . And my husband said Look there's a million books or more already written in the world and all of a sudden along comes this writer who figures he's going to blow a hole in the world figures he's the one everyone's been waiting for the champion of the covered courts who'll write something to move heaven and earth But darling let me tell you something all it takes is one little book just a little missive something along the lines of *The Sorrows of Young Werther* just a little tome like *Vita Nuova* or a little collection like *Season in Hell* or a little novel like *The Silence of the Sea* I know that every writer crosses over to the other side of himself bridges the divide with words that are his and his alone that have the biological structure unique to the solitary individual And look darling both Vladimir and I know we're in a kind of hunter's blind waiting with bated breath for that writing that will be mine alone to show itself for that graphic that will be Vladimir's alone to show itself And for that darling it's worth the effort And this education of mine? Merely so I don't write something that's already been written by someone else it's the reason I read so much to find the niche the free space that will be mine and mine alone And Vladimir? He's attempting to cast that factory of his in a new light something no one's ever done before something only he can do . . . And so darling why get too worked up over it? Either we do something that will top the charts or we don't but the best thing about art is that no one actually *has* to do it So my husband went on in the steam and the smoke while I stepped into the courtyard which was littered with his socks and his shirts and my under-things and there in the cauldron boiled the curtains I'd received as a wedding present and now my husband opened the lid of the washing machine and together we fished out the nearly scorched sheets and together we carried the laundry basket out to the courtyard where the sun had long since swung over the machine shop wall and we looked at that tall wall and both of us froze for what if at that very moment a chunk of plaster was to peel away from the wall yet again and come thundering down onto the roof of the shed below showering bits and pieces of plaster all over our prized laundry so highly prized that we were never doing this laundry thing at home again . . . I'd sooner take everything to the Laundromat . . . But what if the plaster tore away at that very moment? So with trepidation we hung out our sheets and fastened on the clothespins and to distract us from the thought of the plaster crashing down on us my husband continued with his sermon . . . Darling if you treat me nice I'll teach you to write too It's nothing you couldn't get a handle on look here every love-struck boy or girl writes love letters and those love letters are actually ad hominem communiqués and everyone who's written those reams of love-struck letters in a certain sense is already a poet because those romantic missives are filled with such a profusion of drivel that here and there some of that nonsense resembles beautiful literature I'll wager you wrote that Jirka of yours a novelful of letters admittedly not quite like Goethe's own *Sorrows of Young Werther* but you were in love and perhaps still are and those sorts of love-struck letters those love stories that end up tucked away somewhere tied in a little ribbon are the genesis of great writing so darling this is what ties all of us together even as kids we wrote little

messages and stuffed them into the chinks of the tombs at the cemetery and in summer we wedged those letters into the cracked earth
because those letters were the real McCoy for our eyes only and that's
the beginning of real writing . . . I write a sort of love-struck correspondence myself not to women or to the objects of my own romantic erotic desires anymore but I write letters addressed to the elements
I send them out to the beautiful little animals and to the trees and to
the buildings and to those pubs of mine like I was writing to a beautiful girl . . . I write like a hairdresser in love or like a mechanic in love
or you take your pick because when people come across those letters
years later they can't believe their eyes the beautiful images they created the beautiful emotions they were capable of expressing But a
writer continues with those love-struck letters he spends his whole life
writing those love-struck messages to the world . . . My husband went
on and I was weak in the knees and my nose itched and I needed to
sneeze and my back hurt . . . the prospect of another laundry day like
this was beyond me I'd rather swing from the rafters than go into this
Sisyphean task again I'd already lost my high heels and my slippers
and sacrificed my best skirt . . . I'd been under the mistaken impression that laundry work was easy and comfortable at least that's what
the laundry detergent commercials said . . . And still we weren't finished with our laundry and I didn't even want to think about what
was still left and then I had a vision of myself setting off for the Laundromat on a lovely afternoon little parasol in hand my husband accompanying me both of us nicely dressed both of us smiling and then
we arrive at the Laundromat and it's our turn in line and we give the
clerk our ticket and she disappears into the back of the store to return
with a big beautiful package and we pay forty crowns with a
fifty-crown note and the rest will go toward a nice little coffee and my
husband and I step into the street and make for Mr. Vaništa's pub
where we order a couple of cognacs and glow over how cheaply and
beautifully the communal Laundromat laundered our clothes . . . But
for the moment here we are in the laundry room up to our knees in
steam and now my husband and I see the light at the end of the tun-
nel for we're on the last load two sets of curtains which we fish out of
the cauldron and throw into the washing machine and then my husband goes on . . . Look darling the other thing that binds us all to-

gether is the keeping of a diary a little diary people used to keep diaries and they functioned as yet another sort of intimate internal monologue and a diary was shown only to the closest friends and it contained the most sensitive subjects all the writer's hopes and fears a correspondence strictly with oneself After a while though people give up writing diaries but a writer is one who continues with this secret and intimate act one who keeps writing that internal monologue his whole life So darling in the beginning we're all geniuses writing our romantic letters our secret little diaries . . . so who then is a writer? The one who must continue with that writing until he has a book until he suspects that what he's written no longer concerns himself exclusively . . . his love-struck message his most intimate of diaries is suddenly open to everyone and this thing that was strictly subjective now becomes objective and this manuscript becomes an attempt at a contract with the reader . . . So said my husband obscured in the steam of the laundry room and I held on to that Swedish laundry machine which rattled and rolled like the curtains inside were doing battle and all of a sudden I remembered those washwomen who used to do our laundry back when our whole family still lived in Hodonín I remembered how awfully raw and worked to the bone their hands were and how drenched they were as they worked those washtubs but that was their fate doing laundry day in and day out for hire the same awful wet drudgery day after day I remembered they used to bring their kids along too and Mother brought them their lunch in the laundry room and by the end of the day those women were worn out they moved like they had sciatica or rheumatism and only now after having gone through it I understood the level of drudgery the fate of those washwomen whose children came round at lunch to get a share of their mother's food but no free lunch could compensate for that awful toil And my husband had just about enough of it too he mumbled something to himself probably dreaming about how beautiful it would be when this laundry day was over when he'd be off to his nice warm pub for his little pint of beer followed by a stop at his favorite bistro just past Palmovka . . . And he said . . . Darling don't you think it's the same with Vladimir? Those matrices and graphic prints of his are simply a continuation of his own love letters . . . there in the machine shops and tool shops he prints his messages addresses them to the myriad of seemingly insignificant items scattered about the ČKD workshops and through his graphic prints he infuses everything with romantic meaning shows his love for all the things the rest of us fail to notice ordinary things like water for example no one takes note of water in a puddle and water in a ditch and water in pools and swamps on the outskirts Therefore darling I'll say it again the foundation of true art is a never-ending love/hate relationship with oneself a search for that ray of light wherein we find our purpose and the reason why we are here That's why for Vladimir and myself there's no such thing as the future we don't concern ourselves with whether or not we'll have a studio or a writing desk one day with whether or not we'll be famous enough to live off the proceeds of our art because we're not even making art in the old-fashioned sense of the word our art rests upon the nonartistic elements of any given day and from those splinters and fragments and odds and ends we create a collage that's not always what we expect it to be and therefore every graphic print and every one of the pages I write wants nothing more than to be a marginal comment upon the beautiful things we come across at work or on our way to work or on our way home or over a beer at the pub Who knows how we'll continue with this serial love letter with this diary of ours that's never finished? And as if to punctuate this discourse of his which I barely heard anyway he punched the off button on the washing machine and when I opened the lid an angry cloud of steam boiled out and I managed to dislodge the first set of curtains with a long wooden spoon and then another angry cloud of steam leaped out and I barely had time to pull my face away and then my husband helped me get the second set of curtains out of the machine and into a tub of clean water and as the curtains expanded in the water I couldn't believe my eyes and my husband couldn't believe his eyes either he rolled up a sleeve and got hold of the curtains and fished them out of the water and lo and behold those curtains were perforated like they'd been soaking in battery acid or like some crazy dog had chomped down on them and I bolted from the laundry room and into the yard and the steam rolled off my dress and there on the clothesline I saw what I'd hoped not to see both our bedsheets punctured the same way so systematically perforated the pattern appeared almost deliberate My first reaction was the blood rushed to my head and then I looked around at my neighbor's flats to make sure no one was watching and then I quickly tore down those bedsheets and ran them inside our flat and when the steam lifted and my embarrassment eased I checked the rest of the laundry and to my relief it seemed okay and then somewhere in the depths of all that steam I heard the rattle of the empty spin-dry and my husband fiddling with the wet curtains and fishing them out of the water and letting them slosh back into the washtubs and I returned to the laundry room and waved away those clouds of steam as thick as smoke and sure enough there was my husband chuckling with pleasure inspecting those punctured perforated curtains . . . And he said . . . This is going to be beautiful when Vladimir sees this he's going to bust with envy . . . But darling you must tell him we did this to the curtains deliberately as artistic expression you understand as artifact And suddenly I felt a weight fall off my shoulders the shame and displeasure were gone and suddenly I could care less all I wanted was to get it over with and now my husband went back to our flat to stoke the fire in the cast-iron stove and I hung those old curtains of ours on the line they were just like the curtains my papa had managed to take with him from the old house and then I doused the fire in the laundry room and opened the window and wiped down the washing machine and dried the floor and let the water out of the tub and as twilight settled Mrs. Slavíčková went to and fro ostensibly to fetch coal but she loitered in the courtyard just to get a kick out of my sheets and out of my curtains and each time she passed by I bid her a good evening and in the twilight my husband started to perk up he whistled to himself and made trips to the pitcher for beer and the next time Mrs. Slavíčková went by I fluffed out those perforated curtains and I offered Mrs. Slavíčková a feel of the fabric and said proudly . . . Feel that quality they don't make curtains like that anymore . . . And then evening rolled around and the fire roared in the cracked cast-iron stove and I went back to the laundry room to take a bath for there was still some hot water left and my husband went to fetch more beer and then he got changed and made the bed and when I came in from my bath I felt stronger somehow having accomplished that major laundry and perhaps for the first time since I was a little girl I understood through my own exhaustion what those washwomen felt and what a difficult job they had . . .

Though while I never had to do it again those washwomen were sentenced to it for a living And then my husband and I lay there stretched out on the bed next to each other and neither my husband nor I wanted to do those things doing it didn't even occur to us All we wanted was to lie there the pleasant feeling of fatigue suffusing our bodies and we switched off the light and watched the shadows thrown by the cracked cast-iron stove flicker on the ceiling and I closed my eyes my whole body pressed against my husband's . . .

■ □ ■ □ ■

CHAPTER FIVE

Usually my husband met me at the tram stop after my shift at the
Hotel Paris Sometimes though he wasn't there which of course meant
he was at home in bed because he'd drunk too much and was ashamed
of himself That was my husband's thing post-binge shame and crawling into bed so I couldn't see how wobbly he was Tonight he hadn't
shown up to meet me and so I walked along Na Hrázi Street alone
The street was deserted and so when I turned the corner and saw that
gas lamp in front of our building I breathed a sigh of relief and fished
my keys out of my handbag When suddenly a man flew toward me
out of Ludmila Street his fly was open and he held his member in his
hand I broke into a run my legs barely able to carry me and the man
was right behind me practically breathing into my hair and spewing
all the things he was going to do to me in a hoarse whisper and the
things he said were terrible . . . sometimes when we were intimate my
husband would say awfully vulgar things too and come to think of it
most men liked to talk dirty including that jewel of mine Jirka when
we were doing those things he liked to lead off with dirty talk he was
randier than a stud pig but I guess it was all part and parcel of that
thing called love but this man behind me continued to hurl his filth
and finally I made it to our door but I was so terrified I couldn't work
the key into the lock and the key rattled around and the man was directly behind me now up close masturbating hurling his awful invective promising to kill me and in my terror I lunged at the door and
turned the handle and mercifully the door was unlocked and I lurched

forward into the murky hallway and when I spun around to close the door behind me the man was already shooting his semen onto the door handle I heard the slap of his hand wipe his semen on the door and with my last ounce of strength I managed to slide the key into the lock and lock the door and then I just stood there and leaned on the door and out in the street the man knew I was still there he stood against the door and hurled his foul tirade he threatened to kill me after he rapes me and I stood against the wet hallway wall and then I started up the stairs but I was so drained I practically had to crawl up on all fours and then I made it to the courtyard and there was our light shining in our window and when I opened the door and staggered into our flat it was just as I expected . . . my husband lay in bed smiling sheepishly the covers pulled up practically to his chin and he began to happily relay who all had sent their hellos . . . Vladimir says hello and Stan and Vladimir Vávra say hello and Mr. Vaništa and Pepíček say hello . . . And when he was done listing off all the people who had sent their hellos when he saw the way I collapsed into the chair and dropped my purse and keys the way I shook all over well that husband of mine sobered instantly and he sat up in bed and all I asked was that he take a rag and go wipe the filthy thing from our doors and while my husband put on his shoes I simply fell back onto the bed fully clothed I just lay on my back and the fire roared inside the cracked cast-iron stove and I started to shiver and my teeth chattered and my husband staggered to the door and I heard the key turn in the lock and presently my husband returned and then he drew it out of me in bits and pieces what had happened out there in that street of ours . . . And my husband sat on the footboard and as usual promised to never again let me walk home alone late at night he'd wait for me at the tram stop just like he used to and then he simply sat there and I knew the self-reproach was coming . . . Look darling what does this life of mine really amount to? Every single day I have to put myself together again over and over from the time I was a kid just piecing myself together again If I didn't write if I didn't keep those intimate diaries of mine those marginal observations I'd probably be forced to throw a noose around my neck but for real and not like Vladimir because darling today just like any other day of the week I've gone down in flames I get all hopped up on the beauty of this life and then the drink lands me flat on my face and I must reassemble those broken and scattered limbs of mine those *disjecta membra* of mine for today I've hit rock bottom again I can't shake the feeling of those bad report cards coming home with me from school those B's and C's for conduct I don't know what to do with myself anymore my stomach aches all the time fear stirs up my guts and instead of a belly I've got a bubble like I'm a carpenter's level Please forgive me for asking but the man chasing after you wasn't by any chance Vladimir was it? As my husband rambled on I lay on my back fully clothed regretting that maybe I'd married just to secure a permanent residence in Prague . . . After all I'd had plenty of older suitors decent men who owned their own little villas but I'd been involved with Jirka that jazz guitar–playing playboy of mine I'd loved him and in fact I loved him still even now when I heard a guitar on the radio or anywhere else for that matter I instantly saw my Jirka in his tuxedo playing in some club with his band Jirka could play the piano too he could switch between piano and guitar at will that's how good he was and despite his predilection for cheating on me with other women I had to hand it to him he was always immaculately turned out . . . Not to mention that he never drank to excess he always knew when it was time for a little cup of coffee he was a bit like the Italians in that he liked to have a drink but getting plastered like my husband was simply out of the question . . . And so I lay relaxing on my back and my husband beat himself on the chest and beseeched me Darling please forgive me for turning this building of ours into a drunk tank forgive me now that I've hit rock bottom for reciting the ten commandments of the psych ward to myself I know them by heart but what good is it when tomorrow as soon as I sober up I'll have one glass to quiet the shake in my hands and as soon as I have a second I'll be king of the world again happy as can be with life and delighted to be starting life anew In fact darling what has this life of mine been all about? This tiny slice of eternity? He beat his chest with both fists and the repulsive beer-stink poured off him and he was yellow around the lips like that drunk Haňta that disgusting unshaven drunk who always looked like he just ate an egg yolk he was so jaundiced around the lips just like this husband of mine who sat here next to me But Jirka now there was a guy who sported a clean shirt every single day who had to have everything just so straight from the pages of a fashion magazine and his hair was like spun sugar and when he was at the hairdresser he was as touchy about it as a woman and he owned two tuxedoes one silver and one black and when he wasn't playing in his band he wore gray slacks and a brown leather bomber and a nice little shirt or sweater and matching socks to boot And Jirka looked good in anything he wore while this husband of mine looked like he crawled out of a ditch somewhere even in his wedding clothes and now he was off and running again with his monologue Darling what exactly is this life of mine? Nothing more than a blacksmith's bellows an inhalation and exhalation a giant euphoria followed by hangover like night replaces day like storm clouds follow fair skies and now I finally realize I'm the type of person who must live here in Central Europe in a country where the cold and rain take over for eight months of the year and therefore in the argot of the Swedes and Sudetenlanders I'm a *wetrkrank* just like Vladimir that's why those people drink so much why so many suicides And the same goes for me the weather gets to me it's why I always manage to say something people will find unsavory I must offend several people a day but even that wouldn't bother me so much . . . Now I realize it's mainly myself I must offend in spite of myself I continue to dredge up events from my past I thought were long ago dead and buried but they rise from the dead and I find myself helpless against all those poor little kittens that I had to put down at home helpless against all those girls whom I offended and deserted and I'm helpless against those years at school when I carted home those terrible report cards and everyone wailed and cried What's to become of you? My husband went on with his lamentation but did he care one shred what I thought of the whole thing? I who was forced to turn away from him because he stank to high heaven with the alcohol and mainly because in the heat of that drunken blather he resembled anything but the image he had of himself as a writer as a best seller as someone given to dispensing wisdom as if his magnum opus were behind him already and all that remained was to shell out advice on how easy it was to be a writer and an artist And here I was with him in the one room in the one bed next to the one stove and the one toilet out in the yard that was plain bad luck because going at night meant facing a draft of cold air that blew through the courtyard and so here I lay truly violated as if that man out in the street had in fact carried out what he promised as if he had violated me raped me and in the end I might have been better off than having to sit here listening to my husband go on about himself like he was some kind of laureate when in fact he worked at a paper salvage on Spálená Street and spent his free time at the pubs and everywhere but at home at the typewriter writing down the things he blathered on about Now Jirka there was a professional who when he wasn't playing with his band spent hours practicing the piano and composing new songs And so here I lay like in some train station waiting room in Chust and truth be told I'd rather be in that train station in Chust because then I could just climb aboard any train and take it anywhere just so I wouldn't have to be here in this one room on Na Hrázi Street with this drunk person this husband of mine who gave a start when he saw the way I was looking at him I sat up and leaned on my elbows and looked at him with disgust like I'd just seen one of those sow bugs that lived under the rocks and overturned bricks of our courtyard My husband clutched his head in his hands and shouted This life of mine is nothing but purgatory daggers of constant reproach I'm even afraid to look in the mirror but in spite of myself I do look and now I'm able to see things from the other side I peer through a keyhole into a desolate room and there I see myself as the boy afraid to go home But now it's even worse I see I'm starting to be totally alone no one takes pleasure in me anymore and what's worse no one gets angry with me anymore no one sheds a tear for me anymore no one curses me anymore or gets worked up over me anymore it's because I've been written off it's like everyone has given up hope I'll ever start a new life ever realize my potential because I've probably prematurely smashed and squandered that talent of mine to bits . . . And I got the shakes and an awful chill and I pulled up the covers and my husband lay down next to me fully clothed too and he made no attempt to crawl under the covers with me for he probably knew that I'd find it intolerable that I'd kick him out of bed that maybe I'd sooner go back out into the street and be with that lunatic who'd chased me and masturbated and shot his semen on our doors at number twenty-four Na Hrázi Street . . .

■ □ ■ □ ■

CHAPTER SIX

I really had it this time My husband claimed to be a born handyman that no job was too big or too small So I asked him to build me a little shelf a sort of pantry that might fit into the small rectangular kitchen window and we could keep the window open a crack from the outside and I'd keep my bread and my tub of goose fat and my butter and my preserves there on the shelf And so my husband brought along a helper this character named Pepíček and Pepíček made a drawing of that future pantry of ours and my husband sliced open a bag of flour and sprinkled some on the floor and together with Pepíček they drafted their plans on the floor and my husband reveled in the fact he'd finished high school and his professors had taught him geometry and mathematics And so my husband and Pepíček made their drawings and quaffed their beer from the pitcher and when they drew their little girders and their little crossbeams they congratulated each other and drank a shot to their drawings But I was forced to get out my tape measure and measure the width of that window frame and everything else for that matter because as I watched those two dither on the floor it was clear even to the naked eye what they were drawing was nonsense And several times I almost tripped over Pepíček who had the strangest of mannerisms First of all when he was lost in thought he squatted on his haunches and sat there like some kind of giant bird Pepíček was tiny and when he went into his bushman squat he was hardly taller than a chair or a stool and what's more he never took off his hat That hat of his was velvet and looked like something out of the

44
▾

nineteenth century Pepíček wore it mashed down over his eyes and he had a perpetual smile and he smoked constantly and he probably shaved but once a week given the stubble on his face But his eyes were always smiling though it was a rather sheepish sort of smile . . . And so my own personal hell began thanks to the two of them having a surplus of time on their hands for that carpentry work they were always setting off to some lumberyard or other to have boards cut but smiling and smelling of beer and alcohol they never came back with any boards And before my husband even got home from work Pepíček was already there on our stoop squatting smoking elbows propped on his knees that hat of his so huge he might have used it as an umbrella Once when I ran into Mr. Vaništa the pub owner he asked me quite seriously what we were up to at our place if we weren't by chance putting in a new wall or renovating our kitchen and when I appeared confused and asked what led to such a question Mr. Vaništa told me that Pepíček was a regular of his had been coming in for years but lately he'd been acting awfully excited and ordering drinks on the doctor's tab and quietly discussing the monumental carpentry project that he and my husband were engaged in back at our flat And so nearly a month passed before my husband and Pepíček brought home four scrawny boards approximately the height of the window where our future pantry would be And when they saw the boards were cut just about right they were so overjoyed they broke out a bottle and poured themselves a round and then they put the pot on for coffee and Pepíček hopped onto a chair and squatted there like he squatted on the ground and his hat was mashed on his head and he chain-smoked and my husband congratulated him for being a heaven-sent little handyman And then my husband absconded to borrow a hammer and to buy some long nails and it took an eternity for him to return and when he did he stank of beer but meanwhile Pepíček perched on the chair like a cormorant like some kind of vulture his elbows resting on his knees and apparently he was asleep because he was all folded up into himself like an umbrella And naturally my husband didn't start to assemble the pantry right away As was his wont he turned his attention to something completely different and this time it was to sweeping out the stopped-up stovepipe he said the draw on the chimney was insufficient and therefore the stovepipe must be taken outside and the soot deposited directly into the dustbin

It's good to do it while we have Pepíček here he said there'll be two of us for the job And I knew another farcical episode was on tap because before I'd married that jewel of mine he moved the cast-iron stove from one end of the room to the other in order for the whole room to have heat but because the original smithy chimney was in the opposite corner my husband bought sections of stovepipe and ran them across the room and he hung the stovepipe from wires attached to the ceiling But Pepíček said why bother carrying sections of stovepipe outside when all they simply needed was for my husband to get a stepladder and a chimney brush and Pepíček using a long wire would ram that chimney brush down the length of stovepipe and push the soot all the way to the elbow joint where the powerful updraft would take over and carry the soot up the chimney because this used to be a smithy with a smithy furnace And to prove his point about the power of the draft Pepíček hopped down off his chair and threw open the stovepipe vent but as soon as he did the soot poured out into the kitchen practically up to Pepíček's knees and he stood there smiling delighted by the fact it was no longer necessary to sweep the stove since all the soot was already on the kitchen floor And I stood there red-faced while my husband happily ran out to the courtyard and came back a minute later with a tall stepladder which he propped under the chimney and then he undid the section of stovepipe connecting to the chimney and the entire wire-hung stovepipe apparatus swung wildly and my husband came down off the ladder to get some newspaper and matches and then he lit the paper and stuffed it into the round black hole of the chimney and that chimney really did have a powerful draw it sucked the newspaper up with a roar and Pepíček Sviatek and my husband listened to the roar and delighted in the draw of that chimney And just to be on the safe side I stepped out into the courtyard to watch the chimney cleaning operation through the window because everything my husband did ended up going awry like the time he shortened the legs on our rooftop desk and chair to account for the angle on the shed roof but all that did was make the angle worse and so he had to measure over and buy a new desk and new chair down on Novák Street Ditto when he sawed through my closet shoe rack he busied himself with drawings and measurements and boasted of high school diplomas and geometry and mathematics but after he polished off his pitcher of beer and cut a new shelf it was good for nothing because the board was shorter than the width of the closet And so my husband and Pepíček decided to reconnect the stovepipe to the chimney section and to stuff a kerosene-soaked rag into the stovepipe and light it up the idea being the chimney's strong draw would suck the remaining soot up the chimney and over the roof and into the sky . . . So Pepíček wadded up some newspaper while my husband who was pleased as punch with the plan madly reconnected the vertical section of stovepipe that went straight to the chimney and then he shot up the ladder to disconnect the horizontal section of pipe at the elbow joint and Pepíček as per my husband's instructions went outside to the WC and soaked the crumpled newspaper in kerosene and then he trotted back into our flat and when he tried to hand the newspaper up to my husband who was perched on the ladder even on tiptoes he couldn't quite reach . . . and so my husband came flying down headfirst and landed on Pepíček and they lay there on the floor for a moment all tangled up but then my husband collected himself and went back up the ladder with his newspaper steeped in kerosene and then he slid the kerosene-soaked newspaper into the stovepipe and struck a match and with the chimney brush he stuffed the burning newspaper as deep into the stovepipe as it would go And Pepíček listened and my husband listened and outside in the courtyard I watched through the windows and listened and just as my husband pulled the stovepipe closer to get a better look at what was happening an explosion rang out from the depths of the stovepipe and it swung wildly from the ceiling as far as the wires would allow and soot shot from the mouth of the stovepipe straight into my husband's face and enveloped my husband's clean white shirt . . . Incidentally another one of my husband's quirks was whenever we went to Nymburk and he was dressed in his clean slacks and clean shirt and new shoes the first thing he did was start to garden to fertilize the vegetables with manure and it only occurred to him to change into his work clothes once he was completely filthy and today he was dressed in his gala wear a clean shirt and gray slacks because every time he and Pepíček went to buy wood for that pantry of ours they stopped off for a drink at the La Paloma Bistro . . . So now my husband was covered in soot which wouldn't be so bad except his face was pasted in soot and he could barely see and Pepíček Sviatek had to help him down from the ladder and I ran into our flat and got him some water and my husband flushed out his eyes and then he was back up the ladder all black and soot-covered his ear to the stovepipe listening to the draw and it seemed the soot really was blown out and he scampered back down the ladder for some matches and he tore off a section of newspaper and when he lit that piece of *Red Justice* and fed it to the open end of the stovepipe that chimney really did draw beautifully it sucked up the burning newspaper with gusto and my husband stood there on the stepladder and took a theatrical bow and then he rushed down to accept his congratulations from Pepíček Sviatek And then my husband climbed back up the ladder to reconnect his patented stovepipe system at the elbow joint and Pepíček Sviatek fetched the stove shovel and scooped up about four buckets of soot at the base of the chimney but that still didn't seem like enough to him so he knelt down and stuck the shovel through the stovepipe vent and after rooting around for a while he withdrew his soot-covered arm and shook his head doubtfully and then he took the chimney brush and fed it through the vent as far into the stovepipe as it would go and then there was a dull rumble and all that built-up soot that hadn't been cleaned out of the chimney since they'd shut down the smithy came roaring out of the chimney to bury Pepíček Sviatek hat and all and even my husband looked worried and he carefully stepped over to that heap of soot and reached in and helped Pepíček out of that flood of soot and then they stomped their feet and circled the table and spread the soot around the whole room and the soot whirled under the glow of the droplight it was like twilight had descended like I was peering out at my flat through black organdy through a mourning veil And those two congratulated each other and decided to make for Mr. Vaništa's taproom to raise a pint but first they'd have a little stroll along Žertvy Street air out some of that soot and my husband asked if I wouldn't mind sweeping up the soot and making a fire and putting a big pot of water on the stove for him and if I wouldn't mind getting a fire going in the laundry room because he wanted to have a bath And I couldn't say no I had to indulge him he had a score to settle with me on account of something that happened yesterday . . . I'd run out of ground pepper and paprika at home so I mooched a little off the cooks at the Hotel Paris who wrapped up the spices for me in some paper napkins When I got home in the evening I emptied the spices from the napkins and then without thinking I took the four paper napkins and cut them into smaller squares and put them into that courtyard WC of ours Later that night when my husband went to use the toilet a shout rang out followed by a stream of invective and I sat up in bed and rolled my eyes and then I went out to the yard and flipped on the light and there was my husband running around torn pants down around his ankles wailing and hollering and at first glance I thought something terrible must have happened like maybe the cracked toilet bowl had finally given way and sliced open my husband's rear end or even worse his bits and pieces and he went on shouting until he was out of steam and upstairs the Slavíček family appeared on the balcony in their underwear and across the way Liza's window flew open and there was Liza and Slávek silhouetted against the light and then my husband got his second wind and shouted Who the hell put paprika on the toilet paper? So today my husband was returning the unintended favor . . . And just as I resolved to get on with the cleanup who should appear in the window but Vladimir and his eyes gleamed at the chaos before him he stood there in the open window dumbstruck and when my husband caught his look of amazement he cried Come in Vladimir come on in! Take a good look at what an ordinary rube I am to use your words All that's missing is my bathrobe and my little slippers! Come have a look at something only an Allan Kaprow could pull off . . . The little wife and I thought we'd have ourselves a little happening do you even know what a happening is? But now that Pepíček Sviatek and I have had our fun we're all decked out and we're on our way to the La Paloma Bistro but that wouldn't be to your liking it's down by Palmovka lovely woman works there it's where soldiers bring their girls in behind the bistro there's a fence that reads HAY OATS STRAW and people who don't have the cash for a hotel . . . well the soldiers go back there for a shag with their girls but that's not for you dear Vladimir so bye-bye for now but if you like you can help out the young missus here And Vladimir who was almost as tall as those gas lamps out in the street now seemed to shrink somewhat to wilt from what he saw in that flat of ours and he mumbled something to himself and circled that pile of ancient soot in the corner . . . I wouldn't have said the doctor had it in him . . . Madame I lived here I burned the midnight oil here writing those diaries of mine I can't believe it madame this is something not even I could put myself up to What a beautiful little mess what a lovely mess look how beautiful the soot is madame have you ever seen anything lovelier than this soot? And you know what? In your honor madame I'm going to create a soot graphic a graphic print a series of graphic prints to celebrate the occasion . . . You don't have to do much just assist me I'll collect all the soot and take it away just run along with the pitcher young lady and get us some beer and meanwhile I'll revel in the beauty of this soot So said Vladimir and he mumbled to himself and dropped to his knees and reached out his hands and worshipped at that mound of fine soot as soft as ground coffee as delicate as a little molehill And at first I was aghast someone might look into our flat and catch Vladimir kneeling at that pile of soot Vladimir whose nose was already lightly dusted with powdered soot And when I came back there was Vladimir in the same position prone before that pile of soot scooping it up gently with his hands holding it up to his eyes and now he took his glasses from his briefcase and examined the soot and smiled to himself and now I wanted Mrs. Slavíčková or Liza to pass by our window to get a load of what a mess our place was but also to see how moved Vladimir was by that soot how he searched for the right words to describe what the soot meant to him and what he would create from it And sure enough I got what I wanted . . . As Vladimir and I knelt on the floor and shoveled the soot into buckets Liza appeared in the doorway primping her hair with her fingers and looking shocked For God's sake what happened here? And that was just what I was waiting for so I said Nothing much Vladimir and I are just playing around admiring how beautiful even soot can be Isn't that right Vladimir darling? And I got up and carried the bucket of soot past Liza and she jumped out of the way so I wouldn't smudge her little bathrobe and then she whined . . . Ach . . . if only your papa could see this! And whereabouts is your husband? And probably because Vladimir was watching to see my reaction I said like it was no big deal . . . He and Pepíček Sviatek went to the La Paloma Bistro . . . the place where soldiers go to shag their girlfriends . . . What's that? Liza gasped . . . I said shag their girlfriends . . . And Vladimir looked at me with enchantment and Liza caught the admiring glance and I gave them both a coquettish little wink . . .

CHAPTER SEVEN

My husband liked kids it seemed they were drawn to him as soon as we stepped out of our building A kid would lock onto him from a distance already and my husband would smile and occasionally to my great embarrassment just cuff the kid on the head unprovoked just box the kid on the ear and during our walks along the Rokytka River he'd say to kids at random Look you want a cuff on the head? And when the little kid nodded my husband would give him a friendly little swipe and every one of those kids closed his eyes and smiled sweetly because my husband liked kids he meted out those gentle head-cuffs because he loved them and related to them and perhaps it's why he looked at the world through a child's eyes And so in the afternoon sunshine we set off on our weekly stroll that jewel of mine and I and in fact that husband of mine was very much like a child always running off while I kept politely to the path he bolted down to the Rokytka River into the sunshine and while everyone else strolled along in the deep shadow of chestnut and linden and poplar my husband squatted by the Rokytka and splashed about and threw water on his face and then he darted back up to join me only to dash off again to talk to some kids and cuff them on the head and a few kids made a break with my husband and ran off through the crowd of kids playing in the big meadow below Šlosberk . . . Beautiful trails rose along the hillside there trails that wound their way through the trees and hedges and flower beds and in the meadow was a big sandy playground and benches scattered about occupied by mothers and grandmothers and everyone who brought their kids along My husband most enjoyed the kids in the baby carriages because when their mothers weren't looking he made faces at them and sent them into fits And they leaned out of their carriages to watch my husband practically hung upside down in their baby harnesses and sometimes my husband actually managed to get the kid to tip the carriage over and then he hurried over to help right the carriage and assure the mother that when he was a kid he'd been dropped on his head many times by the nanny and nothing all that bad happened to him . . . And my husband had another vice occasionally he'd swipe some kid's buttered bread and before anyone was the wiser swallow it hungrily and while I was left to apologize to the mother my husband would already be laughing and paying the kid off with a five-crown note and sometimes even a ten for eating the kid's buttered bread or roll And so I had my own big kid along for the ride I who was yet to have a child and who probably never would have a child because whenever my husband and I did those things he never used protection and still I never got pregnant and subsequently I was not too interested in having children and what's more I never felt the same connection to them my husband did So it was like my husband became my child But my husband had a rather different take on children It killed him to watch them play with their plastic revolvers and their plastic rifles and their plastic machine guns In those beautiful palace gardens he watched them climb trees and shoot at each other and crawl on their bellies toward each other through the bushes And when he saw groups of little girls hiding behind tree stumps and mowing each other down with their all-too-real plastic rifles my husband cleared his throat and snickered and looked around at all the mothers on the benches who could care less about these games their kids were playing . . . And he whispered in my ear . . . Check out those hundreds of kids how they've got it down from watching the movies just look at the little brats cover each other look at the way the little buggers respect the rules the way they go down when they're shot the way the shooter or group of shooters slowly approaches the wounded the way they keep their pistols at the ready just in case he's faking it Just look how this whole beautiful garden is laden with children playing at war and what a knack the little buggers have for it And look over there that takes the cake they're playing at concentration camp kicking the guy on the ground in the head dragging him into the bushes see how those innocent children have got the SS drill down pat And sweetheart my husband whispered it's the same wherever you go even on the tram some little kid will pull a plastic pistol just like that and calmly take aim from behind his mommy's shoulder and pull the trigger and Bang you're dead! And as far as that innocent little kid is concerned I am dead But they are only just playing those brats of ours those dear little children of ours and Lord knows why shouldn't they play when it's so beautiful out and when will they get the chance to play if not now? That's what the mothers say to me . . . Except that what children play at is what they later become Little girls play with dolls and dollhouses and grow up to have real children and all those brats of ours playing at soldier and cops and robbers since time immemorial how'd all those generations end up? Just look at those buggers make their war their merciless battle against their enemies look at them play at concentration camp while the adults prattle on and doze on their benches and watch their little treasures at play and no one sees how serious the kids are the relish the zeal they bring to battle even now as little children . . . So said my husband and he smiled and shrugged like what can you do and I didn't really understand what he meant and then he stood there next to the sandy playground a place where time stood still and a few kids played with their buckets and shovels aimlessly dug their little dirt piles while others made little gardens and fenced them off with branches and decorated them with pebbles and my husband watched them closely and then he came back over and sat beside me and whispered . . . Take a good look I can already tell you what these kids are going to be when they grow up take that little girl over there at seventeen she'll be in a family way already she's the kindhearted type and that boy there he'll never make anything of himself he'll be a clerk soft and timid take a good look at him standing off to one side already he doesn't know what to do with his hands but the boy over there jumping out of the tree firing his plastic pistol he'll be a success both in his personal and professional life So said my husband and for the first time I noted how engrossed the children were how real it was to them and how unfriendly and cruel their faces were as they blazed away at each other and it sent a shiver up my spine because when I was young the boys had played like this too they'd even had paper caps and carried fake weapons and all those boys had ended up first in the *Hitlerjugend* and then in the

Heereswaffe and finally out on the Eastern Front And so I sat there with my husband and it was a beautiful afternoon the sun dipped over the Rokytka and the boulevard of chestnut trees threw us in shade and everywhere the sun shone hundreds of children glittered in their brightly colored scarves and denim jackets and colorful baby carriages were scattered about like boats at harbor in a deep green meadow and towering over that meadow was a tall poplar at its base a spring water well and a number of people milled about with their little pitchers a figure leaned over its red sweater gleamed just a headless sweater and then it straightened again and carried away its little pitcher of spring water and the people watching the children and the people strolling through the park at their leisure were at odds with the children themselves who occupied the bushes and the trees and the branches the entire hillside swarmed with kids and now and then one of them would freeze behind a branch or a bench and take aim and blast away with their plastic weapon and the victim would drop to the ground arms splayed and that beautiful chateau garden turned working-class recreational area was filled with warfare and I got up and took a little walk around and studied the faces of the mothers and fathers and grandmothers and grandfathers but all of them just smiled or stared off into the distance or dozed sweetly and no one gave it a second thought or was upset by it like my husband was Not that he was upset in any real sense he just liked to reflect on what he saw and say there was nothing you could do about it anyway since people were inclined to indulge their loved ones their treasures their precious jewels when it came to games of this sort My husband stood there in that beautiful meadow arms on his hips and he watched the whole big picture the children and the adults and when I came up to him he pointed his finger and stabbed at the air and said . . . This kid will be a number one and that kid over there'll be a number one too And no one can stop them from becoming a number one because it's already in them . . . And the following week my husband came home from work early and off we went on our walk to Šlosberk and my husband hurried on ahead and then hurried back impatient wanting me to pick up the pace and he kept one eye on the chateau tower clock and presently we came to the beautiful meadow and there were throngs of people everywhere and they were excited and filled with great anticipation and the majority of visitors to the chateau garden were decked out in their Sunday best and my husband pushed his way through the crowd turned around in midstream and waved for me to hurry along but I didn't want to go any farther because large crowds terrified me I even hated riding the packed tram everyone pushing at me and at each other and then the smell of roasted kielbasa and sausage hit me and a brass band sounded from the loudspeakers and my husband waited up for me and then he took me firmly by the hand and pulled me along and when we pushed our way through the crowd there it was! All the kids assembled in the beautiful meadow every one of them with a number on his back and their mothers beside them holding on to their kids' scooters and stretched across the alley of chestnut trees was a large START banner and the race organizers arranged the first category of children for the scooter races and the starting line was packed with spectators mainly the mothers and relatives of the children who'd soon be in the big race and everyone sort of joked around since there was still time but here and there a mother droned at her kid pestered him and it was obvious from her body language that she was dead serious about the whole affair imploring her kid not to blow his big chance at a kick start in life as a future champion of the scooter race And then the moment arrived and everyone grew serious and the hushed spectators locked eyes on the checkered flag and I saw how dead serious the mothers of those children were as they watched that flag And then the flag dropped and the kids took off and my husband clutched my hand and watched intently and some of the kids were already savvy enough to force their way through they had no qualms elbowing someone out of the way while others gave up even before they started and still others simply maintained their position in the peloton and when the pack of racers spread out a little I saw the mothers running alongside the front-runners spurring their children on calling to them and in fact those women were in a race too just like their children maybe even more so and when one of the children refused to let another pass the mothers started to yell and cuss at each other and the whole race was filled with shouts and exhortations and curses peppered in here and there and I ran alongside to hear what those mothers said to each other and what they said to their children for the love of God please win the race and as the race neared Bilá Skála where the Rokytka widens out near Maniny and flows into the Vltava there was the finish line and there was my husband cheering everyone along and then the first kid crossed the finish line followed closely by the runner-up and the third kid went down in a heap just shy of the line and his mother knelt down beside him and hissed in his ear until the winded little boy with the scraped knee dragged himself into a third-place finish whereupon his mother embraced him and burst into tears of joy . . . My husband said to me quietly So this is how the champions of the covered courts are created this is how future number ones are born This is how Vladimir and I compete and we're no better off . . . And then the second race started the five-year-old category followed by the six-year-olds and I decided to go back to the starting line and there I really saw what was going on behind the scenes . . . The children were perfectly normal when they first got to the scooter races but the minute a volunteer pinned a number on them they grew serious and then the mothers came along and adjusted the numbers to make them stand out a bit more and every kid seemed to age about ten years the minute they got their number pinned on the number that was like a confirmation an anointing and some of the kids their eyes just rolled back in their heads I thought they were going to faint or have some kind of fit not because of the number but because of the look their mothers gave them the look of concern that said What my little son is to become of you? And those were the children my husband patted on the head he knew they had no idea what was going on had no reason to race had already given up in advance their little shoulders slumped and their faces guilty and those children were actually still children But then I saw the malevolent glares of the boys with the custom scooters they even wore special racing shorts and clearly their mothers hoped that a win here at the scooter races would launch their kids into a future racing career where they'd have a shot at being number one in the world and champion of the covered courts And the more my husband watched those races the more he seemed to age he had circles under his eyes and he sighed and wiped at his brow and waved his hand before his eyes like he was trying to stave off a bad dream an ugly vision as if he couldn't believe what he was seeing . . . The races ended and a number of mothers became so upset they got into fisticuffs . . . A handful of children were beaten by their mothers and as a result really did go into fits . . . Husbands and wives got into arguments because their kids came in last place they screamed at each other and threatened to file for divorce come Monday . . . Mothers of winning children happily carried off their happy children to the cake shop for their just deserts while the mothers of children who'd lost crept off home through the back streets . . . And as soon as we got home my husband turned down the bed and crawled in under the covers and I was left to stoke up the fire and to fetch a pitcher of beer But after those kiddie scooter races my husband wasn't even up for a sip of beer or a bite to eat he just lay there under the covers quietly moaning . . .

■ □ ■ □ ■

CHAPTER EIGHT

For one reason or another my husband and I started going to Jirka
Šmejkal's studio he was this diminutive painter who lived on Žertvy
Street in a basement studio so enormous it could probably accom-
modate a tennis match or a hockey game and all you could see of
people walking past the windows was their legs . . . and in one corner
of his kitchen Jirka Šmejkal had a pile of coal which he used to stoke
his coal-fired cast-iron stove and he walked around in a white smock
and smiled secretively for he did have a secret his gigantic painting
entitled *Dream of My Father* a painting he'd started last year and on
the canvas lay Jirka's father asleep and above him fluttered a butterfly
and Jirka leafed through an atlas of world butterflies and confided to
me he was going to paint all of those butterflies on his *Dream of My
Father* and that in twenty years he would surprise the public with his
magnum opus . . . But for the time being Jirka had a giant graphic
press in the adjoining room of his giant basement space it was as large
as a tram and the lone item in that basement but Jirka had plans for
the future this was to be his studio as well as a private gallery . . . And
somehow Jirka took a shine to me not because I sympathized with
him or anything but I just couldn't stand how Vladimir and my husband looked down on him how they underestimated what Jirka was
doing But there was no doubt Vladimir liked Jirka they'd attended
graphics school together and Vladimir when he worked on his larger
format copper or duralumin matrix used Jirka's press to stamp out his
graphic prints . . . And Jirka worked for a magazine called *Universe*

and Nature he was quite excited about it and he gave me a demonstration of how he made his butterfly graphic prints and the process amazed me Jirka would take a tiny copper plate and slide it into that gigantic press and the press rattled and made a racket as Jirka cranked the copper plate through to the other side . . . That giant press made such an incredible noise down there in Jirka's basement and the way Jirka stood there and smiled he reminded me of Chaplin in *Modern Times* standing in front of those giant gears a tiny engineer standing in the shadow of a giant locomotive . . . And Jirka smiled at me as happy as a child while Vladimir and my husband went on poking fun at him . . . but Jirka was undeterred for he knew the future was his and that he would attain number one status once his *Dream of My Father* in which his sleeping father was to be surrounded by all the little butterflies of the world was complete . . . And so Jirka demonstrated how that gigantic machine of his gave birth to those little butterflies for *Universe and Nature* magazine . . . and now he pressed a button and the clamor ceased and from under a giant roller Jirka extracted a tiny plate no bigger than a box of matches and he peeled off the felt backing and then using a pair of tweezers he peeled a tiny graphic print off the plate and presented it to me and truly that graphic print was no bigger than a postage stamp and it was adorned with a beautiful little butterfly . . . That's something huh? Jirka said and my husband replied . . . Jirka I don't want to get ahead of myself but you are a future national treasure . . . And Vladimir said Look Jirka how about you send that collection of butterflies to the Crooked Wheel Gallery in Warsaw How about sending it to curator Davis in Miami? Take those Americans down a couple of pegs a poor kid from Europe from the Czech lands shows Mark Tobey and Roth and William de Kooning a thing or two . . . Jirka now that I look at that artifact of yours even I might just have to call it quits with my active graphics . . . And I just sat there on the chair and rolled my eyes at those two champions of the world those two number ones those two men who'd declared themselves best in the world . . . I happened to like Jirka's butterflies and I got up to look at a sensitively rendered oil painting Jirka had made of his mother and turned my back on those two men And Vladimir went into the kitchen and came back with his briefcase and then he and my husband brought a table into the studio and Jirka smiled and cursed them in a friendly way called them a couple of rascals . . . But I won't be deterred! Just wait until I finish *Dream of My Father* . . . but Doctor! . . . Onward and upward! I turned around to see Jirka Šmejkal looking intently into my husband's eyes punching the air with his fist trying to buck up his own courage . . . And Vladimir said to me quietly . . . And now madame I am going to show you something that your husband and I and Egon Bondy first toyed with back when I lived in the place where you live now where in fact I slept in the very same bed where you and your little husband sleep . . . If you please I call it Vladimir's epidiascope . . . And as dusk settled outside Vladimir closed the blinds and plugged in his contraption and suddenly a picture of a cyclamens blossom appeared projected on the white studio wall and snaking over the flower were colored threads . . . my husband put his hand on my shoulder but I shrugged it off and watched that giant blossom on the wall that multihued glowing flower and my husband squeezed my hand and nodded and then we just froze completely amazed because suddenly a large bubble formed on the blossom the bubble bulged and frothed like when milk boils over like when one of those large weeds that grows in a ditch forms a sort of spittle on its leaves like flecks of foam on an epileptic's lips like whipped egg whites and now the foam on Jirka's studio wall expanded and cracked and morphed and dissolved and now the blossom grew another bubble and began to shift form again and the colored threads swelled and steamed and liquefied and expanded and I just watched and I couldn't believe how Vladimir had pulled this off and Vladimir knelt beside me and put his hand on my knee and said quietly . . . Young lady this is such a simple thing any child could do it even you could set it up at home on Na Hrázi Street provided your husband gives his permission Take any sort of flower and press it between two small pieces of glass and when everything heats up thanks to the epidiascope it starts to bubble and create beautiful unexpected pictures protean shapes . . . So said Vladimir and he kept his hand on my knee and I looked to see as did Vladimir if my husband noticed but my husband's eyes were fixed on the picture on the wall and now that the temperature reached its peak the flower seemed to want to break out of that glass threatening to burst . . . But the sheets of glass held fast and now the blossom loosely dissolved and changed color like cooked preserves like melting plum cobbler plums dripping juice over the side of the pan into a red-hot oven And Vladimir knelt beside me his curly locks almost touching my face and I saw his sharp and noble profile his softly curled lashes and I gave a sigh and once again looked over to see if my husband noticed the curly head in close proximity or the hand on the knee But now we all watched what was happening there and all of us were moved and thrilled by that picture by that scorched cyclamens and its baked-in whorls and threads . . . And then someone opened the door from Žertvy Street and someone descended the steps to the basement someone walked back and forth we heard the door to the kitchen open but Jirka and the rest of us were enthralled by the spectacle on the wall by the tragic theater of the poor cyclamens blossom and the fate of the writhing threads And then the door to the hallway opened and two figures entered the studio and Jirka nodded hello and put a finger to his lips and then he went back to watching the wall and two more sets of eyes joined us and we watched until that wretched blossom finally gave up the ghost and dissolved and melted across the wall and all that remained was a frozen slag of scorched matter shot through with dissolving threads And Vladimir took his hand off my knee and Jirka turned on the lights and we all looked at each other like we'd just seen the most beautiful film ever Even Vladimir was struck by what he'd seen but I think he was even more struck by how moved we all were with his epidiascope with his wall creation And then we finally noticed those two people recently arrived It was a handsome young man in a denim suit accompanied by a young woman dressed like a stewardess and she had a boyish haircut and carried a little suitcase the kind little girls carry their dolls around in and Vladimir and the man in the denim suit knew each other they shook hands and his name was Burda he worked as editor in chief of an arts magazine and he introduced the woman as Tekla and then Jirka said we should all go back into the kitchen and Vladimir put away his epidiascope and they brought the table back in And the editor got straight down to business he told us this young woman from Slovakia whose name was Tekla Holényová had just arrived and that she wanted to attend a visual arts school and the best thing would be to get her into the academy . . . and she had brought along samples of her work for us to critique samples she'd provide to the selection committee . . . And Tekla opened up her little suitcase and passed around samples of her work like she was passing out promotional brochures and then she knelt down in front of that young man placed her clasped hands on his knee and gazed at him with eyes full of admiration and that young man went on how talented the girl was how eventually her work would grace all the galleries . . . And Jirka was first to opine on those fifteen watercolors and he smiled guiltily and looked at Tekla with those canine eyes of his and said I think she does have talent I think she should focus on learning to draw exclusively And Jirka stood there in his flecked white smock beneath his mother's portrait surrounded by flawless butterfly drawings and then added . . . If the young lady likes I could coach her at drawing . . . and the young editor nodded and rubbed his hands together and he glanced at the ceiling and sighed like a weight was lifted off his shoulders and then he said affably I know you're the famous graphic artist Jirka Šmejkal everyone is amazed by those butterflies of yours in *Universe and Nature* magazine . . . and he looked at Vladimir but Vladimir was spellbound by that Slovak girl by that Tekla who knelt there leaning on Burda's knee and I could tell already it was love at first sight for Vladimir he had fallen for that stewardess or whatever she was she wore some sort of blue ensemble and her shapely form filled out that ensemble to the point of bursting and she had shapely legs and a slender face as if she held to a diet and when she smiled a sort of diminutive blue dot appeared in one eye . . . And Vladimir set aside her watercolors and gazed at the young woman he stood there staring unable to tear his eyes from her face and my husband who now held the watercolors examined them again and shrugged his shoulders and said . . . First impressions are good undoubtedly there's talent I think when I first saw the drawings of a seventeen-year-old Vincent van Gogh one could argue if he'd presented those drawings to the professors at the academy they'd have thrown him out but wait just a second! In the end Vincent broke through and surely no one doubts his Borinage or Paris or Arles drawings and paintings anymore . . . but what does my wife have to say on the subject? And I said . . . You're all nuts! For me it's nothing more than doodling! And Tekla got up and just then I realized she was a fair woman indeed a woman capable of driving a man crazy and certainly she'd driven both Jirka Šmejkal and Vladimir instantly head over heels And Tekla knew it too and the young man named Burda pulled a flask of French cognac from his pocket and poured everyone a shot and we all raised a toast to the success of this young woman this Tekla Holényová who'd come all the way from Slovakia to study painting in Prague . . . And then they started to show off and to drown each other out and the names van Gogh and Munch and Salvador Dalí flew around that Žertvy Street basement Only Vladimir was quiet and he stared at the dirty floor but not one single move of the young Slovak girl escaped him he took her completely into his heart and into his soul and I knew I'd have to settle for that brief moment when his hand had rested on my knee when those curly locks had been so close to my face because Vladimir and it was becoming more obvious by the second had fallen in love at first sight with this woman and this woman was to be his fate And just like that Tekla seemed to snap out of her melancholy and apprehension and she said in Slovak that although Jirka had a beautiful head of hair the cut was no longer in style and if he wanted she'd update him to a Canadian crew cut And Jirka laughed and raised his head and trumpeted at the sky he just couldn't believe his luck and he went and got a pair of scissors and Tekla wrapped a towel around his neck and Jirka sat on the chair and kept raising his head and Tekla kept pushing it back down as she cut his long hair and she seemed to know what she was doing and Vladimir finally seemed to relax and he laughed very carefully as if his teeth were broken and although he'd been incapable of looking her in the eye he now watched Tekla from behind as she leaned over Jirka . . . And then Tekla pulled off the towel and Jirka stood up and looked at us to see what we thought and Jirka looked very handsome indeed he resembled a professional Canadian hockey player and I saw everyone else had the same impression and Tekla took down the hall mirror and brought it in and held it up for Jirka and Jirka suddenly saw himself as we all did . . . And he shouted We have to frame it! And he ran into the alcove and brought back a bottle of brandy and he topped everyone off and we all raised a toast to his new hairstyle and indeed from that moment on Jirka seemed a different man he ran out to the hallway mirror every so often to check himself out and presently the editor glanced at his watch and gave a start and said . . . I have to get a taxi right away and get to a meeting but look here Jirka Tekla's got no place to sleep tonight in fact no place to stay period so look here Jirka I'll put those butterflies of yours in my magazine I'll write something about them let her stay here for a week just for a little while until I can find her a sublet . . . And Jirka laughed and went all giddy at the luck and without a moment's hesitation said Look my friend anything for you I've got an army cot here she can sleep on I'll stoke up the stove for her and I can even take the army cot into the next room and she can have the bed . . . And Jirka Šmejkal was jubilant and then we said our good-byes and when Vladimir went to shake that young woman's hand he was pale and couldn't meet her eyes he was so head over heels surely he would have fainted dead away . . .

My husband and I went to his cousin Milada's place once a week for a proper bath . . . she hailed from Brno as did my husband and she was fond of talking in the Moravian dialect in the Brno slang . . . she was born on the outskirts in Pekanda in an apartment building whose gallery-like balconies made it look like a big prison . . . The Germans in Brno called Pekařská Street Pekanda . . . To get to Milada's place in Holešovice my husband and I would cross the Libeň Bridge where there was always a pleasant breeze from the water and a nice view of Bulovka hospital . . . Mainly at night . . . My husband liked to trail his hand along the stone parapet of the bridge and breathe in the night air and gaze at the river at the surrounding landscape and the lighted hospital pavilions reflected in the water's surface and he was quiet and I had to be quiet too . . . It was always fun at Milada's place Milada's husband Mr. Kocián loved to eat and early every afternoon he was on the phone to Milada down at the paper salvage to make sure she didn't forget what to buy for dinner and to remind her not to go drinking slivovitz with the drivers at Svozil's pub . . . And when Milada failed to arrive home at the appointed time Mr. Kocián watch in hand would wait for his wife in the entranceway . . . I often caught him standing there with a worried look on his face and I kept him company . . . And by the time even I started to worry there was Milada stepping off the tram shopping bags in hand only to be met by a livid Mr. Kocián who marched beside her and swore at her and pointed at his watch and cried . . . Where were you? I can smell slivovitz on your breath . . . And before we even made it up the stairs to the door of their flat Milada was in tears claiming she'd simply eaten three rum pralines earlier that afternoon . . . And on it went inside the flat with Milada crying and Mr. Kocián endlessly repeating how he had rescued her how he had pulled her up from the gutter . . . and only when Milada began to prepare dinner did Mr. Kocián settle down . . . and in a quarter of an hour everything was back to normal Mr. Kocián singing an opera aria in his falsetto . . . Darling Marta . . . Oh darling Marta . . . I enjoyed dining at the Kociáns' . . . Mr. Kocián went apoplectic whenever gravy was on the menu because Milada ate with such abandon she never failed to spatter her blouse . . . It's obvious you're from Pekanda! Mr. Kocián would holler . . . Mr. Kocián was chief officer of Kabeš a firm that manufactured central heating systems . . . every year he went abroad and he loved to travel and depending on whether he was going to northern Europe or to the Mediterranean he wore a sailor's cap or a Panama hat . . . He packed the sailor's cap or Panama hat in a paper bag and only put it on once he crossed the border . . . When the mood struck him he described his travels with great relish . . . he liked to tell me that he was the illegitimate son of Count Lánský of Růže . . . And he dressed like it too especially on Mondays when he attended the Monday Nighters Club along with a host of actors and former politicians and other famous characters . . . it was men only and the closest a woman could get was a peek through the door a wave of the handkerchief . . . and there Mr. Kocián's friends Jaroušek the Bolivian consul and Fryb the news anchor would wrap up the important global political events of the week . . . And on those Monday evenings Mr. Kocián shaved twice and applied color to his hair and slid a hairnet over his hairdo and powdered himself and shined his shoes and picked out a necktie and laughed and glowed with pleasure and sang in his falsetto . . . My darling Marta . . . darling Marta . . . I came over to their place once to find Mr. Kocián collapsed in his armchair and Milada in tears . . . obviously something terrible had just happened . . . The thing is Milada forgot to buy red beets to accompany the šunkaflek they were having for dinner . . . and šunkaflek without red beets was a prospect so awful Milada had to go back out to the main street . . . but everything was already closed . . . and when she returned in tears Mr. Kocián reminded her yet again that he had rescued her from the gutter . . . And through her tears Milada told him he could kiss her in the ass . . . whereupon Mr. Kocián promptly collapsed and lay there up until my arrival when he said to me in a weak voice . . . my wife suggested that I kiss her *in* the ass that's not even proper Czech . . . imagine she suggested that I the illegitimate son of Count Lánský of Růže kiss her *in* the ass . . .

Milada and I often played a little game where we tried to use as much Brno slang as possible . . . in Brno slang lunch was *šnicle* and cabbage was *kel* and purse was *perza* and people who liked money were *žgrgoňs* and heart was *hrzna* and a liar was a *hompál* and a stove was a *šporhert* and the kites the boys flew in fall were *rachlas* and we swam in the Brno *švimbec* and sister was always *švica* and a bouquet of flowers *pušna* and a cop was always a *hemon* and a lilac a *holr* and Židenice was *Dinice* and King's Meadow was *Krpol* or *Kénig* and we called Pisárky *Šrajvold* and a bald man was a *glocňák* and a bald head a *glocňa* . . . cousin Milada and I loved the Brno slang and when my husband was around we went on for hours because he was as fluent in the Brno dialect as Milada . . . And my husband would take his pitcher and walk over to the Battery Tavern for his beer and sometimes he went all the way to The Sailor or to Hájek's because their ten-proof according to him was by far and away the best . . . At that time my husband dreamed of the one book that was to be his future he dreamed of its publication and of how we would get all dolled up in our finery and set off for Prague for National Avenue and then Wenceslas Square at twilight where that famous book with his name on it would be in the display case windows and we would make like we're just out for a stroll and that first book of his the one that brought him fame because it was a knockout would be in the display case window of every single bookshop . . . And shortly after we married I often spied my husband practicing his signature it was almost like he was in a hypnotic trance like when people doodle nonsense along the edges of a newspaper or on the back of a restaurant bill . . . so my husband practiced his signature in those unguarded moments . . . and in about six months he had a fine signature it was his surname capped off in the same stroke with his first initial . . . And his distinctive signature was scrawled on all our newspapers and all our magazines and I had to admit it certainly was an impressive signature the likes of which you could find only on a banknote . . .

■ □ ■ □ ■

CHAPTER NINE

The machine shop directly adjacent to our little flat did not irritate me half as much as that Perkeo typewriter . . . it had two rollers and keys like bared teeth and the letters were in German only since the typewriter hailed from Deutschland My husband typed like a virtuoso even when it was getting dark he hammered away at the machine with those stumpy little fingers of his pounded at it like he wanted to knock its teeth out but the machine withstood and overcame everything he threw at it My husband had a strange way of writing he fed in the paper and then gazed out the window ten fingers typing away like he was playing a sitar and he wrote so fast it was hard to believe so I'd check for myself and sure enough he really was writing and everything did make sense but for all the horrible typos But that was because the machine had no diacritics my husband never bothered to add them he played that machine like an instrument it was grown into him like an artificial kidney like a pacemaker and he told me that when he dreamed of the text he saw the Perkeo machine in his mind's eye and what's more the machine in his mind's eye merged with his fingers and when he dreamed of the text he saw the keys leap out and smear words onto the page saw the keys like scattered musical notes and those notes created words and those words appeared to him across the keyboard both ordered and chaotic and he plucked his thoughts from thin air and transcribed them his ten fingers hammering away at the keyboard and the keyboard ordered those thoughts into sentences and the sentences flooded page upon page upon page until finally he was left exhausted or the thoughts just scattered and disappeared . . . My husband called his machine the Perkeo atomic *schreibmachine* . . . Egon Bondy coined the name when my husband read him his work up in Kladno . . . My husband seized the opportunity to write when I was at work or when I went to cousin Milada's for a bath or when I was over at Liza's knitting mittens or working on my needlepoint . . . If I got home early he'd continue to write and signal me to keep quiet and I'd sit there hating that Perkeo machine because he merged with it body and soul without it he was lost my husband was incapable of writing by hand like a soldier on horseback a lancer a dragoon is incapable of walking straight when he comes down off the saddle and when my husband wrote something down for me on a piece of paper it looked like it was written by a child . . . sometimes his handwriting slanted off to the right and other times to the left and he even stuttered when he wrote by hand he was incapable of writing anything nonliteral by hand he stuck strictly to the facts . . . but when he sat down at that *schreibmachine* of his the images just poured out of him and he wrote and he wrote and sometimes I stood under the window and eavesdropped on his furious writing but if I said anything he'd slow and stop and look at me angrily and then take a few more keystrokes like he was adding periods and then he'd wrap it up and come down off the roof those flowing thoughts suspended in air those glowing sentences in his mind's eye extinguished and he'd shrug and take the pitcher and go out for beer his writing on hold for later But sometimes he continued to write furiously it didn't matter if I talked to him or if someone came over he'd simply go on smiling at the images at the sentences nothing could distract him and he wrote and he wrote because as he said if he didn't get it down now it would disappear from his mind's eye forever . . . So in the second year of our marriage I bought my husband a new typewriter it was also a German make a Torpedo and when I put it on the table next to his Perkeo atomic *schreibmachine* the ancient machine looked more modern and straightforward than the new one The Torpedo came in its own little case just like the Perkeo except that my husband had thrown the old case out and carried the Perkeo bound with a couple of straps like a school kid carrying his books . . . that Perkeo machine was indestructible . . . he took it down to the river and it wrote wherever he put it no matter if it was on an angle or a level surface and one time he even dropped it into the Vltava and it went on writing just like his Austrian Roskop alarm clock went on ringing when Mr. Vaništa dropped it into the sink went on ticking underwater just like the Perkeo machine dripping water went on even stronger than before . . . and so when my husband came home to find that Torpedo machine I dared buy him he stared at those two machines for a while and then he sat down and gave that new typewriter a whirl but somehow he couldn't quite get the hang of it the keyboard was higher and wider and had an extra row of those diacritics the other machine was missing . . . He had to practice but in order to get any work done at all on the new machine first the old one had to go into the closet and under a blanket so it wouldn't get jealous of my husband's infidelity with the new machine the opponent that had suddenly appeared in our Libeň flat on Na Hrázi Street Nevertheless my husband hammered out the first of his early drafts on the sensational old Perkeo typewriter he petted it like it was a little critter and because he never cleaned it it was all dusty inside and dust crumbled off the black ribbon and the keys were stopped up with ink and the ink stopped up the hollows of the letters and the inside of every letter was filled in with black so those letters stamped on the white sheet of paper were like bricked-in windows outlines only but none of that mattered to my husband because he was essentially a slob . . . he liked things neat but only superficially he liked to sweep up but he swept everything under the bed he liked to tidy up to the extent he threw a tablecloth over his papers and writing supplies threw an art nouveau blanket over them like he was making a bed . . . but the tea towels were the most excruciating my husband used tea towels for everything when he washed his hands he dried them with a tea towel to shine his shoes he used a tea towel he even blew his nose into a tea towel and wiped his sweat off with a greasy tea towel and when the tea towel got too filthy and I wasn't looking he stuffed it into the cast-iron stove Although we did have a WC in the courtyard by husband preferred to pee and this truly drove me mad onto a dirt pile in the courtyard that sprouted thick vines of Virginia creeper and that was my husband's thing to pee in the courtyard at night the same dumb expression on his face all men have when they pee And it became like an unwritten rule . . . when my husband thought I was at work he peed in a corner of the yard he even started doing it during the day but I often caught him at it and gave him such a start he peed all over his trousers and then I walked past him angrily and pretended to be sick to my stomach . . . He got me back though . . . when I was at the basin doing my personal hygiene that is to say washing down there he suddenly came in and caught me completely off guard . . . Horrified I yelled at my husband not to look and then he got his licks in by pretending to vomit pretending to be sick like what he saw had scarred him for life . . . he went outside and yelled for me to hear . . . What a way to start the day! Just my luck to see the old lady on the piss-pot first thing in the morning! Despite the fact I never used a chamber pot or even kept a chamber pot in our flat . . . it disgusted me . . . even in the snow I'd sooner cross the courtyard in the freezing cold to use the WC with the icicles hanging inside . . . My husband was unbearably messy with everything including that Perkeo typewriter of his When I caught him at his writing it was similar to when I caught him peeing in the courtyard it threw him off guard and he started making mistakes and even his Perkeo typewriter seemed caught off guard and the keys jammed up in the gate but my husband in mid-stroke reached in with two fingers and unstuck and separated the keys and in that regard the machine was indestructible any other machine the keys would have snapped right off but this one took the brute force even when the keys bit into each other and locked together my husband's strong fingers pried them apart and the whole machine jumped up like it had sunk its teeth into my husband's fingers jumped up angrily and hung in the air and refused to let go until my husband shook it off and the Perkeo machine clattered to the floor and then my husband picked it up and caressed it with his fingers which were black from constantly reaching in to unstick those keys and as he touched his face while writing even his face got smeared with black but when the machine fell to the floor he just picked it up and dropped it on the table and fed it a fresh sheet of paper and the machine went on like nothing at all had happened . . . Egon Bondy said that machine really did run on atomic power . . . Nevertheless my husband decided to retire the Perkeo machine and use it as decoration . . . alongside the large split pine tree stump he kept in the flat a stump that had once housed wild bees my husband had wheedled the stump from a group of Russian soldiers billeted at the old brewery and over the years it had followed him everywhere to

Old Town Square to the building where the Schönbach funeral parlor was and then to Jáchymová Street across from the Jewish school and then to the dormitory in Dřín by Kladno and now the old tree trunk stood here crumbling inside and next to it was a tea doll stripped of her crinoline dress her pink arms splayed and she sat beside the tree stump and stared in wonder at the moldering beehive gnawed into the pine wood . . . And now the tree stump and the tea doll were joined by the Perkeo machine its rollers clasped together like teeth in a firmly set jaw its keys mute inside the collapsible typewriter that now stood on its stool next to the hairless dressless tea doll And whoever came over was most smitten with the typewriter they caressed it and held it in their lap like it was a little animal and they opened it out stunned at how beautiful and modern and compact the machine was with its one row less . . . A guy named Frank used to live in our building in the flat facing the street . . . Frank was retired on account of his huge heart which was so massive in fact the pathologists couldn't wait to get at him with their postmortem . . . as Frank said proudly with a heart like that you went into retirement because it was the biggest heart in all of Central Europe . . . Frank had worked as a stove-fitter he fixed bakers' ovens and his area of expertise was the door and mouth of the oven he inlaid those oven doors with quartzite set in a mixture of cement and other stuff . . . and he had a beautiful stove in his flat and because my husband often admired it Frank built us a similar stove the mouth inlaid with small stones set in a mix of fireclay and water glass Frank often made my blood boil because he talked endlessly about intimate subjects and about how great he still was at it and how he could do it twice a day thanks to his giant heart As soon as he saw me he'd start talking about those things but I got him back by pretending to be sick and one day I actually managed to vomit on his trousers for real So Frank and my husband engaged in their smut and although my husband was reluctant to talk about sex he certainly didn't mind hearing about it And Frank had this idea he was going to write down everything he knew about that heart of his everything he'd observed and particularly he wanted the doctors to know about his risk-free twice-daily sex romps So my husband lent him that typewriter that atomic Perkeo *schreibmachine* and Frank pecked away at all hours like a woodpecker practiced his typing skills and in three months he had the hang of it except for the grammar which was botched because the machine had no diacritics And then Frank began to write his work on the largest heart in Europe the heart that Professor Vondráček himself couldn't wait to get his hands on But as Frank described his ability to have sex twice a day with no side effects he was compelled to increase his sexual activity to an occasional three times a day as a result of which his heart finally succumbed and he no longer pecked away at that typewriter he just lay on the floor in an upended armchair because that was the most comfortable position for him . . . my husband said that Frank lying there in that overturned armchair looked like he was screwing a goat . . . he visited Frank and they'd joke around and my husband would take his yellow tape measure along and measure Frank and then look around the room and say How do you expect the undertaker to get around in here with the coffin? And Frank laughed so hard he'd squeal my husband was always joking around with him and Frank took it as an enormous favor on my husband's part And so the jokes went on about the coffin and about the armchair since he was screwing an armchair now could he do it twice a day or three times a day? Until one morning Frank whose voice had grown progressively louder as his blood vessels popped one after the other yelled at my husband . . . Look here Doctor you take back that typewriter! Take it take it! But my husband put his hand on Frank's back Frank who lay there in that upended armchair and said . . . Just hang on to it Frankie and practice hard . . . You are practicing aren't you? After all Frank as soon as you get the hang of the typewriter you have to write all about that big heart of yours the biggest in Europe you have to get the information out there you've got it in you for Christ's sake Frankie just start writing you'll be a number one writer Frank understand you live in Prague and that Prague is the heart of Europe and only you can write a report about the largest heart in Central Europe only you hold the key and all the papers and diagrams and X-rays on the heart that sent you into retirement . . . for the love of God Frankie quit squealing and start writing There's no better time to start writing than when you start to see things from the other side Hang on to that Perkeo *schreibmachine* . . . I wrote my strongest stuff on her . . . So Frankie keep up with your writing focus more on that report about your heart . . . practice

Frankie practice but practice while you're getting something down already . . . And Frank replied that as soon as he felt a little better he'd get down to writing he'd talk about his life as a stove-fitter and about his visits to the faculty of medicine about how the professors used sound and pictures to lecture the medical students on the largest heart in Central Europe Frank's own and with his report Frank would include the contract he'd signed with the university which stipulated he mustn't swim or ride in airplanes or even take express trains because Frank had sold his heart to the university and Professor Vondráček couldn't wait to get to the autopsy to get a load of that giant heart for himself . . . So said Frank and the blood vessels in his heart continued to pop and he made it all the way to that beautiful stove of his inlaid with quartzite set in fireclay and water glass . . . and in the morning when his girlfriend arrived Frank was already dead . . . He hollered before he died but no one heard him if anything the people upstairs probably thought it was the neat lady Beranová hollering in her sleep the lady who washed down the hallway with buckets of water and swept the water into the gutter who yawned so loud when she retired to that twilit room of hers it sounded like she was howling . . . Or perhaps Liza and Slávek and even the Slavíčeks upstairs thought the howling had come from the woman who lived across from the neat lady . . . she was a recent widow and every now and then when she realized she was indeed a widow that her husband was gone for good she sat in her chair by the stove and wailed and moaned something awful like a dog tethered to a doghouse for life who finally realizes he'll never run across the village green again never bound off through the fields with the rest of the doggies again . . . So some time after Frank's death and after the funeral my husband caught up with Frank's girlfriend at the flat and asked her to return the Perkeo *schreibmachine* he lent Frank for his writing . . . But the girlfriend said she didn't know anything about any machine and my husband pleaded with her and offered her cash but she insisted she knew nothing about it and in fact had never even seen it . . . And my husband was miserable twice he got drunk on account of he missed his Perkeo *schreibmachine* so much he'd written hundreds of pages of his life on that machine and when he looked at that split pine tree stump its insides eaten away by wild bees when he looked at that hairless tea doll beside which his Perkeo machine used to sit . . . he hurled the tea doll into the trash and took an ax and chopped that tree stump he got as a gift from some Russian soldiers to smithereens he even chopped the stool which had housed his surrealist still life to bits and now and then when he began to cry and moan in his sleep I soothed him . . . There there don't give that Perkeo atomic *schreibmachine* another thought . . . there there . . .

■ □ ■ □ ■

CHAPTER TEN

My husband and I spent a week in the Krkonoše Mountains We lived in the Jilemnická Chalet in Upper Mísečky . . . my husband used to come to Lower Mísečky as a student he showed me the cottage where he always stayed owned by Mr. Scharf and below Mr. Scharf lived Mr. Donth and lower still lived Mr. Berauer . . . All of them had worked in the forest and had plenty of kids my husband said that every year when he came for winter break there was always one kid more at Scharf's place because when Mr. Scharf was in the forest Mr. Donth was likely to come over to his place to borrow an ax or a saw and Mr. Donth was a redhead and wouldn't you know it every second kid of Mr. Scharf's was a redhead too And my husband showed me the Waldheim Tavern with its green logs where he'd always gone for dinner after his ski trips there were never more than one or two guests at the Waldheim and everyone drank bottled beer and to go with the beer my husband ate buttered bread and salami for dinner and it was always hot inside the restaurant thanks to a huge tiled cast-iron stove . . . But that was all in the past . . . not a single German was left here in the Krkonoše after 1945 some fell in the war others were beaten to death with shovels and the rest were shipped out . . . And aside from the exiled and fallen Germans even the local cattle population was wiped out my husband told me there used to be six hundred head of cattle in these mountains and now there were only four cows left up at the North Star above the town of Pec . . . back when the North Star was still run by a German woman she'd milk her cows in the evening and offer up fresh warm milk with a shot of rum . . . and now most of the cottages were held by state-run companies and reserved solely for the leisure of their employees . . . My husband reminisced on the days when the Germans were still around when practically every cottage served up a meal of buttered bread and *bauernschmaus* a platter of bacon and salami and white pudding and smoked meat and there was always fine bottled beer to go along and the best thing was the woodstove heat in those cottages in winter And what made my husband saddest of all was the departure of those six hundred cows and the departure of those worked-to-the-bone Madonnas those gaunt women who'd disappeared along with their beautiful dialect But my husband never failed to add that most of those Germans had been Nazis and all of them had celebrated the losses suffered by the Czechs and therefore it could come as no surprise that when the Germans lost the war it was two eyes for an eye the full jaw for a tooth because you reap what you sow and to the victor go the spoils and heaven help the vanquished We went for hikes along the marked snow-covered trails we left our skis behind and set off in our ski suits and our backpacks and our ski poles to help in the snow and my husband went on with these long monologues he was terribly angry at all the Germans in Bohemia and Moravia because it was the Sudeten problem that had triggered the Second World War and with the German's betrayal of our republic and with their rallying cry of *Heim ins Reich* they'd sealed not just their own fate their own future resettlement but the fate of the Czech lands because the loss of the war had ushered the victor into Central Europe and with him a new epoch where everything was different So we hiked the marked trails one of our favorites went down to Špindler's Mill and my husband looked around as if in a dream because all the names of all the hotels and cabins were changed and when my husband saw the piles of garbage and cinder behind the hotels and cabins when he saw we could get nothing to eat in those former hotels because they'd been nationalized and reserved for the use of their own employees . . . he carried on loudly with his monologue he decried the Germans because if not for the war they'd still be here and he'd still be going to those overheated cottages and drinking that beer of his except that with their *Heim ins Reich* the local Germans had spoiled these Krkonoše Mountains for my husband and they got what they deserved and it served them right to end up as terribly as they had because back during the First Republic it was the Germans who'd first trampled on the rules of a civil society and in fact what had befallen them was not nearly enough to compensate for their crimes and for the loss of that beautiful mountain dialect which decamped along with the Sudetenlanders . . . And their betrayal led to the loss of that beautiful Prague German and the beautiful German dialect of Brno and Opava and Jihlava and the lovely dialect of the Spiš Valley disappeared too the *Cipldeutsch* of the Spiš Germans and the Cheb *Egerlanders* And my husband lamented the loss of this twinned language which disappeared along with the six hundred Krkonoše cows and along with the woodstove hot cottages and restaurants But so what? The Germans had no idea how to behave and wherever they went with their banners and their concentration camps and their ideas of pure race they brought misery and ruin and death Therefore they deserved what happened to them they had it coming and in fact they got off easy considering what they brought down on Europe As a student my husband took his winter breaks in Mísečky he used to be so fond of the people here . . . forty crowns lasted him a week and five crowns put him up at Mr. Scharf's place in *Dreihauser* and it never would have occurred to him not in his wildest dreams what was coming in '37 the degree to which the Germans would change . . . swastikas appeared in attic windows and many of the Germans cooled toward my husband in fact some of them stopped talking to him altogether and suddenly those forest workers swelled with pride and raised their voices and rolled their eyes toward Prague and all of them started to wear white knee-highs and those Madonnas started to wear dirndls and in the pubs they sang martial German songs most especially *Wacht am Rhein* And those Germans made me ashamed particularly for their conviction that all their social problems all the ills of the world were the Czechs' fault Prague's fault and that everything would change once they achieved their big dream of *Heim ins Reich* . . . And we ascended the glittering trail up the Golden Knoll and my husband stopped to gaze out over the weather-beaten spruce trees at the landscape and it was a beautiful sunny day and we decided that after lunch we'd head over to the Chalet Elbe and so we took our time hiking the trail through the spruce and dwarf pine and now we left the thicker forest behind and up ahead the trail was marked by weathered spruce and by trail markers buried to the hilt in snow . . .

My husband stopped and pointed with his ski pole . . . Over there we found the schoolteacher from Hradec frozen and five meters away from her the husband frozen too and each of them was holding a frozen orange Back in '34 when I came here on winter break we had a two-day blizzard blow through and when those forty-eight hours were up we went out to find the missing Down by Chalet Elbe they found two officers barely thirty meters from the chalet . . . in the blizzard they'd gone around in circles . . . and below the Golden Knoll the others and I found that schoolteacher curled up clutching that frozen orange in her hand and we brought her and her husband down to Renner's place just as they were like a couple of armchairs like those statues of a seated Christ that's how frozen they were because when a snowstorm hits the Krkonoše it's worse than the Tatras . . . But the Tatras on the other hand have the advantage that every year several dozen tourists are killed are dashed to bits in the gorges and against the jagged cliffs . . . they say if you've got to go then drowning's the best way . . . But how could the Germans who'd lived here before who'd been decent before be surprised . . . after they left twenty million or more dead on the front lines after they left six million tortured to death in the concentration camps . . . how could those Germans be surprised that after they lost the war a tooth for a tooth became a whole jaw? How could they be surprised that former leaders of every village had to dig their own graves and were then shot? How could they be surprised that as they were being rounded up into camps and shipped off for relocation thousands more were killed even after war's end? With great pains I killed blind kittens because it had to be I killed rabbits at home because it had to be and with great pains I might even kill a man if it had to be But those people whose loved ones were tortured to death by Germans in concentration camps and prisons . . . it certainly never surprised me that as payback those people might demand not a tooth but a whole jaw . . . take what happened in the Krušný Mountains it was after the war they put two SS men on a trailer and forced them to tear each other limb from limb to gouge each other's eyes out and then an arm and then a leg and then another arm until the only thing left on the back of the trailer being pulled through the village by a tractor were a couple of torsos and one arm and the one arm remained simply because the man with no arms had nothing left with which to maim the other . . . but they still had their lips and as they were thrown into their graves they screamed Heil Hitler . . . And my husband was breathing hard because we'd left the trees behind and now we climbed along a narrow glittering plain and I felt faint not from my husband's story but from something I'd never experienced before . . . looking into the depths of the valley I was overcome with vertigo . . . as long as I had the tree trunks and the dwarf pine and the tops of the spruce trees as reference I was okay but now as I continued to climb and the spruce and the dwarf pine slipped away I was sure I was spinning along with the whole planet and the Golden Knoll and the whole valley pitched over and fell into the depths like the whole world was on a giant mill wheel and around it went and all the cabins and spruce trees and dwarf pines below me reeled up again and grazed the mountain peaks and then everything whirled past again like a carousel and the vision and the feeling of great anxiety brought me to my knees and I clung to the snow tooth and nail and now I was spinning and I cried out because I felt sure I was spinning through the air sure I was in motion and I cried out again from the vertigo from the feeling I'd spill out and go tumbling down off this glittering sunlit mountain into the valley below and my husband stood barely three meters away and reached out his hand and I crawled toward him slowly like I was crawling through a blinding snowstorm I crawled to him on all fours afraid to reach up and grab his hand . . . and now my husband who was at first amused called out to me as to a skittish horse and now when he saw me crawling toward him on all fours screaming this was to be our last few minutes to-gether he knelt down and put his arms around me and I glued myself to him and closed my eyes and my heart pounded inside my throat and my husband coaxed me to my feet but I fell back into the snow immediately and I moaned and whimpered and then he had to lead me by the hand back down the trail and when I opened my eyes the whole world pitched over again and spilled its contents and again the feeling overtook me that I and everything around me was lashed to some sort of gigantic invisible mill wheel . . . And when I felt the first trail marker the first weather-beaten tree when I wrapped my arms around the first spruce tree only then did I open my eyes . . . and there was the dwarf pine and the spruce descending along the slopes of Golden Knoll and there were the skiers ascending the crooked trail and the roofline of Jilemnická Chalet jutting out of the dark forest smoke rising from the chimney . . . and that sight didn't quite calm my nerves but it did help stop the spinning in my head the feeling I was upside down on an invisible mill wheel And I started to cry I was so upset I felt like I was choking and my husband led me down carefully his arm around me and he held me by the hand and meanwhile our ski poles were back there somewhere stuck in the snow along the trail which rose beyond the spruce and dwarf pine to merge with the blue sky and I looked up to where the thin ridgeline of snow split the azure blue sky and again I was overcome and I tried to get my legs under me by looking into the valley for reference but again I fell to the snow and hung on tooth and nail because the ground spun away and the Golden Knoll went with it and the cottages and the cars and the buses in the valley below pitched and rolled upside down somersaulted and even my husband's legs went out from under him like he was on ice and he was ripped away from me and I felt like I was in a structure whose foundations had suddenly flown into the air while its roof collapsed into the cellar and at the last minute I tore my eyes away from that thin azure blue line separating heaven and earth and locked onto my husband's eyes and in that way we carefully descended step by step almost as if I was drunk until finally we made the spruce trees again and when I looked around there was just the snow-covered trail marked with ski tracks and boot prints . . .

On the second day we wanted to go for a walk through the snowbound and sunlit landscape down to the patisserie in Špindler's Mill But when we got to Renner's place where the ski runs on Mount Šerých meet my husband stopped and pricked up his ears Gathered there was a large group of skiers and they even had an outdoor buffet with tables and stools set up and a banner that read START on one side and FINISH on the other in big red letters and all the skiers were covered in logos like they were World Cup racers and some of them warmed up and worked their shoulders while others got set and practiced their start positions and the race organizers checked their names in earnest and apparently it was an Old Boys race divided into two groups of competitors sixty and below and sixty plus and there were some pretty old gentlemen among them and these Old Boys looked most serious as they prepared for the big race . . . one of the organizers told my husband the race was held once a year and was a gathering of old friends who'd raced together back in the day as well as locals who

wanted to participate in the annual championship and some of them
actually trained daily for this race cycled and ran and in fact a few of
them who were already into retirement even cross-trained because to
them this Old Boys race was a life-and-death test of their mettle of
whether they could still not only participate but win one of the ten
prizes . . . And before the race started everyone smiled and clapped
each other on the back before the race started they were the best of
friends and they ribbed each other and inquired about their prostates
and how much mineral water they drank each day and they were
joined by their wives and their friends and some of the more hard-
core racers even had a little oatmeal prior to the race while everyone
else ate wieners with mustard and this whole giant group of Old Boys
acted like little kids I never saw a happier bunch of old fellows and
from their faces it was obvious some of them had competed and won
at the national level it was obvious from the shape they were in and
from their top-of-the-line Austrian and Italian ski gear . . . And then
the time came for the organizers to check their lists and assign the
racers their numbers and from the moment their wives and friends
pinned their numbers on their backs from the moment the last number was pinned on the last racer all conversation stopped and the
ribbing ceased and it seemed like the competitors didn't even know
each other in fact they gave each other dirty looks And then one by
one the racers were released onto the race course onto the slopes of
Mount Šerých and my husband took me by the hand and we ran
down a side trail to where the course looped and turned back toward
the START/FINISH line . . . And the track was littered with spectators
mainly relatives and now the racers pushed themselves to go as fast as
they could and I saw by the set of their faces they took the race deadly
serious and when one of the racers went down he got up again heavily
and with great shame . . . many of the racers were probably doctors
and engineers by trade and people who belonged to ski clubs and
back in the cities they came from they were probably considered ex-
perts in ski racing and no doubt when a World Cup race was on
television they provided expert running commentary . . . therefore
when one of them took a header it was an awful humiliation and up
he came as fast as possible to catch up with the rest of the pack . . .
And from their dog-tired faces and from the way they moved my
husband could tell exactly what they were thinking . . . and down at

the turn we witnessed one racer wanting to pass another but the guy wouldn't let him by in fact he tried to block his way and so they screamed at each other . . . Let me by! . . . and the guy blocking his friend yelled . . . Never! . . . And thus the Old Boys race turned into a matter of life and death . . . Some of the racers were already dead tired when they reached our position at the turn the sweat poured off them and their haggard faces reflected a sense of dread that they were on their last legs and that perhaps they wouldn't even finish the race . . . but their wives and friends were there and they ran alongside and spurred them on and offered them drinks in plastic cups to perk them up . . . And the wives and friends of the racers no longer took this race as a friendly little get-together now it was flat out a question of prestige . . . And the racers as they passed one another cussed and hurled the most awful insults . . . And inevitably it happened one racer tried to pass another and they got tangled up together and they tumbled into the spruce trees and the powdered snow settled down on top of them and while they'd been the best of friends and full of smiles back at the starting line now they lay there arms and skis and poles all snarled up even their faces were stuck together and they bellowed at each other with contempt and the fellow who'd been knocked down flew into such a rage he sank his teeth into his friend's ear and the blood came spurting out . . . and then they managed to disentangle themselves and the one fellow took off in an attempt to catch up with the others while the fellow with the bloody ear just lay there and shouted . . . You bastard I'll file a complaint . . . you'll be disqualified! And he lay there in his top-of-the-line ski gear like a bug flipped over on its back and wiggled his skis back and forth but he wouldn't allow anyone to help him up he simply refused and kept trying to get back up on his skis so he could at least finish the race and file a protest . . . and my husband looked at me and I knew what he was thinking I was getting to know my husband well enough so that we understood each other without saying a word . . . I could see it in his eyes he was remembering the kiddie scooter races in Šlosberk the kiddie races that had also turned into a matter of life and death for the kids and especially for the mothers . . . and so we took the trail the long way around and eventually made our way back to the START/FINISH line . . . And now the Old Boys were hitting the homestretch giving it everything they had they were all pretty much one step away from a heart attack . . . two old fellows were neck and neck and running alongside screaming were their wives and their friends and they spurred them on and shouted at them and kept pace with them and in fact it was the wives and the friends racing now and they could care less whether or not the winner collapsed across the finish line dead from exhaustion . . . and so in the end one of the old fellows did make it across the finish line first and when the runner-up crossed the line right after he bent over the winner lying there in the snow and said bitterly . . . If you'd let me past I'd a shown you . . . And he too collapsed in a heap tried to catch his breath he cooled his face in the snow and the snow glittered and the sun shone and now other racers started to cross the line and the race officials clocked their times and marked down their names and the wives and the friends of the first six across wrapped them up in little blankets and surprisingly the wasted faces those dog-tired runners-up started to relax and started to smile . . . and those smiling faces took on the look of a little child overcome with joy at the sight of a blazing Christmas tree surrounded by presents . . . And then the tenth-place finisher crossed the line and he stood there bent over double the sweat dripping off his bowed head and when this tenth-place finisher raised his head suddenly he too was happy suddenly he too was still an Old Boy a competitor and he accepted the congratulations of the other men and they shook hands and beamed at each other and clapped their arms around each other's shoulders awash in the good luck they still had the stamina to complete a race as tough as this . . . and then the rest of the old fellows dribbled across the line the ones for whom there were no prizes left and they crossed the line guiltily even though they might have put more into it than the men who finished in the first ten . . . and as these men crossed the line no one welcomed them no one cheered them on and no one ran alongside them in the homestretch . . . and when they crossed the line their wives ashamed and angry threw them their blankets and from the look in their eyes it was obvious that it was in fact the wives who'd lost the race . . . and so two groups formed . . . the first ten finishers all aglow at their phenomenal luck . . . and the rest of the pack . . . and the members of this second group looked sad and guilty and ashamed . . . one fellow who came in twentieth even tore off his skis and ran for his car which was parked nearby the forest . . . he peeled off his gear as he ran and then he strapped his skis to the roof of the car and jumped in and rolled down the window . . . and the race officials ran after him and cried . . . For God's sake Doctor what are you doing! . . . and the doctor who was almost in tears yelled back . . . You'll never see me here again! Good-bye! And he stomped on the gas and for a second his tires spun in the snow . . . and then he was off race officials on both sides of the car tapping on the hood but he made the road and took off in the direction of Jilemnice . . . and meanwhile other officials unloaded trophies from the back of a small truck and lined them up in the sunshine on a long table covered in white cloth and the winner's trophy lorded over all . . . and then those first ten Old Boys stood in line to accept the official congratulations of the chairman of the Old Boys race . . . and the rest of the pack stood off to one side and hung their heads still shell-shocked they'd come away without a trophy . . . My husband whispered . . . This is a total cakewalk compared to how jealous poets and writers are of each other . . . darling they can be so foulmouthed it's practically criminal they're so jealous and backstabbing they make those gossiping busy-bodies in the Libeň tenements look like amateurs . . . except that what you see here is child's play compared to how painters go at each other they'll stop talking for life if one gets a state prize and the other doesn't But take note darling what you've witnessed here symbolically represents not just a picture of our society but of humankind in general . . . according to Hegel it's history's driving force and therefore the wellspring of the world's greatest ideas . . . the only people the only society with the right to bask in the sun . . . is the society capable of maintaining its youth capable of victory . . . My husband blathered on and I barely heard what he was saying I felt sick from what I'd seen . . . And I said . . . I don't feel like going to the patisserie anymore I just want to go home . . . And then it was like someone waved a magic wand . . . shortly before the trophies were awarded the old fellows who finished outside of the first ten suddenly perked up suddenly their tragic expressions melted away and they looked at each other sheepishly and as if by some secret signal they finally went over and joined in with the winner's circle and they congratulated the winners most sincerely and the wives and the friends of those men shook their heads as if to dispel the regret and the petty complaints and they crowded together and everyone shook hands and voices rang out and corks popped on chilled champagne and the sparkling wine flowed . . . and even the man with the punctured ear came over to congratulate the man who punctured that ear and bottle of champagne in hand he swore he'd take a bite out of his friend's ear at next year's race just to even the score . . . And my husband went on quietly lecturing me . . . Darling when I take you to Berlin to East Berlin we'll pay a visit to the Pergamon Museum . . . there's a frieze there depicting the Greek victory over the Gauls . . . the frieze has an almost cinematic quality . . . but the most beautiful scene is where a young Gaul upon realizing the battle is lost takes his sword and kills his wife and then runs himself through . . . And the capacity of the sculptor to relate to the vanquished enemy . . . is the most beautiful element of that Greek victory over the Gauls . . . By rights the Old Boys winner's trophy ought to go to the fellow with the ear bitten through . . . you understand?

The next day I stayed in bed while my husband set off alone into that winter wonderland on his way to indulge at the patisserie in Špindler's Mill and I lay there in bed and gazed at the ceiling and I kept picturing that Gaul stabbing his wife and then himself . . . And I imagined the sculptor who'd had the courage and sympathy to render a sense of wistfulness to a sculpture that should have been strictly a celebration of victory . . . I lay on my back and gazed at the ceiling and it occurred to me that maybe societies back then were crueler than today but maybe they also had a greater sense of nobility given the sympathy they displayed to those they'd conquered . . . And so I lay on my back and replayed my own fate . . . Though I had in no way participated in the war I nevertheless belonged to the ranks of defeated Germans and therefore I'd been sent to a camp and no one showed me an ounce of sympathy . . . even when I was put to work in the fields . . . at lunch I had to sit off to one side with the other German women . . . the regular labor women sat at a distance like we had scabies or something . . . and one day I was so hungry and those women ate their buttered bread and one of them caught the look in my eye . . . she reached out her hand with the bread in it and when I went to accept that slice of buttered bread . . . she yanked it back and went on eating . . . and I stood there shamefaced and the German women glared at me and the labor women laughed at me and no one showed me an ounce of sympathy . . . *Jedem das Seine* as my husband liked to say . . . even I who was innocent took the blame . . .

and the scene with the bread stays with me to this day . . . And then my husband returned scented with beer and he sat on the footboard and said . . . Darling that Old Boys race came to a sad finish last night . . . the competitors and their friends were celebrating raising a toast to everyone who won and lost and around midnight the winners decided to go for a sauna . . . and the fellow who won the race . . . after everyone else went to bed he thought he'd stay a bit longer . . . and in the morning there was no sign of him in the hotel so they went to check the sauna and found him half scalded to death . . . seems he fainted and fell on the hot rocks . . . and when they lifted him up the meat just fell off his bones . . . darling this world is no cakewalk . . .

■ □ ■ □ ■

CHAPTER ELEVEN

Everyone thought my husband was a happy person that a husband like mine must make me the envy of every woman that life with my husband must be nothing but fun and games But it was something else entirely My husband was a very restless person he tended to want to go off on his own he always wanted to be someplace other than where he was and whatever he did he did as quickly as possible just to get it over with just so he could move on to some other place where he wasn't satisfied either and where his one desire was to be back in the place he'd just run from My husband always gave the impression he had a train to catch or that he was late for a show And when he dressed it was just the same he'd be dressed but never really dressed even his mother said he was always missing something he dressed on the run and he had to be careful not to poke out an eye or put on his coat while it was still on the hanger he even ate while standing up and staring out the window He was forever looking somewhere else and as I came to learn after being married to him for a while he looked some-where else just so he wouldn't have to look at me And when he did look at me when our eyes did happen to meet I could tell I made him very unhappy he wanted nothing more than for me to be gone for me to be anyplace but where he was This despite the fact he had so much time to himself . . . I worked until late in the evening every day and therefore my husband after he got home from work still had several hours undisturbed to focus on his writing But it was the same old story . . . When I was at work he wandered around Libeň he came home only to go out again he sat down only to get up again and he paced the courtyard and fumed he couldn't make the most of his time . . . In fact that husband of mine was plain useless He knew how to start something but not how to finish it . . . he liked to garden liked to plant vegetables but often when we came to Nymburk those vegetables of his would be overgrown with weeds and so his gardening never amounted to much more than pulling weeds . . . despite which he regaled everyone on the train within earshot with his horticultural stories and the women held him up as an example to their own husbands see how adept he was at raising such cabbage such lettuce such dwarf apple such spindle-shaped greengage plum . . . But everything was overgrown because rather than engage in actual gardening my husband preferred to read about it in his *Předmostí Guide to Gardening* and therefore he was forever catching up to what he neglected to what he allowed the weeds to overrun And our lovemaking was along the same lines I always implored him focus strictly on the lovemaking and nothing but the lovemaking forget about what tomorrow's going to bring . . . But my husband was incapable of staying in bed he never lingered after lovemaking never stayed to talk or perhaps to just lie there and watch the firelight from the cracked cast-iron stove flicker across the ceiling Before we engaged in those things then yes certainly he was like a wild bull relentless and he tore the pajamas off me and everything had to be right now and it would seem he loved me terribly and just had to have me . . . But afterward when his desire waned when he began to come out of that trance when the lightning flashing through his mind and through his limbs quieted when he came down from that fierce lovemaking and returned to the here and now of number twenty-four Na Hrázi Street he simply got up out of bed and wiped his privates in a towel or in a handkerchief or in the tattered curtains . . . and he rolled away from me and looked anywhere but at me and I knew that he felt even more alone and even more unhappy and wanted nothing more than to get dressed and to strike out for Šlosberk or anywhere as long as it wasn't here . . . and he had the same habit of wanting to be somewhere else when he was at work . . . whenever I went down to Spálená Street he was always somewhere else either coming back from Husenský's with a pitcher of beer or on his way to get some meatloaf to keep him going with his paper baling barely an hour passed before my husband was off again to somewhere else anywhere but the paper salvage My husband also liked to cook but even that cooking of his never lived up to the claims he made to people as he lectured them on the fancy recipes he'd studied in cookbooks or learned from his mother And my husband had a reputation as an excellent cook but I knew better . . . he found a way to ruin whatever he made he managed to burn everything because while he cooked he liked to read or pop down to the pub to inquire is Pepíček Sviatek around? Because his food was always burnt and always missing something my husband had to smooth everything out with a ridiculous amount of spice he managed to turn plain old goulash into something resembling Chinese food and when he burned the goulash he liked to say a proper goulash has to be a little scorched in fact some of his friends who were cooks used a trowel to scrape their burnt goulash off the bottom of the pot My husband liked to hear people's recipes for goulash he'd listen and nod his head and close his eyes and then say But what about the last step? And when no one had the answer my husband said with erudition . . . Finish it off with just a dash of vinegar just a flick of the holy water off your fingers And so my husband was considered a number one cook which I found quite amusing until he ruined the goulash at home so many times it stopped being funny except maybe in the sense that I had a special child at home instead of a husband or maybe a husband who I only saw on weekends when the mental institute in Lower Beřkovice loaned him out to me So my husband was perpetually rushing off somewhere in the hopes that some vision would appear some sentence would strike him and that one sentence would save him and make him a number one crown him Champion of the Covered Courts And as I came to learn after about a year of our magnificent marriage my husband's eating habits were much the same . . . He never ate like other people never went to bed like other people at work he ate his lunch in the morning or on his way home in the afternoon and he never ate breakfast at home and in the event he was forced to sit there with me he just sipped his coffee and smoked his three American cigarettes and turned pale and felt sick But in any case he always brought a thick slice of bread slathered with lard to bed with him and wolfed it down and sometimes he got up in the middle of the night to slather a slice of bread and devour it . . . hungrily like he made love . . . and then he lay there gasping for air and I lay there next to him in sheets littered with breadcrumbs but he just smacked his lips and both our pillows were greasy from those lips of his . . . Liza and Mrs. Slavíčková told me that when I wasn't around my husband liked to come home and throw back the covers and climb into bed and he slept as sound as a newborn swaddled in the luck I wasn't at home and he could just crawl into bed . . . some afternoons he was so dog-tired he didn't even bother to take off his clothes he just dropped into bed and fell dead away . . . Liza and Mrs. Slavíčková tried to cheer me up by telling me that before I had come along my husband sometimes went to bed as early as noon in anticipation of those late-night parties of his those infamous in-house weddings that kept the whole building up at night . . . And just like my husband made love and just like he cooked and just like he did his job down on Spálená Street and just like he went at his gardening is just like he wrote . . . He rushed along clumsy fingers hammering away at the German Perkeo typewriter the machine that had no Czech diacritics and was so small it reminded me of Vladimir's rolling press the one he used to create his graphics which were not exactly beautiful but which did have an ethereal quality sort of like Vladimir himself Anyhow my husband hid his writing from me but when I did happen across a few pages I never saw such a mess my husband wrote so fast he got ahead of his own thoughts and as a result every line brimmed with so many typos it made no sense and my husband hammered that machine so hard he perforated the pages like a ticket punch and he raged at those pages and filled every inch of space and he was always in such a hurry it was just like when we made love . . . and he tore a chunk off each page as he ripped it from the machine that's how much he couldn't wait to get on with his writing . . . And I was under the impression that he wrote all afternoon while I was at the Hotel Paris But both Mrs. Slavíčková upstairs and Liza across the way knew better they listened to that future number one of mine typing away and wondered why he was always in such a hurry as he wrote where was he racing off to? And when my husband was at his writing those two women would stop what they were doing and listen to that wild writing come through the walls and through the open windows they enjoyed the sound of a writer like that at work And they heard my husband curse and shout and give himself courage And my husband went at it like he was driving a team of horses cussed and swore like a brewery drayman And when half an hour passed my husband drenched in sweat took the pitcher and went off for his beer and he was always in a lather and exhausted and he'd run a hand over his brow and fling the sweat to the courtyard flagstones The only time my husband was truly relaxed in his writing was when the weather was nice when the sun was shining . . . typewriter in hand he climbed up onto the shed roof where his two customized chairs waited and that typewriter was so small it fit just so onto the seat of the chair . . . and as both Mrs. Slavíčková and Liza who had a clear view of my husband through her window liked to say . . . When the sun's shining there's no pleasanter person than your husband . . . and sometimes my husband climbed up on the shed roof in the afternoon and stayed up there writing until sundown . . . the only reason my husband wrote up there was so he could get a tan . . . the thing is my husband was under the impression that he was handsome only when he had a tan and so on his days off he was up there at ten in the morning already and as the sun advanced his chair advanced along with it he followed the sun and moved his writing as the sun moved and he didn't mind if I sat next to him with my needlepoint or reading he didn't have a worry in the world as long as he could bask in the sunshine and when he sat there in the sun writing he was oblivious to my presence wholly absorbed and when he was in the grips of that fever I was convinced he really would make it he would write something after all because even as he sat there beside me in the courtyard he was off in another world it was just like his mother said from the time he was a kid he was always off somewhere else . . . and when the sun was shining and he was at his writing I knew he was somewhere else . . . inside that writing of his enraptured like he was part of some cult of sun worshippers and what's more when my husband wrote in the sun he didn't even have to look at what he was writing it was like he wrote simply to be in the sun And when the sun set behind the clouds my husband came out of his trance and collected his typed pages and took his Perkeo typewriter home and then he grabbed his stein and off he went to somewhere else again to Lyška's or The Brewery or maybe down to Douda's or to The Merkur and sometimes to Vaništa's and The Old Post Office but it was always him and his stein on the move to somewhere else simply because the sun had set and the environment was no longer conducive to writing And when my husband sat up there writing in the sun it almost seemed to me like he was playing the piano . . . And so I never had the wherewithal to look at what he wrote it sort of scared me and besides he never offered me a look at those pages of his and so I learned never to show an interest in those improvisations of his . . . But one thing that always got to me . . . when he finished writing out there in the sunshine when he was done pouring out practically everything he had inside . . . he'd pluck up the nerve to gaze at me to take a good long look and I was able to return his look and gaze into his eyes and in those moments I was happy I married this man . . . And my husband had this ability to look at himself objectively to see himself as I or his mother or Mrs. Slavíčkova or even Liza saw him He was acutely aware of his own faults and he suffered for it but at the same time he knew his shortcomings made him who he was made up his style and besides that's just the way it was Somehow he knew if he kept up this particular tempo for a few years this rhythm of his with the pedal to the metal he'd capture something that was uniquely his and his alone . . . kick a hole in the drum as he liked to say And my husband knew how to observe the things around him he was adept at singling out whatever related to himself When we walked along the Rokytka River my husband said that all the stuff people had tossed into the little stream was akin to his own writing . . . when we peeked into the factory yards in Libeň and Vysočany my husband felt a kinship with the pervasive mess he saw there he said his writing resembled the scattered junk the hodgepodge of machinery . . . and when my husband and I peered across the fence down by the La Paloma Bistro the place where he liked to say with a laugh soldiers took their girlfriends for a shag behind the wall . . . we saw a mess of dilapidated planks and boards and beams and all of it my husband likened to himself he said his own soul was strewn with the same kind of mess like the boards and beams scattered about the courtyard An extraordinary amount of junk and scrap littered every factory yard and my husband was struck by this scene because he said the whole picture was a precise rendering of not just his own writing but of his thinking as well he said he belonged to this epoch and was in fact a child of the times . . . And on our walks back from Šlosberk we liked to stop here and there and window-shop my husband's favorites were the prepared foods the kind you had to finish off at home according to your own taste he said his own work was akin to these prepared foods that it was up to the reader to take the work home and add his own spice his own input . . . everything that was open to interpretation was symbolic of and a key to modern art said my husband and what he wanted to write what he was truly after with his writing was to leave some space open for interpretation . . .

I just couldn't get it through my head that back when my husband was still a young man and living in Nymburk one of his greatest pleasures was to step out on the promenade . . . like his mother said he even did his own ironing the perfect crease was a must for the promenade and he shined his own shoes of course the best shoes from Kabele one pair patent leather black perforated the other pair suede perforated and my husband kept a whole arsenal of neckties and little shirts and when he dressed for the Sunday promenade he took an eternity to select his shirt and his socks and as he dressed he wore a hairnet because back then his hair was so thick he had to oil it just to get a comb through and once he was all dressed up in the latest style and latest colors with great care he took the hairnet off in front of the mirror and his necktie simply had to go with his shirt and with his shoes and he smiled at himself in the mirror and took forever to arrange his white pocket kerchief according to the style of the day and then he picked out a hat that of course was from Čekan and then the deerskin gloves with the little opening up top and if it was hot outside he just held the gloves folded over each other in one hand and then it was time to set out from the brewery and stroll into town onto the promenade and in the afternoons he liked to take boat rides with his beautiful girls or go for walks in Tyrš Park on the island and in the evening it was off to the hotel on Knight Avenue or to the Grand Hotel or perhaps a game of cards at Šafránek's and he was always dressed to the nines except in summer if it was too hot he made an exception and draped his jacket over his arm . . . These days however the last time he was well dressed was at his wedding and even then he'd worn his beautiful suit and hat more like it was a costume he simply wasn't himself in those clothes . . . Something happened not just to the way those factory yards looked but to the way people looked as well back when I worked at the veneer factory come Saturday night everything was put away and organized and the place was swept clean and Saturday nights people in the country and in the cities came together in the village squares and in the city plazas and in the restaurants and in the taverns and back then all the buildings and all the courtyards were spotless and anyone dressed the way my husband and for that matter most people dressed today was considered a bum a good-for-nothing because back then you couldn't step out on a Saturday or a Sunday without a tie without a hat without shoes highly polished . . . I had to admit my husband was right he was in fact a child of his time a reflection of the environment in which he lived and come to think of it so was I .·. .

■　□　■　□　■

CHAPTER TWELVE

That sonny of mine my Nymburk mother told me after four years of studying law at Charles University he got tired of it and then as if on cue the Germans rolled in and occupied Bohemia and Prague and they even shut down the universities and that sonny of mine was delighted the schools were closed happy to have the perfect excuse not to finish his law degree it was the evil Germans responsible for taking over the university for preventing him from completing his studies and instead of becoming a lawyer my sonny started work at the notary copying entries to the land registry . . . And then he got a job at the Railway Cooperative as a clerk he did their books and when he was done with his work he just sat there and stared out the window he could sit there for hours with his pencil poised over the paper just in case the boss walked in and if he did there was my sonny scribbling away and the folks at the cooperative were very satisfied with him because he pretended to be a hard worker and he even learned to sleep with his pen poised over the ledger and in the afternoon he took catnaps but as soon as someone came in there he was scribbling away like he'd never stopped . . . But that wasn't really his thing either and so he went to work on the railway proper putting down ballast on the Poříčany to Nymburk section of track and that was his golden era to be outside to be in nature with the rest of the fellows shooting the breeze and swapping out ties and pouring ballast and then to pause for a moment to stretch his back and look around at the fields and pine groves and forested meadows and off in the distance the Sázavský hills or the town of Louceň glittering on the hillside and to the west Mount Semity and the white slopes of Mount Přerovská and my sonny was smitten by all this he didn't even play the piano anymore he was glad the Germans had shuttered the universities and one of the fringe benefits was that his work with pickax and hoe made his hands so calloused his fingers so battered he couldn't play the piano anymore and he'd hold up those laborer's hands of his and say it was the Germans' fault for making him work on the railroad putting down ballast . . . and so to the outside world he was a poor little thing and a victim of the Nazi regime but as far as he was concerned he was a number one because once a fortnight he got to put a handcart onto the tracks at the local station and while he and another worker pedaled it down the tracks the corpulent trackmeister sat splayed across the bench in front of them watching the rails his whole body tuned into their condition and so my sonny just couldn't wait for that day to roll around once a fortnight when he'd ride the handcart to Poříčany and back again to the local station and come rain or shine my sonny the romantic was wholly absorbed by that countryside running along the River Labe and he was mortified that come war's end he'd have to go back to Prague and resume his studies at the faculty of law . . . there he was on the handcart him and the other fellow pedaling away their elbows knocking together while up front the trackmeister dozed on his bench his whole body tuned in to the rails . . . and in the evening over a beer at the station pub the trackmeister would lament the arrival of the Germans and how instead of working to further our nation our country's best and brightest were under the jackboot of fascism . . . And so on the days my sonny carried the trackmeister aboard the handcart people turned out to watch my sonny go by and they felt sorry for him but that sonny of mine was all aglow at the luck and as he passed those folks trackside between Poříčany and Nymburk he raised a suntanned arm and threw them a friendly wave . . . And something which pleased my sonny to no end was his weekly walk along the same set of tracks . . . striding along with his track wrench over his shoulder making sure all the bolts were tight . . . And he walked all the way to Poříčany and then took the train back he got an extra day off for this work because he always left in the evening and didn't come back until after midnight and then it was straight to the Pub by the Bridge where my sonny regaled them with tales of the resplendent countryside he knew every forest glen and every pine grove and every village and every guard house along the tracks that happened to have a beautiful young woman in uniform working the crossing gates . . . there was my sonny amid all that beauty and he even got paid for it . . . and at night the guard houses were so nice and warm . . . and beautiful girls in uniform made tea for my sonny and he signed his name in the logbooks and whenever he felt like it he set off with his track wrench over his shoulder and a can full of torpedo signals and one time just for the heck of it he put one of those torpedo signals on the track and dropped a rock on it and it went off with such a racket the stationmaster was forced to file a report and that was all she wrote for my sonny and his handcart all she wrote for working on the tracks shoveling ballast and so he went to work as a clerk at the *Signalmeisterei* in Nymburk and my sonny was even prouder of this latest function he had a strange way of finding pride in things no one else would be proud of . . . and so he was extremely proud of the credentials that allowed him to travel the entire Nymburk district to ride aboard those machines in the company of signalmen and switchmen because young lady from a locomotive one can closely watch the semaphores note their condition mark down repairs as necessary but the kicker for my sonny was that he got to ride aboard those locomotives aboard those machines he dreamed of as a little boy when they chugged past the brewery shunting malt cars back and forth to the brewery along the spur . . . he'd get so excited he couldn't sleep and my sonny's favorite thing in the world was to go down to the main station in Nymburk to watch the express trains thunder through and some of those giant locomotives even stopped in Nymburk and my sonny would stand there on the platform along with a gaggle of local boys because boys in Nymburk lived for those locomotives the boy whose father was an engineer that was the same as if he was a footballer or even the president today . . . and my son stood there on the platform and what a sight when that express locomotive ground to a stop and the engineer climbed down to run his hand over the machine to give it a swipe here and there with his rag to check the couplings were secure . . . and some of the engineers out of Hradec Králové wore white shirts and bow ties and chauffeur caps and smart vests with pocket watches and chains and while the fireman climbed down the steps and ran into the station pub for beer . . . the engineer put on a show for the boys and then the fireman came back with a quart of beer dripping foam and then the dispatcher appeared and gave the all clear with his paddle and that express locomotive pulled out hissing and steaming and my son and the other boys just stood there speechless for another fifteen minutes because to a boy from Nymburk a locomotive like that was a revelation . . . And so my sonny had the good fortune to get into a dispatcher training course in Hradec Králové . . . And the thought of wearing a uniform made him weak in the knees not that he'd have rank right away but he'd still get to wear a uniform . . . And he managed to narrowly avoid the ax when he decided one day to use the executive washroom on the second floor of the main station in Hradec Králové . . . there was my sonny peeing away when in runs an officer of the railway and shouts What do you think you're doing? To which my son replied . . . Taking a piss . . . And the officer grabbed him by the shoulder and said . . . What did you say you were doing? And my sonny who has no choice but to spritz the tips of the officer's patent leather shoes said . . . As you can see I'm taking a piss . . . And the officer shouted . . . I'm going to put you on report! And my sonny said . . . Go cry to your momma . . . After which the *Reichsbeauftragte* himself put my sonny on report but it was of no use since all the dispatchers who took the course were sent up to the Reich to work as dispatchers on the Görlitz–Breslau line . . . and so the incident on the second floor of the Hradec Králové station brought my sonny a certain amount of fame and when he completed all his tests when he was finally able to don that uniform with the insignia and the gold apprentice pin well that sonny of mine put on his uniform on Mánes Street in Hradec Králové and dressed in his beautiful uniform waltzed down the promenade barefoot and when I learned from the Nymburk stationmaster my sonny had the audacity to step out barefoot in his uniform well I knew right then and there he'd make something of himself . . . you watch darling that sonny of mine will amount to something yet . . . my hunch is because he's always off in his own mind somewhere he'll be a writer . . . not to mention the fact he always failed Czech language at school . . . Anyway my sonny worked as a telegraph man and then finally as a dispatcher I already mentioned that darling but what I didn't mention was the time my sonny took the test at Kostomlaty station the test that would allow him to serve unsupervised . . . so the gentleman who struck fear into the hearts of all stationmasters and dispatchers arrived at Hradec station . . . And Railway Inspector Chmelec asked my sonny . . . If the semaphore and switch boxes are out how do you know a train is approaching? And my sonny said . . . Visually . . . Correct and in case of fog? And my sonny all dressed up in his uniform pulled a white handkerchief from his pocket and placed it on the ground next to the tracks and then knelt down on one knee and put his ear to the track he listened for a while and when he stood up he told Inspector Chmelec Train number eight-o-four just passed through Kamenný Zboží . . . And an astonished Inspector Chmelec said . . . And what manual did you read that in? And my sonny said . . . I saw it in an American western Gary Cooper played a tracker . . . he used the technique to scout for Indians if they were coming on their mustangs or if a herd of buffalo was on the way . . . And Chmelec praised him for his initiative and told the commission my sonny would make a fine dispatcher on account of he took such pride in his uniform . . . And so my sonny made dispatcher and there never was a person more proud of his uniform and the more he prayed to keep that uniform for life the more mercilessly the Soviet army pushed back the Germans and my son was sad but happy at the same time because he rooted for the Soviet army and each day they got closer to the Czech lands was one day closer to victory one day closer to the universities reopening and then my sonny would have to relinquish that beautiful uniform which by the way darling he looked just smashing in . . . twice he was almost shot in that uniform first when the partisans blew up a munitions train near his station and then just before war's end when the partisans took out a section of rail the local SS commander nabbed my son and took him for a ride on a locomotive and it was only down by Ostré the commander let him go again . . . but my sonny was sad because he feared what would come when the last German was captured when the last German fell on the battlefield when all of Prague would celebrate the victorious Soviet army and the end of that horrible war . . . my sonny was sad because he knew he'd have to complete his studies and accept that law degree and that would be it for his splendid uniform and for his being a hero and for blaming it all on the Germans he'd have to start his life over again and differently . . . And do you know darling he was so in love with that uniform he served in it for two months after the war ended . . . they practically had to tear it off him and force him back to law school . . . And then my sonny went back to being a civilian and nothing ever did suit him finer than that dispatcher uniform . . . as a civilian my sonny was a rather ordinary fellow and so he didn't look back on the Protectorate as those who'd been imprisoned or those who'd lost relatives in battle or to the concentration camps . . . and that was his paradox . . . my sonny viewed the Protectorate through the prism of that uniform of his and when he recollected those days he lit right up . . . And if you asked him when was he happiest and if he had the chance to do it all over again what would he want to be? Without a moment's hesitation my sonny would tell you . . . A dispatcher . . .

■ □ ■ □ ■

CHAPTER THIRTEEN

My husband's past revisited him in installments Out of nowhere he suddenly perked up and shouted The arbor! The arbor! Darling an image just came to me of that arbor in Židenice wrapped in climbing ivy and tucked away in a back corner of Grandmother's garden . . . Grandmother had every sort of flower in her garden . . . and every Sunday we attended the big church mass . . . and Sundays during the holidays Grandmother brought lunch out to the arbor . . . the thing is darling I lived at Grandmother's until I was four years old and then for two months every year during the summer holidays even when I was at university Two summer months at Grandmother's and that arbor was like my chapel I read in there and Grandmother and I ate our lunches and dinners in there and during the holidays there was a tin plate adorned with strawberries and strawberry leaves . . . And right next door to our garden was the Turečeks' garden and it too was filled with flowers and below us was Mr. Musil's parcel and he had flowers galore and now I've got it! Now I know whose photograph that was hanging over the bench in the arbor! It was Wagner in his beret a profile of Wagner . . . So shouted my husband as he finished off a slice of buttered bread and the second installment to the story came as we were on the tram crossing the river on our way to cousin Milada's place my husband got this faraway look in his eye and just like that he was off and running again with memories of Židenice . . . Now I've finally got it! After all these years it's come to me! Darling the rear wall of our arbor bordered a property that stretched all the way up from Poděbrady Street and through this property wound a tree-lined path and four times a day the Stanovský stonemasons came and went along this path . . . Stanovský was their name! So shouted my husband inside the tram much to my embarrassment and I pretended he was not my husband at all that I had nothing to do with this person causing a commotion But my husband eagerly pressed on . . . Only now it's coming to me picture's as clear as day . . . Those Stanovský stonemasons came and went along that path four times a day up to their workshop by the cemetery and down to their house at the foot of the hill . . . And I'd hear their heavy boots and their voices but I never actually saw them because of where I sat near the back wall of the arbor And Grandmother told me once as we listened to those heavy footsteps pass by and fade away that the youngest Stanovský had tuberculosis from carving all those large stones him and his father and brother made into headstones So one time I decided to go up to the cemetery gate and have a look at the stonemason shop myself . . . its open front faced the cemetery presumably so people passing by who'd lost loved ones could look inside at the sample headstones . . . And darling I saw those stonemasons working in there cloths tied around their mouths and the headstones lay on sawhorses and the stonemasons wore aprons and work hats and they worked with hammers and chisels and one man chipped away at the raw stone and another chiseled the name into the smooth face of the headstone and another polished the face of the headstone and the workshop swirled with dust and it was open to the path that led to the cemetery and the workshop itself was housed inside what looked like a huge aviary a cage and I figured that was so no one could steal one of the unfinished headstones But later I realized the aviary with the thick wire mesh was there to protect passersby from flying shards of stone And day in and day out the Stanovskýs labored there carving headstones from first thing in the morning and at noon they went down the path to take their lunch and then back up again the sound of their work continued late into the evening and when Grandmother had the kitchen windows open the sound of their chisels and their tools and their hammer blows reached us inside . . . And darling now it's coming to me after all these years the whole picture's filling in again even with respect to the youngest Stanovský . . . I used to watch him because one of his eyes was sort of an opaque blue Grandmother told me he lost use of the eye from an accident at work and what's more he had this strange barklike cough that was always with him not just at work but even when he walked the path behind our arbor wall with his brother and father And that youngest Stanovský he had a girl and they were engaged to be married and she often sat on a chair in front of the workshop while her fiancé worked inside always coughing just a little bit and I often saw young Stanovský and his girl strolling quietly through the locust trees and they both seemed quite sad and when I said hello and Stanovský looked at me I saw his dead eye bluer than a forget-me-not or a periwinkle and it's only now I realize why the Stanovskýs never smiled why they were always sad . . . they made headstones and sold them to the bereaved and they shared in the sadness of the grieving family and after so many years even the way they spoke was sad and subdued sort of the way people speak when they're inside a church And in winter Grandmother wrote to me at the brewery to tell me the youngest Stanovský had succumbed to tuberculosis not even a year after his wedding . . . So my husband went on with the story but he wasn't telling it to me so much as he was telling it to the rest of the tram and a couple of old folks who wanted to get off several stops back stayed on board just so they could hear my husband go on about the Stanovský stonemasons . . .

We were to expand our flat into the adjoining room and on the day the landlord gave us the key Pepíček Sviatek came over daydreaming and smiling to himself and wearing that hat several sizes too big for his head and he squatted on a chair on a piece of newspaper and rocked back and forth on his heels . . . he brought a stone hammer and chisel along with him and my husband went into the adjacent room where he'd lived before he and Vladimir swapped flats and he opened the windows to air the place out it was much darker than our own flat because the window was in the shadow of the circular stair-case that led up to Mrs. Slavíčková's place And my husband made a fire and the cast-iron stove roared and I knew if we had another room to our flat there'd be three fires going in three stoves because fire was my husband's thing And so Pepíček Sviatek went up the ladder I'd rented and using his hammer started to loosen the bricks from the wall and that part of the wall had a frame around it because it was actually a walled-in doorway And soon the first brick came out and then my husband carried bricks outside and Pepíček Sviatek perched on the ladder engulfed in mortar and plaster dust and I sat on a chair in that kitchen of ours and looked out at the sliver of sky over the slanted shed roof and I was in a sulk because I kept pleading with my husband to change into some old clothes and barring that to at least change out of his clean white shirt But my husband was much too absorbed in what he was doing he emerged with a bucket of bricks and then plunged back into the clouds of crumbling plaster and mortar and only half of Pepíček Sviatek was visible there glowing in the clouds of dust and luckily the dust stayed in the room with the two men and my husband's footsteps echoed throughout the empty room and suddenly his voice rang out happily . . . Now it's come to me! The reason I'm partial to funerals . . . it's so obvious! There in Židenice the windows of Grandmother's house faced Balbínová Street and every day three and sometimes even four funeral processions went by! With music! And there the street was on a sharp incline and suddenly the cart carrying the coffin and the funeral wreaths was too much for the horses and they had to stop to rest practically right under our windows and I was always there to watch as a pallbearer chocked the wheels with a brick and right under our window was the coffin and all the mourners and immediate relatives contorted in tears and I could never understand why people when they lost someone were so wracked with tears and prone to such fits! And all through my childhood all through those twenty summer holidays there it was right under the windows an arm's length away I saw those black horses strain at the reins and the procession ascend the hill until it reached the first turn in the road where the wheels were chocked and the procession paused again before it made its way to the cemetery gates and passed the Stanovský shop where the three stonemasons stood with their caps doffed and paid their respects to the deceased as the procession passed through the cemetery gates and it's just now occurred to me! Standing there the Stanovskýs were also in effect advertising their own stonemasonry . . . you could buy a headstone for your loved ones right there at the cemetery gate . . . Come on over here darling come give us a hand my little dove with these buckets of plaster! And my husband stood there in the center of our new room and almost all the brick was cleared from the doorway now and my husband reached out his hand and he was covered in white dust from head to toe and he smiled at me but I was still ticked off with him and I turned away to stare out the window at the sliver of blue sky . . . Suddenly Vladimir appeared in the courtyard and as if to rub it in he was dressed in his Sunday best the clothes he'd worn in the May Day parade when he carried the state flag and my husband stood in the doorway to the adjoining room and begged me to come and give him a hand but I was thinking about how Vladimir had fallen for that awful girl from Slovakia how he'd given me the brush-off since he always pretended to have a bit of a crush on me and how dare he fall in love with that Tekla and because I was in a sulk over what happened between Vladimir and Tekla down there in Jirka's basement I got up and went into the new room just as Vladimir came in and he was left alone in our kitchen . . . And I grabbed a bucket and started filling it with plaster and Pepíček Sviatek carried out the ladder and loosened the last few bricks and then he squatted on his haunches next to the stove and gazed at the new doorway and then Vladimir joined us and he looked around and seemed surprised at what he saw and my husband put on an apron and fetched a bucket of water and as he began to wash down the doorframe he said happily . . . And now another picture's come to me! I remember how unhappy I was back then because nobody had died on me . . . the tears I shed over having no headstone of our own in Židenice cemetery! And so over the holidays for a crown a day I watered a certain grave and oh how I loved watering that grave! And I had a little rake to rake the sand around the grave just so . . . And the sexton paid me thirty crowns a month to water that grave! And then I sat there on a tombstone and listened to the women talk about their loved ones who passed away! So my husband shouted and he washed down the doorframe and Vladimir stood there taking it all in and then he said to me . . . You know what your husband should be? Madame that husband of yours now it's finally come to me he should have his own funeral parlor He certainly is inclined to it I'm sure it would suit him well . . . You know what would suit you Doctor? Running your own funeral business that's what And Doctor do you realize how good you'd be at selling coffins? Those quotations of yours would be perfect for that! Pepper your speech with quotes from the great poets and you'd be rolling in dough! So you're adding an extra room to your flat? Well won't that be something! And here's where the great writer will have his little desk and here's where the library will be! Just like Jirka Šmejkal! First he sets up his studio and then he stokes his little stove and leafs through his monographs and then it's off to see his friends to engage in lively conversation about Munch and Picasso But mainly Picasso because he's all the rage these days . . . trumped only by Vincent van Gogh lots of very thoughtful conversation about him even though his prints hang in every restaurant and no one even notices them anymore but wait just a minute! We mustn't forget . . . Bonjour Monsieur Gauguin! Bonjour . . . So said Vladimir testily but my husband only smiled and went on with great enthusiasm . . . Ach now I'm thinking clearly! Dearest Vladimir excellent of you to mention I should have my own funeral parlor! It's true I watched every single funeral procession out the window of our little house in Židenice But do you know why even my grandmother watched every single procession? You'll never guess because only now it's come to me after all these years it's finally dawned on me You see the horse dung dropped by the funeral horses belonged to the house it was closest to and after the procession made its way up the hill . . . if Grandmother was lucky enough to find horse dung in front of the house she'd scoop it up with a shovel and carry it off to the yard and there she saved it for her most beautiful flowers to make them blossom more beautifully make their scent that much sweeter . . . And Pepíček Sviatek rocked back and forth on his heels and smiled and smoked and he was covered with dust which settled lightly to the floor and my husband brought in a broom and with a theatrical flourish wrapped a wet rag around it and began to clean out the cobwebs in the corners and Vladimir stood in the middle of the room and then he took the bucket of mortar and plaster from me and said with a smile . . . Let me help you madame . . . and he waited for a second bucket and then he carried off those two heavy buckets like they were nothing like they were a couple of kiddie pails filled with sand . . . And I watched him through the window saw his legs were as straight as a young lady's except that he buckled at the knees a bit but that was probably because he was almost two meters tall . . . And then he ran down the steps and presently two thuds rang out from the buckets being emptied and then Vladimir came up the stairs again first his curly head appeared and then the rest of him like a swimmer coming up a ladder out of a pool . . . And my husband added wood to the stove and swept out the corners of the room and in between the windows and then he brightened at a memory . . . My grandpa the one who always went around with a flower in his lapel was someplace else every day . . . one night it was singing one night playing cards one night the firefighters' social and Saturdays and Sundays he was off hunting and on Sunday we went out to visit him and he played cards with the hunters . . . Grandpa used to walk me to school to first grade in Nymburk and both of us wore flowers in our lapels and Grandpa no matter what he was doing shining his shoes or ironing his clothes was always whistling to himself he was always in a good mood . . . my mother used to say her father had a restless streak and when he came down with his annual fever and was forced to stay home for one night it was just miserable for the whole family and everyone breathed a sigh of relief when he went back to work at Heinrich Pisco's on Bratislava Street cutting cloth made to order . . . So said my husband and he ran his wet rag around and rinsed it off again and then he went at the cobwebs which were stippled with moist plaster and mortar dust . . . And Vladimir smacked himself on the forehead and said . . . Look Doctor I just remembered one of my mother's old boyfriends left his housecoat over at her place You know what I'll bring it over for you and you can lounge around in it in your new flat . . . A shame you don't have any kids! You'd be a model daddy You'd look after the kids like no one else I can just see the kind of model pappy you'd make what do you have to say to that madame? It was obvious Vladimir was making fun of my husband but at the same time it struck me my husband would make a good father because he loved lecturing me just like he loved lecturing Vladimir and I was always beside myself with frustration because when we were together my husband lectured at me morning noon and night even when he was just recounting some story it was part and parcel of the ongoing tutelage and it just drove me mad because I never had an appropriate comeback to those stories of his . . . And now there was no holding him back he was oblivious to whatever Vladimir threw in his face to those insults and on he went with his lecture . . . And so one day my grandpa lay down and he simply never got up again . . . he died of hunger emaciated by cancer And a telegram came to Nymburk it was in the heat of May and Mom and Grandma were already in Židenice and the telegram came announcing Grandpa's death and so Dad and I drove out and by the time we got there it was already dark and we hammered on the neighbor's door and he gave us the key to the house and told us Mom and

Grandma had gone to Obřany to see Uncle Bob and so we unlocked the door and there on a board on the bed I was born in lay Grandpa dead and he was yellow and emaciated and he smelled sweet and my father lay down on the ottoman and I lay down next to my dead grandpa and I couldn't get to sleep I kept having to look at the body and the more I looked the more I knew this wasn't my grandpa this was a corpse and nothing more . . . And then it was time for the funeral and the same men from the funeral parlor who I always saw in the procession passing by our windows came to put Grandpa in a coffin and then the relations arrived there were hordes of relatives and they crowded into the room where Grandpa lay in a coffin and they wept and lamented and flung themselves at the body kissing it and I stood there and leaned against the coffin and then there was nothing you could do anymore they put the lid on the coffin and carried it out but they couldn't make the turn in the hallway on account of the stairs so they accidentally tipped Grandpa out of the coffin and like a collapsed puppet put him back in again and then we went out into the sunshine and I was assigned my place in the procession and then the music began to play and everyone was dressed in black and then we went up Balbínová Street and the procession and the cart bearing Grandpa's coffin came to a stop not just so the horses could rest but because we were in front of Grandpa's house and the band struck up Grandpa's beloved Moravia Moravia! and I stood there and looked up at the windows of the little house and now it was me who was torn up and wracked with sobs and I was struck how different it was to be in the actual funeral procession how different it was to be the kid standing there rather than the kid watching from the window And back then it hit me that the only real misfortune is the misfortune that visits *you* . . . Even the horse dung thudding to the ground from the giant hindquarters of the black funeral horses couldn't move Grandmother . . . she stood there wracked with sobs while normally she never passed up the opportunity to collect the horse dung from the funeral procession to make her flowers more beautiful . . . And then our procession turned the corner and the horses stopped at the cemetery gates and there in the stonemason workshop stood the two baldheaded Stanovskýs father and eldest son but I saw the younger brother too the one who died of tuberculosis and he doffed his hat and bowed his head and gave us his condolences and wouldn't you know it shortly after my grandmother paid a visit to the Stanovskýs and ordered a headstone which old Mr. Stanovský inscribed Tomáš Kilián . . . The irascible grandpa Tomáš Kilián was a hunter and way back when on that Sunday my mother came home to announce to her parents just before lunch she was in the family way Grandpa Tomáš dragged her out to the yard and rifle in hand yelled Now get down on your knees because I'm going to shoot you! And my grandmother my wise grandmother Kateřina came outside and said Come on in and eat before your food gets cold And so they went in to their lunch and thanks to my grandmother neither I nor my mother was shot . . . Look here Vladimir you said someone left a housecoat over at your place and that it'd look good on me and I could walk around and pretend to be the model daddy So Vladimir when are you going to bring me that housecoat? And Vladimir stuttered and apologized he said that rain was on the way he could feel the giant nail in his head that was an accurate gauge of barometric disruptions and now that the nail was piercing the roof of his mouth and through his lips mightn't it be better Doctor if we all went for a drink I should come along too as well as Pepíček Sviatek for today was Vladimir's payday and therefore we were all invited down to Mr. Vaništa's not to mention our new room was cause for celebration . . . My husband was in the middle of wiping the floor down with a wet rag and he said as if to himself . . . Dearest Vladimir sure we'll go have a drink but lately I've heard through the grapevine you like to indulge a bit too frequently and why beat around the bush dearest Vladimir you've got a drinking problem I'm not saying there's anything wrong with having a few beers fair enough you've got something to celebrate so you drink your ten beers but apparently you're celebrating every single day All right fine so you drink your ten beers a day like old man Nohejl And then maybe someone down at your shop is having a birthday and fair enough you put back fifteen beers and then maybe a big holiday rolls around so sure you have another ten beers But I'm begging you on my knees don't turn to the drink Don't keep up what you've been doing all year with the home brew and the hard liquor Look Vladimir let's be straight with each other Braque wrote it is noble to suppress one's urges . . . You think I'm lecturing you again but you must also consider your dear mother why do you insist on making her suffer so with your incorrigible drinking! Have a little dignity Suppress those urges of yours Even your friends complain to me about your drinking They say they wash their hands of you they say they're worried you'll get carted off to the drunk tank at Skála and those who are fondest of you say they're worried the drunk tank at Skála or the Apollinare detox ward might not be enough maybe it's straight to the Bohnice Asylum with you And now instead of setting an example you're leading us down the path to drinking to getting completely plastered And I don't mind saying Vladimir that hurts You mean to say you don't have an ounce of willpower to pull yourself out of that cursed passion for the drink? Take a look at me I was standing at the precipice but the strength of my will won the day Today I'm a different person and that rubs salt in your wounds Vladimir I implore you don't drag me down into the muck too come to your senses before it's too late! So said my husband and he took great care wiping down the dust with the wet rag he'd tied around the broom and now he unraveled the rag and dropped it in the bucket and rinsed it out and then as he knelt there he spread the rag on the floor and proceeded to wipe down the floor with excruciating thoroughness And Vladimir stood there looking around the room the color completely drained from his face and down on bended knees my husband went on . . . But you know who I feel really sorry for? You already carry enough shame around to last you a lifetime To you nothing is sacred anymore But again I beseech you to consider your dear little mother Give up the drink give it up I'm down on my knees begging you . . . And Vladimir threw back his head and let out a bloodcurdling scream and in two strides he was across the room and at the stove knocking Pepíček Sviatek off his chair along the way and before we could react he picked up that incredibly heavy stove which happened to have a fire going inside he picked it up with immense strength and shook it free of the stovepipe he picked up that kitchen stove like it was an empty five-liter bucket and the stovepipe knocked Pepíček Sviatek on the head and clattered to the floor and Vladimir ran out to the yard carrying that hot stove I barely managed to get out of his way and he plunked the stove right in the middle of the courtyard and dusted off his hands and then he ran down the steps and slammed the door to the street behind him and my husband went on wiping down the floor and humming to himself like nothing at all had happened and Pepíček Sviatek and I went out to the courtyard and I brought some old rags along and

when Pepíček and I tried to move that stove it wouldn't give an inch
And then my husband came out in his completely destroyed outfit it
was the last decent one he owned and the knees were soaked through
and his shoes were ruined but he was still humming to himself and so
Pepíček and I took one side of the stove while my husband took the
other and together we managed to get the stove to the doorway stopping to catch our breath about ten times along the way and although
Vladimir was already long gone he was still with us in spirit because
not even Pepíček Sviatek could comprehend how Vladimir had managed to run through one door into the hall and then a second door
into the courtyard so smoothly so effortlessly while carrying the
stove . . . we got stuck twice as we tried to negotiate our way through
the doorways we banged up against the walls and it was only when we
decided to slide that stove across the threshold that we barely managed to squeeze it through . . .

■ ▫ ■ ▫ ■

CHAPTER FOURTEEN

When I was on afternoon shift I liked to set off for work a little
early . . . I'd get all dressed up and grab my little parasol as usual
and go down to visit my husband at the paper salvage on Spálená
Street and as usual the minute I stepped into the passageway there I
felt like someone had slapped a cold compress on my back it was so
cold and drafty and there was my husband working away under the
bright glare of the bare bulbs and he always seemed quite proud of
the work he did baling books and papers and the finished paper bales
were lined up against the wall and the garage was littered with books
and out in the yard rose a giant pile of scrap paper and two cats kept
my husband company at the paper salvage and my husband drank
his pilsner beer all day long for nothing else could keep him as warm
certainly not tea . . . he drank his beer by the liter from a tin mug and
he had an earthenware stein too . . . and sometimes when I stopped
by they were loading a truck with paper bales and my husband liked
to show off how strong he was and together with the driver's mate
he tossed those bales into the back of the truck like they were nothing and my husband always sent me down to Husenský's with his
mug and his stein to get him his beer and the first time I went in
there the barmaid said to me coldly . . . That's the doctor's mug . . .
but I told her I was his wife and from then on the barmaids and the
pub owner always smiled at me and called me sweetheart . . . and I
was careful not to get run over crossing the street with those pitchers
full of beer at the Palace Diamant . . . and I passed Saint Tadeus and

the Church of the Holy Trinity where the parish wall was covered in thank-you notes and in the corner was a statue of Saint Tadeus and a kneeler . . . and one afternoon I caught my husband and Haňta there drunk and down on their knees praying and they had red stars pinned to their hats and to their overalls and as they prayed crowds of pedestrians streamed past and I stopped to overhear two elderly gentlemen watching those two kneeling men say with satisfaction . . . It's a good thing the Bolsheviks are finally crawling to the cross . . . and I continued past in my brand-new outfit and my little parasol pretending not to know my husband . . . it was only later at home that I said to him What sort of nonsense were you up to? And my husband laughed and said someone had accidentally dumped a bag of discarded police red star insignia at the paper salvage and he and Haňta had pinned those red stars to their caps and to their overalls and done up like that had made the rounds of the pubs and the secondhand bookstores where they sold the rare books that had been ditched at the paper salvage . . . and with a laugh my husband continued . . . and you should have seen it darling when Haňta tossed a handful of those red stars into the pissoir over on Charles Square . . . guys coming in and taking one look and running out again with their flies undone better to go piss in the bushes . . . that's how bad those red stars in the urinals shook them up . . . And every time I visited my husband down at the paper salvage he sent me to fetch him a pint of beer at Husenský's . . . and the barmaids called me sweetheart and said Say hello to the doctor! We're expecting him for lunch . . . And sometimes I accompanied my husband to lunch at Husenský's . . . we never ate in the pub but always in the narrow taproom with its row of little tables and two chairs each . . . and they really did know how to cook at Husenský's I just loved their pheasant or their partridge with red cabbage . . . and my husband liked to show off and horse around at Husenský's there was no place he was happier and the barmaids whenever they had the chance liked to give my husband's shoulder a little touch and the patrons in the taproom always called out to him but there was one lady who was especially fond of him she was a sort of hunchback and she always wore a hat with a bunch of cherries on it and my husband would engage her in these long conversations like he was in love with her and as always when my husband thought he was relating something truly exceptional he shouted at the top of his lungs and the hunchback lady shrieked with laughter and always managed to reciprocate as if she too were in love . . . and sometimes her husband was there as well a tall mustachioed gentleman who worked as a guard at the Pankrác prison and his role at Husenský's was to pretend to be jealous of his hunchback wife and these theatrics went on day in and day out at Husenský's and somehow my husband always managed to play his role a little differently And I'd just sit there and shake my head and roll my eyes and the barmaids would call me sweetheart and be in hysterics over the antics going on and then to top everything off Haňta would walk in and start drinking his shots . . .

My husband managed to tame a little pussycat over there on Spálená Street and she was so in love with him that when he squatted down and held out his apron he wore a big burlap apron at work she ran at him and leaped right into his apron and my husband nuzzled her and she closed her eyes and rubbed against him she was probably the reason my husband loved to work at the paper salvage she never left his side and when he went to Husenský's that pussycat stood there and stared into the passageway and the minute he appeared she ran for him and my husband held out his apron and in she leaped . . . It was practically a circus act . . .

There was always a grand time to be had with Mr. Haňta but I was getting a little sick of it . . . One day I went down to Husenský's before lunch to get my husband his beer and there sat Haňta in the taproom like he was sitting in a barber's chair and I could barely watch the way the whole taproom was making a fool of him . . . One of the patrons tipped a jar of mustard onto Haňta's bald head and then the patrons eating wieners at the bar took turns dunking those wieners in the mustard dripping down around Haňta's ears it was like they were dunking them right into Haňta's head and he just sat there with his hands on his knees and smiled and the whole taproom roared with laughter and the barmaids wept and squealed . . . Haňta was a magnet for people who liked to have a good time . . . My husband told me how Haňta had been carted off by the police once and tossed in the St. Apollinare detox ward . . . Haňta was throwing some in-house weddings of his own and around midnight decided to accompany his friends to the tram stop . . . and since it wasn't far to go all he wore was a tea towel but the wind blew up from the river navigation and whisked that tea towel away but it was only a hop skip and a jump to the tram stop so Haňta soldiered on covering his privates with his house keys . . . and at that very moment a paddy wagon rolled by the one that hauled off drunks and gypsies and muggers and they threw Haňta and his keys on board and off they went to Žižkov to round up more drunks and it wasn't until the afternoon of the next day that Haňta showed up at work still stunned at the beautiful events that had caught him up . . . And every time I stopped by to meet my husband this same Haňta the one everyone liked to make fun of would tell me some story I simply couldn't get out of my head . . . Most recently through an awful bout of hiccups and while leaning up against the wall to keep from falling down Haňta told me . . . Madame you're an educated woman surely you're familiar with the Nuremburg laws on the purity of the German race . . . You know what I'm thinking of now that I see you here . . . Nuremburg! I'm thinking about that infernal boy King Vaclav IV . . . madame there was a piece of work! At home he drank his way through his Cheb and Loket landholdings . . . but guess with who . . . his masseuse Susanna! But that wasn't nearly enough . . . So on his way to France he and the royal entourage decided to stop off in Nuremburg for a little picnic . . . and the booze flowed for days and the little picnic turned into a debauchery! There in Nuremburg the king of Bohemia drank through not just his cash but his crown as well . . . he had to pawn it . . . And who lent him the money so he could continue on to France with his crown intact? The Nassau bankers that's who . . . they had dough! And in Nuremburg . . . And madame it is in his honor that I drink through my paycheck today . . . Vaclav IV was a king of kings a world number one and champion of the covered courts a jolly good fellow . . . much like your husband and myself . . . Presidents and kings and sheikhs the world over should take him as an example . . . because after you drink through everything you have there's nothing left for war . . . and peace reigns eternal . . . drink through or pawn off all the state treasuries and treasures all the orders and all the medals and all the crown jewels . . . And who's going to lend you money today? There are no more Nassau bankers from Nuremburg or Fugger families from Augsburg or Rothschilds from Vienna and Berlin . . . madame in honor of that infernal boy Vaclav IV I'm off to drink through my paycheck . . . with Susanna the barmaid no less . . . And I stood there and I had to turn my head away because Mr. Haňta's breath stank so horribly of liquor and beer but at the same time I was rooted to the spot because Mr. Haňta in the depths of his drunkenness was always very eloquent it never failed to surprise me and now Mr. Haňta groped his way along the wall and out into the passageway I saw his silhouette and now his figure lighted in the sun out on Spálená Street and then he lurched off to the left toward Saint Tadeus and Husenský's . . . And I stood there in the cold passageway holding that mug of beer and suddenly I had such a thirst from listening to Mr. Haňta I took a drink and then another and another . . . the beer was beautifully tempered and needless to say back out to Spálená Street I went for more . . . that king of Bohemia certainly had it right . . .

Sometimes when I arrived to pick up my husband he was already done with his shift and in the shower and then his boss Mr. Slezák who was always very courteous would offer me a chair while I waited . . . And then my squeaky-clean husband and I waltzed down Spálená Street and we always went straight to Pinkas . . . and first things first my husband ordered us two beers in the taproom and we drank them down and only then did we go into the pub proper where they brought us a few more beers and after four pints my husband got what he called a savage hunger and the only thing he ever ordered was pork roast and potato dumplings sprinkled with onions and the gravy was always caramel-colored and once a week when I went with my husband I too had the pork roast and potato dumplings and truly there was no better pork roast in town . . . according to my husband one lady had been making this Pinkas specialty of the house for the past twenty years . . . this pork roast with sauerkraut and potato dumplings sprinkled with fried onions . . . And my husband lived in mortal fear of the day that elderly lady might pass away . . .

When we had a little time to ourselves my husband and I liked to go to the movies . . . during the first two years of our marriage the only movie we ever went to see was *Gold Rush* . . . I have to admit I came to enjoy seeing the same movie over and over . . . *Gold Rush* . . . even though we'd seen *Gold Rush* more than twenty times my husband never failed to tear up when the Georgia character appeared onscreen and the more she appeared the more he cried until he didn't even bother to wipe away the tears he just wept openly and people in the theater turned to look at my husband and then at me with pity . . . My husband loved Chaplin because at the beginning of every film he was just a poor little tramp like the types my husband met in the pubs of Libeň and Vysočany . . . and when all was said and done my husband took himself for the same little tramp as Chaplin . . . whose capacity to make a fool of himself actually made a fool of his rivals and thus Chaplin was number one and my husband glowed with pleasure because he too fancied himself a potential number one . . . So my husband and I went to the Čásek Theater in Libeň the tiny movie house beside the variety store they still called Kulík's Place . . . and I too cried while watching Charlie's comedies . . .

■ □ ■ □ ■

CHAPTER FIFTEEN

My husband never took his vacation all in one stretch he liked to take
it by the day He loved to savor every part of his day off morning noon
and afternoon In Nymburk he managed to weed his whole garden on
a day off plus make the rounds of all his favorite pubs and restaurants
In Prague a day like that was no small thing and my husband always
planned his little holiday to correspond with sunshine and he dressed
up in his Sunday best because when the sun shone down on Prague it
was something to behold My husband booked his days off when the
weather forecast said nice weather was on the way And so while everyone else was at work my husband's movable feast began . . . My husband was so intimately familiar with those pubs of his he knew which
one had the best morning sunshine and which one had the best afternoon sunshine take Horký's Pub for example where the sun shone in
from eight in the morning and the place was always full first thing not
just for the great beer but for the morning soups and the goulashes as
well . . . And just before noon at Horký's Pub the sun slipped over the
roof and by one o'clock it shone into the courtyard and into the gentleman's washroom and by two o'clock the sun peeked through the
courtyard window and the pub that was in shade over noon was once
again bathed in sunlight . . . But my husband couldn't stay put in one
pub he'd have one beer and then be on his way again chasing the
sun . . . Klouček's pub had the finest afternoon sunshine the whole
taproom glowed in the light and my husband relished the radiant
sunshine as it lit up the joint and glittered off the nickel-plated taps

off that throne of beer and my husband sat in the taproom in the sunshine decked out in his Sunday best and it was like being in church for him like attending a big mass and the bartenders there in the sunshine were like priests in their ceremonial vestments and my husband thought this must be what heaven is like with all of its hierarchy the waiters as the little angels and the bartender as the Archangel Gabriel and the angels serve up the beautiful beer but it's not beer it's the holy Eucharist and the pub owner in his white smock overseeing the quality of the food and the cut of the beer is Saint Peter and my husband and all of the other patrons drinking their beer bathed in sunlight are true believers a gathering of the blessed that no longer cares about hell or purgatory these people sitting here with their golden glasses of beer have made the finals they're the chosen few the Lord's flock and all of them accept the body and the blood of Christ in the form of this wondrous beer and creamy foam . . . That's why my husband only needed to take one day off at a time because for that one day he was in paradise . . . Mornings my husband liked to go to Vaništa's it was flooded with sunlight first thing and Mr. Vaništa in his white vestments poured those heavenly pints of Smíchov draft and from across the hallway from a kitchen bathed in morning sun came his wife Boženka with heavenly plates of steaming goulash and tripe soup with paprika and plates of pickled herring . . . And so my husband turned a workday into a holiday he knew just how to pick a day with sunshine and he sat in his pubs and he just couldn't get enough of those taprooms bathed in sunlight he alone knew they were heaven on earth in Libeň He sat there and paced himself took little sips of beer to keep from getting drunk before noon he had to make the drink last until afternoon when the sun quit Mr. Vaništa's taps and slipped somewhere behind Palmovka . . . And so my husband would move on to Lyška's where he liked to sit in the taproom and look out the window at the sun and at the Rokytka River and as soon as the sun withdrew from Lyška's he was off to The Old Post Office for a quick little pint because the pub was wedged in between two tall buildings and only received a couple of hours of sunlight before the sun slipped away over the rooftops . . . One day was not enough for my husband to make all his heavenly rounds . . . But my husband was in no hurry he knew another beautiful sunny day would come and he would take up where he left off . . . Another mini-holiday was kicked off at Ferkel's pub where early-morning sunshine streamed into the taproom through a huge café-style window and at Ferkel's my husband's usual was a half-pint and he just couldn't get enough of this gleaming altar of beer and of Mr. Ferkel who despite his prosthetic arm managed those taps as deftly as if he had two good arms . . . And Ferkel's had a garden and when the weather was fine you could enjoy your beer outside at a nice little table with a checkered tablecloth and Ferkel's was also home to Prague's smallest theater you got to it through the garden and it was as tiny as a dining car on a train and you could watch films here catch the latest blockbusters and anytime you liked you could sneak off through a back door to the taproom for a beer and it didn't even have to be intermission . . . Sometimes on his days off my husband only visited garden restaurants he loved a pub that had a little garden and maybe a few tables . . . like they had at Strasburg . . . but by far and away his favorite place on his garden restaurant days was The Old Contrabass . . . The Old Contrabass bewitched my husband with its garden restaurant beneath the giant old trees and its outdoor terrace that resembled the foredeck of a holiday steamer and trams ran past its wrought-iron railings on their way up to Bulovka or down to the Electric Works and just up the street from the Contrabass was a large intersection with tram islands right across from which was the Beggar's Pub . . . my husband had never been to the Beggar not that he forgot it was there but during his first few years in Libeň he somehow never got around to it and so that pub remained a mystery to my husband although he talked about wanting to go there all the time even in his sleep if only to see what the garden restaurant at The Old Contrabass looked like through the windows of the Beggar's Pub . . . and although he'd stood poised on the threshold of the Beggar's Pub on numerous occasions he never could find the strength to go inside as he said for just a little while just to take a peek and have a half-pint in the taproom just to take a gander out the window to see what The Old Contrabass looked like from across the street And so my husband would sit at the closest table to the wrought-iron railing and he always turned his chair around and rested his chin on the backrest and then he stared in wonder like a little kid at the trams ascending from the direction of Libuše's Pub and The Green Tree and then he'd lean out across the railing to watch the trams descend from the direction of The Charles IV and make their way down toward the turn in the road where the green façade of The Green Tree Pub glittered in the sun and my husband hoped against hope that history might repeat itself that another tram might lose its brakes before the turn and crash through the taproom of The Green Tree coming to rest just inches from the taps . . . And so my husband sat in the sunshine and listened to the click-clack of the barmaid's heels as she carried the beer into the sun from the depths of the pub and my husband never went into the taproom of The Old Contrabass because that was his garden restaurant and just like he never went into The Old Contrabass taproom he never went into the taproom at The Beggar . . . he had no reason to because there were so many beautiful things to see in those fleeting morning hours the trams and the cars and the pedestrians and the shops and the build-ings and the façade of The Charles IV and the crowns of the giant old trees overhead and the rustling of their leaves and my husband lik-ened all of this to impressionistic paintings and particularly the paint-ings of Utrillo who according to my husband had such a knack for painting those walls in Montparnasse that all you wanted to do if you beheld one of those Utrillo walls was whip out your wiener and in deep reverie piss all over the wall in honor of Utrillo . . . And so my husband sat there listening to the click-clack of the barmaid's heels he always turned his chair around so he could sit with his arms folded over the backrest and his chin resting on his arms all the better to see the beauty of the neighborhood unfold around him . . . And once he got his fill he strolled down the hill sometimes to stop off at Restau-rant Libuše whose windows faced directly south . . . but my husband wasn't a big fan of restaurants he preferred his pubs . . . and bathed in sunlight at Libuše's he drank his beer and he liked to stand at the bar and watch the water stream from the faucet into the pewter sink . . . and that stream of water rushing endlessly into the pewter sink was carried away by nickel-plated pipes . . . and the barkeep rinsed out the parade of glasses brought over by the waiter and he held each glass up to the sunlight pouring through the arched windows and squinted at it and when he was certain it was clean he drew another pint . . . and my husband loitered at Libuše's and sipped his half-pint . . . while the barkeep rinsed a glass in the pewter sink and drew a third and held it up to the sunlight to make sure the color and the quality and the kick of the beer was still up to par . . . and he stood there like he was blessing the whole joint and my husband might have dropped to his knees if as he said he had the guts because right then the barkeep was as serious as a priest raising the holy Eucharist from the chalice and blessing the worshippers who knelt before him to accept the host as the body and blood of Christ . . . but no one else seemed to see this and my husband looked around the restaurant at the lunch crowd reading their papers or studying their menus or smoking their cigarettes in deep reverie and inside the sunlit pub the smoke rose to the ceiling and gleamed in the morning light like smoke rising from a censer during morning mass . . . and with the glass up to the light the barkeep brought it to his lips and took a little drink . . . and he considered a moment and then nodded his approval and the heavens were appeased and the beer was good and then the barkeep rinsed the glass in the pewter sink where the water gushed from the faucet and then he went on drawing those pints just the way people liked them . . . into pint glasses or old-fashioned half-liter steins . . . And on his days off my husband also liked to visit Jeřábek's over the noon hour . . . the restaurant was inside an art nouveau–style building and you entered through an arched wrought-iron gate adorned with wrought-iron palm leaves and flowers intertwined with the crescent-shaped words GARDEN RESTAURANT . . . And my husband liked to start off with a half-pint here and this was the only restaurant he truly loved because everything was original from the art nouveau sign in the entrance to the walls garlanded with plaster decorations and palm leaves to the two lithe nude women set among little purple tiles and inside the taproom stood a tall art nouveau credenza with sliding glass doors etched with palm leaves and tropical flowers and inside the credenza were antique glasses belonging to regulars from bygone days glasses adorned with leaded lids and glasses decorated with hand-painted violets and marigolds and glasses depicting scenes of poachers and hunters and of girls in dirndls and Tyrolean hats . . . and an old woman worked the taps here and took the lunch orders and she wore old-fashioned clothes and kept her hair pinned up in a giant bun . . . it was Mrs. Jeřábková who lived here on the first floor with her husband and who owned this building and this establishment which was still decked out with Thonet bentwood chairs and round café tables . . . and before my husband sat down on the Thonet chair he picked it up and inspected it and Mrs. Jeřábková watched how amazed he was by this finely crafted chair . . . and he raised his glass and looked into the old woman's eyes and she smiled and shrugged and sighed deeply . . . as if to say what can you do . . . And then my husband took his beer out to the garden . . . and he strolled through that garden restaurant which was all original right down to the little gazebo with the dilapidated roof . . . and inside the gazebo where the music once played were stacks of old chairs and broken tables the original tables and chairs weather-beaten and worn down with age and now they lay here as my husband said thrown together as if in a mass grave and what pray tell did they dream of? Who had once sat in these chairs and what young lady had rested her elbows atop the white tablecloths? And who had danced here and to what sort of band? And what sort of garden parties had taken place and what sort of raffles and what sort of Saturday nights and Sunday afternoons . . . And my husband stood here and looked very much like when he went up to the cemetery in Koráb to pay his respects graveside to Hlaváček the writer and to Müller the hockey player who was buried over by the cemetery wall . . . Müller our greatest hockey player after the war who'd died of injuries sustained during a game in Germany . . . and now he rested there a broken hockey stick on his headstone . . . and with the same air of sadness my husband stood inside that garden restaurant which had managed to preserve just a touch of art nouveau on the walls and in the furnishings just a touch of *Jugendstil* . . . and of course there was Mrs. Jeřábková who'd lived here as a starry-eyed young lady back in the *Jugendstil* period . . . On the days my husband made the rounds of the garden restaurants he liked to follow the Rokytka River over to Vysočany to the Slavic Linden restaurant he liked to get there around nine o'clock in the morning and go straight through the hallway and into the garden beneath the old chestnut trees where he sat at the table closest to the courtyard . . . and the tablecloths at the Slavic Linden were so blindingly white they hurt your eyes and my husband ordered his pilsner and the waiter brought it out into the strong sunlight and then my husband always looked across the courtyard to the portico on the second floor where Mr. Brabec lived the former owner of the Slavic Linden and current part-time bartender . . . and when it was nice weather you could catch the elderly gentleman out on the portico at around nine-thirty taking his time and getting ready for his shift at ten . . . and next to the portico wall stood a floor-to-ceiling wooden statue of John of Nepomuk . . . and on the wall opposite Saint John's statue stood a large mirror before which Mr. Brabec brushed his pomaded hair and he wore black pants and a white shirt and a black bow tie that was exactly the same size as his mustache and Mr. Brabec was small and portly and had a beer belly of which he was quite proud . . . and as a finishing touch Mr. Brabec put on his French piqué . . . and then he walked toward the mirror and inspected himself to make sure everything was impeccable and right before ten o'clock rolled around Mr. Brabec worked his shoulders to make sure his French piqué settled perfectly and then it was time for the final check and he stood before the mirror to look at himself to turn to the right and to the left to lick a finger and run it over each eyebrow to smooth down his mustache and then he smiled at himself and backed away until he was lost in the depths of the mirror and my husband didn't miss a thing because he came to the Slavic Linden after all just to watch the old guard Mr. Brabec prepare for his ten o'clock shift behind the taps . . . and there in the light reflected off the taps Mr. Brabec dressed in his French piqué drew his perfect pints with the same ritual deliberation of one conducting midnight mass . . . of one conducting Christmas Day Mass . . . or the Mass of the Resurrection . . . And when Mr. Brabec was transferred over to Brázda's Pub my husband didn't follow he continued to frequent the Slavic Linden and to gaze over his first pint at that statue of John of Nepomuk at that empty mirror . . . but that mirror wasn't really empty because my husband said he could still see Mr. Brabec in his French piqué taking one last look at himself to make sure he was in perfect trim before coming downstairs . . . But my husband was the sort who attracted not just strange people to himself but strange events as well . . . he kept up with the Slavic Linden not just because of Mr. Brabec who was and wasn't there but because of another patron a gentleman who was somewhat younger than my husband . . . and this gentleman always wore a blindingly white shirt underneath which my husband always said he stashed an entire beer keg . . . but it wasn't a beer keg at all it was his stomach swelled out on account of an inoperable tumor and so the man drank beer nothing but pilsner beer with a salted roll to go along and he said the Slavic Linden was a good place to make peace with one's maker and he spent his days there and in fact even had his mail forwarded . . . and he said with a laugh . . . it might be best if they rolled a cot into the Slavic Linden for him so he could spend the night since he just couldn't wait for the place to open up every day at eight in the morning . . . and so mornings my husband went to the Slavic Linden made his rounds of the garden restaurants and he was always fascinated by the man in the white shirt who sat there in the sunshine drinking his beer and nursing that huge tumor under his shirt . . . and each time my husband came back from the Slavic Linden he reported the man was still alive . . . until one evening he said . . . He came to say good-bye and to tell me that tomorrow he was going to die . . . My husband when he indulged in his Prague days off never ate much . . . but he liked to take a pickled fish and hold it up by the tail and toss it back like a sword swallower . . . and he liked to say when there's drink to be had you must limit the eating . . . and that treasure of mine was partial to nibbling on something in addition to the pickled fish . . . Nearby Jeřábek's Restaurant was Libeň's only horse butcher . . . and my husband liked to stop there on his way back from Jeřábek's to pick up a hundred and fifty grams of horsemeat sausage . . . and then he waltzed up Primátorská Street eating that horsemeat sausage without bread . . . And as his last stop on those days off my husband always ducked into the Tavern on the Corner on Žertvy . . . The Tavern on the Corner was bathed in sunlight all day long . . . it was a strange-looking pub on a corner sort of wedge-shaped and the barkeep drew his pints and gazed out the door at the brush-covered railroad tracks across the street and both the barkeep and my husband were on tenterhooks for the moment the freight or local passed by on its way from Vysočany to Libeň Station . . . that was a big moment for the barkeep and my husband . . . and the whole pub shook with the approach of a heavy freight . . . but for my husband the tremendous shaking couldn't hold a candle to the beauty of the machines themselves old steam engines which ran on coal and billowed thick clouds of smoke and as the freights passed by particularly the ones ascending the grade from Libeň to Vysočany they had to make extra steam . . . and clouds of smoke so thick billowed everywhere that pedestrians were forced to stop and wait for the smoke and steam to clear . . . and through the open doors the smoke slipped into the pub but this was the kind of pub where no one noticed what was going on around them there was always so much smoke and so many drunks that even the smoke and steam sliding through the open doors into the Tavern on the Corner caused barely a ripple among the patrons because this place was always filled with a wall of cigarette smoke . . . anyone coming in had to practically squat to see who they were looking for under that cloud of smoke . . . And when the smoke coming into the pub off the street was so thick my husband could see neither the barkeep nor the street outside . . . he liked to imagine it was akin to the Oracle of Delphi and the frenzied screech of the oracular seeresses as they sat in smoke and prophesied the fate of kingdoms . . . And in about fifteen minutes the air cleared up and the sun shone in again and my husband and the barkeep were on tenterhooks for the next freight train to roll by . . . And at the end of one of these days off my husband would come home thoroughly wretched . . . but I was used to it already . . . he walked up Na Hrázi Street dragging his jacket by the sleeve the picture of misery . . . but he was awestruck and astonished and he sat on his chair and closed his eyes and smiled to himself and relived everything that had happened on his one-day vacation . . . Why write he said . . . when what I lived through today was a whole novel . . . the ordinary life's enough for me . . . because I don't want war and I don't want to conquer anyone I wish a one-day vacation would be enough for everyone to have their own moment of revelation . . . darling I'm not interested in any more beautiful tragedies . . . the ones foisted on me from the outside are more than enough . . . I want the world to stay at least the way it is right now because darling I'm afraid of that great and much-celebrated future . . . I wish the spring could last forever . . . as Mahler wrote . . . I truly wish the world could stay where it is . . . enough already . . . I wish it was according to Mahler . . . the world stays in the here and now . . . And so my husband blathered on the same man who moments ago strode up Na Hrázi Street in a cloud of beer ready to bowl over anyone in his way and as was his wont he walked up the middle of the street to the sound of cars honking behind him . . . and people jumped out of his way and on he strode all lit up like that gas lamp in front of our building . . .

■ □ ■ □ ■

CHAPTER SIXTEEN

I never dreamed the past could be so alive and so painful . . . I stood before the sealed door of my old flat in Pieštany where I'd lived with my parents and my sister and my little brother until my father signed over everything he owned to the state and left for Germany with my mother . . . after that it was just me and my little brother Heini for about a year until the International Red Cross came and took Heini away and then I lived there alone for a while until I fell in love and that jewel of mine Jirka moved in . . . Jirka who'd cast a spell over me with that guitar of his I'd always been a sucker for the guitar and looked on anyone who could play as on a god and so Jirka and I lived there together and we loved each other and had plans to be married and we swam up at the reservoir and went out with our friends and Jirka was my fiancé and we looked beautiful together even though Jirka was a bit of a rogue but that was part and parcel of his calling since anyone who played in a band like Jirka was liable to be the subject of admiration particularly from those women those little sluts who liked to sit in the front row and make eyes at him and Jirka gave as good as he got for he was a professional pianist and a guitarist to boot . . . And as per our agreement my husband arrived in Pieštany with his brother Břeťa at ten o'clock in the morning but since I was unable to get into the flat before my husband's arrival because the flat was sealed I didn't have time to erase all signs of my previous life with Jirka and so the three of us stood there on the second floor and the clerk from the town office unsealed the flat and I unlocked the door and the curtains were drawn and I opened up a window to clear out the stale air it had been more than two years after all and the clerk asked I drop off the keys when we were finished and then he took off rather quickly and much to my dismay I saw why . . . the whole place looked as if it had been ransacked by thieves looking for money stuff was tossed everywhere and Břeťa and my husband who'd left a day early to visit friends in the Moravian countryside were still drunk and my husband looked terrible I could see he'd gotten completely smashed the night before he looked like Haňta unshaven and yolky-colored around the lips like he'd been eating hard-boiled eggs and he stank to high heaven of slivovitz and both he and Břeťa were running on no sleep and they sat down collapsed is more like it and panted and closed their eyes both of them had the hiccups and I was actually glad my husband was drunk because it gave me time to take the framed photographs down off the walls and tuck them away in the laundry basket . . . photographs of me in my bathing suit lying next to Jirka photographs of Jirka looking dapper in his blue tuxedo playing his guitar beautiful photographs of Jirka who'd looked so great it just cut me to the quick how everything had ended and I didn't look so bad myself lying there on the beach at the reservoir stretched out in the sunshine in my bathing suit I couldn't believe how good I'd looked what a beautiful figure I'd had and mainly how happy I'd looked in every photograph it was obvious from my whole demeanor I was in love And now the two drunks managed to get to their feet and to move what I told them to move and though Břeťa had a limp he was still fleeter of foot than my husband who seemed to have aged by about twenty years or more because of what he'd glimpsed in those photographs on the wall and my husband had that jealous look in his eye and he was obviously more floored by those sunlit photographs of me back in the day than he was by the slivovitz and so he put the laundry basket with the photographs in it off to one side under the large mirror that stretched across the entire wall the mirror that reflected the whole ugly room the homicide-like scene . . . I wanted to leave that mirror behind but my husband insisted we take it he considered it the only appropriate wedding present and I looked into that mirror while the two of them moved out the wardrobes and the chairs and clomped wearily up and down the stairs in the heat and every time my husband came back into the room he looked into the mirror and what he saw there I now saw as well . . . it was me looking into the mirror for the last time swallowing a handful of pills and collapsing onto Papa's custom-made sofa . . . That was the last time I'd looked into the mirror that stretched across the whole wall and it was my friends from Piešťany who had found me and now the same couple was here to help me move and mainly to help me with Papa's Empire chiffonier which they had back at their place And the first thing my friends did when they came in was look at the couch they'd found me on was look in the mirror they'd looked in when they picked me up off that couch And both my friends were dumbstruck when I introduced them to my husband and they looked at me as if to say you still had plenty of time to find yourself a husband like this And my husband was sweaty and all covered with dust from carrying furniture he looked simply awful while I of course was dressed the way I'd always dressed in Piešťany I wore my red high heels and my best outfit and I was freshly coiffed and my husband and I couldn't have looked more different . . . and to top it off he appeared on the verge of tears somehow what he'd seen there in my flat had knocked the wind out of him . . . and his brother Břeťa had also recognized instantly that my past was still there that I'd failed to get rid of it in time and he held it against me just like my two friends who were glad they could give me a hand and never have to see me again held it against me and so around noon most of the furniture including the two giant couches and the larch-wood kitchen cabinetry was loaded onto the back of the truck and then the only thing left in the empty flat was the mirror and under it the laundry basket with the photographs inside which my husband had covered over with a sheet . . . And then my friends went to get a screwdriver and for the next hour the men took turns trying to loosen the three-meter-long mirror from the wall but my husband gave up he showed everyone those stubby fingers of his worked to the bone at the paper salvage and so my husband hefted that past of mine that laundry basket with the photographs inside and down the stairs he went and then he just couldn't hold back anymore he sat there on the step and went through one photograph after the other and then he went through them again and again and I was the one who had to climb onto the back of the truck and help Břeťa position the couches so we could lay that giant mirror down on one and cover it up with the other like a couple slices of buttered bread and when my friends carried the mirror down the stairs when they'd placed it carefully just where Břeťa wanted my husband got up and he held the laundry basket with the framed photographs inside and somehow he sobered up somehow looking through those photographs of mine helped him come to terms with it and he smiled and tried to catch my eye and then when he looked at me I saw he understood everything that he'd suffered and descended to the very depths of his jealousy and that he forgave me for leaving that flat untouched exactly as I'd abandoned it and in fact he was grateful for the chance to see into my past . . . My husband handed the laundry basket up to Břeťa in back of the truck and Břeťa wedged it under a couch and then we tossed him up the ropes and he lashed them down and tied them off at one end while my husband looped the other end around the bumper and my friends backed away making hand gestures like we should follow them over to their place if I wanted to collect my black Empire chiffonier And I went to lock up my empty flat and my footsteps echoed throughout and I shut the window and took a last look around convinced I should have followed my first instinct . . . douse the place in gasoline and watch my past go up in flames . . . And then at my friends' place we strapped that beautiful Empire chiffonier to the back of the truck and it was obvious my friends had hoped I'd leave them the chiffonier because before they brought it down they tried to convince me it was practically coming apart at the seams that they were doing me a favor keeping it at their place . . . But I stuck to my guns because it was the only beautiful thing left to me as proof of how we'd once lived and the only fine piece of furniture I had to remind me of Papa . . . And Břeťa strapped the Empire chiffonier to the tailgate of the truck and the way it hung back there reminded me of when the Russians rolled in with rabbit hutches of feverish little German rabbits strapped to their trucks and I thanked my friends who'd grown sullen and distant the minute I insisted the chiffonier was coming with me and now in frustration they sniped at each other that it was time for lunch and they barely waved good-bye as we climbed into the truck and set off for home And I sat in the middle and my husband pulled away from me in the grips of another bout of jealousy and melancholy and every so often he ran a hand over his face and pulled even further away from me and that internal struggle of his continued and I knew full well there was nothing I could do about it because you just can't turn back the clock to the way things were and I watched the road go by outside and then it started to drizzle and my husband and I looked at each other and he said quietly Where's the tarp? And about half an hour later Břeťa jerked his thumb to the rear and replied The tarp's on the bottom the tarp's underneath all the other stuff . . . And the windshield wipers went back and forth in the rain and somehow the rain lifted the somber mood in fact I wanted the rain to turn torrential I wanted it to rain buckets and for everything in back to be in ruins by the time we got home I was glad the rain would drench and obliterate those photographs and seep in behind the glass frames and wash away the dust from the furniture and streams of dirty water would go trailing off the back of the truck and even we would arrive home to Na Hrázi Street in Libeň washed as clean as that furniture as clean as that past of mine Perhaps the rain and the break in the humidity lightened the mood in the cab of the truck and Břeťa rolled down his window and breathed in the fresh air and around us the land was shrouded in mist and light fog And the state road passed through forests and villages and towns and twice along the way we stopped for gas and I hopped out at one of the petrol stations and went over to the butcher shop a chalk sign out front read TODAY'S SPECIAL HOT MEATLOAF And I bought a kilo of meatloaf and ten bread rolls and then we stood there and ate the meatloaf hungrily without a word and around us a light rain fell and steam rose off the fields and the forests and off the warm meatloaf and we ate our bread rolls and meatloaf with great relish glad we could eat and not have to make conversation because even Břeťa was rattled by that past of mine by what he'd seen there in the old flat and every so often he too ran a hand over his face glad he wasn't in his brother's shoes and glad he could concentrate on the drive grateful for the rain which required him to drive more carefully and thus to adhere strictly to the rules of the road a good thing because the last thing he needed was to get pulled over by the police for a breathalyzer And my husband cleared his throat a few times and was off on one of his stories . . . Finally I understand a little of what made me tick! My friends were always boys who were worse off than I Why was it that my friends were always the guys failing grades the guys who were a little soft in the head? Now I finally get it! Because to them and to myself I was a number one! I fed the guys who didn't have any food at

131

home like I did And the guys who didn't have any heat at home I'd sit them down in our kitchen to get warm and I'd show off not just as a do-gooder but as the sonny of the brewery foreman And I'd fry them up ten eggs with buttered bread on the side and force them to eat it which they did and then they threw up and felt even worse than before . . . I also tried to teach them stamp collecting how to paste stamps into an album I bought albums for them but I didn't really know how to do it myself and we pasted gum arabic all over the stamps till they were sort of glassed-in and preserved under a layer of the stuff and these fifth-grade dropouts fellows who were sort of half-wits were in awe of my stamp-pasting skills and when I forced them to try it for themselves they got gum arabic all over their hands and the table and on their clothes and in their hair and I was the one who taught them how to do it who tutored the guys dumber and unhappier and uglier than me because I couldn't stand being in the company of someone smarter or better looking than I was In short I always befriended the guys who made me look better You can probably imagine me as a student nothing but B's and C's and even D's for conduct going around with holes in my clothing and in my socks . . . So said my husband and outside it grew dark and the drizzle still came down and once in a while the windshield wiper on my husband's side just sort of gave up and he had to reach out the window and give it a hand and even this little thing was a welcome distraction from dwelling on that past of mine . . . I had hoped to put some distance between myself and all that but to no avail there it was in back of the truck riding along with us and the closer we got to Libeň the more I realized there'd be no shying away . . . And so we stopped twice more to walk around the truck and to check the load but the rain had lashed the ropes down so tightly it wasn't going anywhere and the rain the constant light drizzle washed everything in back of the truck clean even those two giant sofas looked like they'd just come back from the cleaners and we each stepped off into the forest for a moment and then we climbed back into the truck and got going again and my husband took up his story . . . So what happened is that Famfík Schaniel who was a year younger than me started coming round the brewery with his mother . . . They came to visit the brewery manager a man named Sklenář . . . That Famfík was always decked out in a sailor's scarf . . . and a beautiful sailor's cap with blue ribbons . . . He looked like some American kid from a Chaplin comedy the kind of kid who'd punch you in the nose first with a smile and ask questions later . . . Famfík who lived with his mother and father in a house on the town square . . . Famfík who could build a huge Merkur set and stoke the steam engine and make it go . . . And his father was a retired Austrian major who was bald and who was good at making jams . . . that was his thing hundreds of jars of fruit preserves . . . And at school Famfík was always number one and he never lost a fistfight . . . And when Famfík was four his father started to teach him the piano . . . I took piano lessons too . . . But I only got as far as the Bayer School basic proficiency . . . but Famfík he'd sit at the piano decked out in his white sailor's scarf and tear through Weber's polka . . . and I'd just stand there like a bump on a log shamefaced . . . and so Famfík was just better at everything and it shook my confidence except for when I was around those half-wit dropout friends of mine and then I was all right . . . And then Famfík's family moved away to Prague . . . but over the holidays he still came to visit his uncle at the brewery . . . and I was busy failing grade eight just like I'd failed grade five . . . but Famfík was a first-rate student and when he sat down at our piano and tore through Chopin's nocturnes followed by Weber's polka . . . in the ensuing silence Mother looked at me reproachfully . . . and to top it off Famfík was built like a Greek statue . . . because Famfík along with Štorkán were the national junior swim champs . . . and sometimes both of them were in town together and while we splashed about in the river like little kids Famfík Schaniel and Štorkán practiced their crawl against the current all the way from the railroad bridge up to the stone bridge . . . and not just one or two passes either . . . and when they climbed out of the water they looked like bodybuilders . . . and they wore these tiny bathing suits . . . and black bathing caps . . . and both of them were tanned a deep bronze . . . and like the other boys in Zálabí I always swam in my shorts . . . and all the fellows from Zálabí when they saw Famfík and Štorkán they lowered their eyes . . . like those national junior swim champs were a couple of pretty girls . . . And so they trained the whole afternoon there against the current and after when Mother invited them over to our place . . . She brought them a loaf of bread and a tub of pork lard and Famfík and Štorkán sat there and slowly sliced their bread and slathered it in pork lard . . . and they drank almost an entire keg of our famous Nymburk brewery twelve-proof . . . and they ate and they drank and they drank and they burped and the burping suited them and I was plain speechless couldn't even get a piece of bread down . . . I was frozen . . . and then Famfík sat at the piano and thundered through *Rhapsody in Blue* . . . and then he played Liszt's *Liebesträume* for Mother . . . And another world champion used to visit Zálabí from Prague . . . Harry Jelínek . . . he didn't know how to do anything per se . . . but he was seventeen and he had the same build as Famfík Schaniel . . . and he could swim too not that he was breaking any records but he could swim . . . come to think of it Harry Jelínek had a better build than those two champions and over the holidays he lived at the Hulíks' place . . . they had a garden center in the little glen behind the brewery . . . and Harry knew how to get himself a nice bronze tan . . . I used to like going over to the Hulíks' because old Mrs. Hulíková reminded me of my grandmother she grew vegetables and took them to market in the town square . . . and right next to their garden was a little house where the Weises lived . . . old man Weis used to lie drunk in the ditch . . . and there was probably some bad blood between them and the Hulíks because they put up a fence in front of their windows facing next door . . . I never understood why the Weises preferred to look at fence boards rather than a beautiful garden of vegetables and blossoming flowers . . . and during the holidays the Hulíks' garden was Harry Jelínek's domain . . . and when I was around him I got shy and lowered my eyes . . . when Harry stepped out in the evening to take a stroll around town people looked at him and were speechless . . . and the girls in town when they could muster the courage to look up at Harry striding past like a king just couldn't get over young Harry . . . who was always tanned and looked like a beautiful Swiss bull . . . and to top it off he had curly blond hair always brilliantined . . . and when he spoke his voice was deep and raspy . . . And then I was in high school and in love with a girl named Jiřina . . . Georgina . . . Sundays I took her for boat rides and there we were one Sunday me rowing the boat along and Georgina sitting in the stern with her parasol and as we approached the bridge . . . who should come striding across but Harry Jelínek in his dragoon uniform . . . I forgot to mention Harry joined the army and for me that was the kicker Harry striding along the promenade in his riding boots and his red riding pants and his green tunic with the yellow lining and it wasn't just me but all the students all the young guys were so jealous of him nobody wanted to talk to him . . . So Georgina looked up at the bridge to where Harry Jelínek leaned over the railing and straight out of some American film Harry waved and called . . . Hello! And my Georgina raised her hand and wiggled her little fingers and cried happily . . . Hello! Harry! And I kept rowing and the boat slid under the bridge . . . and all of a sudden I just withered shamefaced and I didn't say another word after that I got the shakes like I was sick or something . . . because Georgina's eyes were half closed as she savored that beautiful greeting of Harry Jelínek's the dragoon who only moments before had leaned over the railing with his tan and his curly blond locks filling out the army cap that was shaped like a little boat . . . Back then . . . I don't know why . . . I shaved my head . . . I was so miserable from the fact that even my Georgina saw Harry Jelínek as a number one as a world champ . . . and not me . . . And then the Protectorate came . . . and Famfík and Harry Jelínek vanished from Nymburk . . . and by war's end I so wanted them to come back during summer holiday . . . for now I had the beautiful dispatcher's uniform and the beautiful overcoat and the shiny summer tunic with the golden high school lapel pin and the gold-embroidered winged badge . . . I so wanted them to see me . . . but they never came back to Nymburk . . . I found out that Harry Jelínek became a pilot and went secretly to England . . . where in a year's time he was shot down over the English Channel . . . As for Famfík Schaniel a few days before war's end he was on his way to meet a girl in Libeň . . . and he ran into a few of his army buddies . . . and they said Look here Famfík you were an army sniper . . . come with us the Germans have occupied the Bulovka hospital . . . we're on our way to defend the Troja Bridge . . . And so instead of going on his date Famfík went with the boys . . . and that's where he got it the Germans up in Bulovka with their machine guns were sniping at partisans defending the Troja Bridge and Famfík took one in the spine . . . And then he couldn't walk for a year and they took him to Canada to a military hospital where they operated on his spine . . . and in two months Famfík was back swimming again in the hospital pool . . . and then he got his engineering degree in Canada . . . and got married . . . and bought himself a Pleyel piano . . . And he did come back to Nymburk once . . . he walked with a limp . . . he brought his wife . . . and he was moved when we reminisced about his father and his fruit preserves and his Merkur set and his little steam engines . . . and how he and Štorkán used to swim against the current . . . Famfík's wife was a Welshwoman and they had their plans all laid out since Famfík was an army engineer and could take his retirement at fifty-five they looked forward to returning to Wales to the house where his wife had been born and they even planned to bring that Pleyel piano along . . . So said my husband and the truck was already making its slow and relentless way through the River Labe country and somehow my husband's story served to relax me because I knew that by way of Famfík and Harry Jelínek my husband was actually talking about my Jirka whom he'd seen for the first time up there on the wall of my old flat and in fact my Jirka had been a playboy too a handsome devil like Famfík and Harry Jelínek and no doubt my husband told his stories to reconcile himself to the fact Jirka was in the same category as his own friends who weren't really his friends at all maybe they were with the passage of time but that Famfík was still a number one today same as back in the day and Harry was a number one too Harry the hero shot down during the Battle of Britain and my husband had nothing left but to put all his money on that writing of his if he too wanted to be a number one and that probably explained why he was so afraid of that writing he was after all forty-five years old already and still not the man he and his friends fancied him to be . . . and I made up my mind right then and there in the cab of the truck that as soon as we were recovered from the move I'd buy my husband a new typewriter I'd do everything in my power to help him quit his job and just stay at home and write and write until he wrote that first novel of his that first text that wasn't going to be published anyway but at least he'd get those big ideas he and his friends dreamed of down on paper and that would vault him to number one status . . . then we dozed off for a while and Břeťa smoked those cigarettes of his chain-smoked them and when I woke up and rubbed my eyes my husband was asleep against my shoulder and it looked like the rain had stopped a while ago and then we were into Libeň and we pulled up under the gas lamp well past midnight and Břeťa hauled himself up onto the furniture in back of the truck and loosened the ropes and untied them and my husband ran around the truck and caught the ropes and carefully Břeťa handed down one piece after the other and the first thing my husband carried to the open doorway and leaned against the wall was the huge mirror and then he turned the hallway light on and the courtyard light on and then we saw Pepíček Sviatek in the light of our flat waiting patiently for our arrival after having spent the day whitewashing the walls of our new room with lime . . . my husband and I had decided to turn that new room of ours into the kitchen while our old flat would serve as the bedroom and house the Empire chiffonier . . . and my husband carried the mirror up to our flat and very carefully leaned it against the wall and then he came back and when he climbed up onto the truck to give Břeťa a hand with the furniture the first thing he handed down to me was the laundry basket with the photographs inside and I carried it up to the flat and shoved it under the bed And so with Pepíček Sviatek's help we carried up the tables and the cupboards and the suitcases and no one talked and when we were done Břeťa didn't want to stay and rest a while he said he just wanted to get back to Nymburk and have his dinner and make himself a little coffee and then crawl into bed beside his wife like he was used to doing and Pepíček Sviatek took his leave as well and said . . . Doctor tomorrow I'm going to have me some shots at Láda's and put it on your tab . . . Later on my husband told me with a laugh . . . You know when I was up on the truck with my brother I happened to look into the second floor of the building next door and what do I see but some guy lying in bed pulling up a woman's skirt undressing her slowly and that was all I needed . . . what if we gave it a shot right now? . . . You see . . . That Harry . . . his name was Vašek Jelínek . . . Václav . . . but all of Nymburk knew him as Harry . . . because he looked like an American actor . . . you see what I mean?

. □ ■ □ ■

CHAPTER SEVENTEEN

In a week's time my husband and Pepíček Sviatek had the kitchen and our old room set up so nicely I actually started to look forward to coming home My husband stopped up our old front door and threw a carpet over it and parked a large table in front of it and from then on you entered that new room of ours through the hallway door . . . Pepíček Sviatek did a beautiful job painting the arched ceiling and he and my husband mounted the large mirror lengthwise and it stretched practically across the entire wall and the courtyard windows reflected in the mirror and you could see everything that went on in the courtyard and every person coming to our place or continuing past and up the circular stairs to the upstairs portico where the Slavíčeks lived . . . I kept the new kitchen cabinetry in the exact same configuration Papa used to have it and once I hung my new curtains in my new kitchen I finally felt like the lady of the house . . . And we had an art deco lamp in our kitchen which shone on our kitchen table where there was always a little flower because my husband loved his flowers . . . I never had the knack for picking the right flower and setting it in a vase I wasn't one for things like flower arrangement because ever since I'd been moved out of our villa and locked up and forced to work at the brickworks I'd lost interest in beautiful things and it had fallen to Papa to take care of everything to try to lift me out of the doldrums and now here was my husband who knew precisely how to hang a wild asparagus in the window and where to place a primrose in a vase and ever since we brought back my parents' furniture from Piešťany a subtle change had occurred in my husband . . . And he certainly was in his element now that he could make his fires in two stoves and the place was always warm regardless of when I got home and my husband bought a cast-iron stove at a bazaar and installed it in our old room and the gypsies brought him buckets of coal and at night he wrapped four briquettes in newspaper and slid them into the stove and the briquettes smoldered overnight and in the morning all my husband had to do was add a little firewood and the fire blazed happily away And since we had a relatively new kitchen stove in our new room my husband moved the old stove into the courtyard and decorated it with wild asparagus plants and primrose blossoms and the stove sat next to the shed where shoots and tendrils of wild ivy cascaded from the roof and down over my husband's death mask the one Vladimir had cast for him way back when . . . And in the evening it was lovely to sit at the kitchen table under the lamplight and under the arched ceiling and the white tablecloth glowed under my hand I liked to just sit there and look at my hands resting on the white tablecloth and there was always a vase on the table with a primrose blossom and a sprig of wild asparagus It's true my husband ruined everything he touched with those stubby fingers of his but he did deserve credit for one thing . . . he always knew exactly where to put a flower or where to put a chair or a little table in this my husband had a woman's touch and above all he loved little flowers he loved to put just one little flower in a mustard jar or in an old-fashioned rye whiskey shot glass And so I came to like being at home in the evenings I looked forward to it and sometimes I just couldn't wait and I'd turn on that lamp with the little flowers on the shade and then it was wonderful to walk through our new doorway into the next room and I always glanced at myself in the mirror that reflected our beautiful flat and the fire in the cast-iron stove in the corner and I was very surprised not just that my husband and Pepíček Sviatek had cut down on the hard stuff and were sticking to beer but that they too took pride in that beautiful flat of ours And my husband was most proud of how he'd set up our bedroom He sent me out to buy a few dozen meters of fabric and then one day my husband and Pepíček Sviatek huddled together in our old room whispering and taking measurements and making calculations and then they took the fabric across the street to Mr. Barták the tailor who sewed them a huge drape in about a day . . .

and my husband and Pepíček sat under the light of the deco lamp at the kitchen table with me and drank their beer and smiled slyly at each other and my husband sewed rings onto the drape with those stubby fingers of his and a few days later I came home to find Pepíček and my husband sitting there grinning and they poured me a shot and then my husband went into our old room and turned on the chandelier and the large table lamp with the beige shade and strung across the whole room at a height of about two meters was a wire and hung from the wire on metal rings was the drape which split the room neatly in two and on this side of the drape was one of the huge sofas we'd brought back from Piešťany and a little round table covered in a blue tablecloth and my husband pulled back the drape and there was the cast-iron stove blazing away in the corner and there was the other sofa at right angles to the first and blankets and pillows were laid out on both sofas and I saw at once from the setup that my husband and I would sleep with our heads almost touching . . . And then Pepíček Sviatek gave me a bow and hurried off to have three shots on the doctor's tab at Vaništa's pub before it closed . . . And that night and every night hence my husband and I slept with our heads almost touching I could hear his every breath and just to level the playing field I drank beer in the evening too and both of us were scented with beer and thus it never again occurred to me to turn away from my husband because he reeked of beer . . . I often caught my husband sleeping behind the curtain in his little lair . . . he loved to go straight to bed after getting home from work outside the sun was still shining but my husband was so dog-tired from his work on Spálená Street he jumped into bed and fell dead away for an hour or so . . . And when he woke up he was like a new man and he set out with his shopping bag on those make-believe shopping excursions of his and shopping bag in hand he wandered along the main street stopping in all those little pubs of his while I was either at work or at home because just then I couldn't get enough of that new flat of ours . . . My husband loved his two cast-iron stoves loved feeding them the busted cupboards and planks the gypsies brought him and he had a woodshed full of paint barrel staves scavenged from the former brush and paint supply next door the place was littered with hundreds and perhaps thousands of empty paint barrels left over from when it was nationalized and my husband had a key to the gate and he'd trundle over there with a baby carriage borrowed from the gypsies and load it up with splintered barrels and the barrel staves were solid oak and burned beautifully and the cast-iron stove popped and roared and my husband added oak staves to the fire and they smoked and exploded like petards and burned so furiously the cast-iron stove glowed red Often my husband added wood to the fire and then ran outside to the courtyard and down the stairs and from there he liked to watch the plume of smoke rise to the heavens and admire the beautiful draw of our smithy chimney And my husband was keen on that smoke and proud of that draw and whoever came over to our place got an earful about that famous chimney of ours and since they always needed convincing my husband took them outside and down the stairs and showed them that strong plume of smoke which he claimed on a windless day was as straight as the trunk of a birch tree And thanks to my husband I was equally keen on that flat of ours It was beautiful and after dusk I often turned on all the lights and went into the dark of the courtyard and from there I looked at our lighted windows at the beautiful planters of blossoming water fern hanging inside our windows and I learned to arrange our curtains in the Viennese style tied together with a big bow in the middle and it was so lovely I thought if I was someone else seeing the place I'd surely want to live there And sometimes I looked in from the courtyard and thought why not just leave the curtains open a smidgeon give people going by a little taste? And I wish I could have seen myself moving through the kitchen at twilight my image reflected in the large mirror that stretched across the whole wall . . . I was so enchanted by that flat of ours I often left the lights ablaze and went downstairs and into the street to stand beneath the lighted gas lamp for a while and I pretended I didn't know this building that I was a stranger maybe looking for someone and I entered that hallway of ours like a stranger passed under Mrs. Beranová's windows on my way to the courtyard and then I climbed the stairs drawn by the flat glowing with light and I paused in the courtyard as if it was my first time here and looked from window to window and took the whole thing in and admired the thick stalks of wild ivy which overgrew the walls and crept along wires strung across the courtyard and tendrils and shoots of ivy fell down to form a sort of veil through which the tall windows of that quiet and trusted flat shone . . . and I said to myself as if I was here for the first time . . . That flat must be beautiful

I wonder who lives there? And in those moments I felt risen from the dead like I'd woken up to begin my life anew like everything that happened to me had happened to someone else and then it was time to finally sever my last ties to Jirka to that love of mine and when I was home alone I retrieved the laundry basket with the framed photographs of me and Jirka together and the cast-iron stove blazed away and I went through those photographs one last time looked into those eyes and into that face one last time and then I threw that beloved face into the fire and watched the fire consume it slowly at first and then voraciously and some of the photographs I had to fold over to get them into the stove and as my husband loved to boast the draw on that chimney really was powerful and the fire simply devoured those photographs like I had soaked them in gasoline and so that fire feasted on my past on those moments I thought would remain with me forever and the last item for the fire was an oval portrait of Jirka and when I turned the photo over there was my own photograph pasted to the other side . . . there was a time I had been under the naive impression our lives would be as close as those two photographs pasted together . . . The look in Jirka's eyes in those photos was altogether different from how I remembered him from how he had presented himself to me and to others . . . And then I remembered celebrating Christmas with Jirka and how it had been quite different to how most people celebrate Christmas . . . Jirka always stayed home on Christmas Eve and he took great pains with his Christmas tree decorations . . . he never hung any candy canes or tinsel or shining stars on our tree and he had to have a spruce tree because he said that only a spruce tree made for a proper Czech Christmas and instead of all the fancy baubles Jirka decorated the tree with little red apples and with plain old gingerbread cookies tied with a white thread and on Christmas Eve Jirka lit the candles and he was somber and serious and I had to fry him up some fish and serve it with a plain old Moravian salad and we were very serious as we ate and then Jirka opened the Bible and every Christmas he read from the Gospel according to Luke . . . how in those days a decree went out from Caesar Augustus that all the world should be enrolled and how along with many others Joseph came to the city of Bethlehem with his betrothed Mary who was with child and while they were there the time came for her to be delivered and she gave birth to her firstborn son and wrapped him in swaddling cloths and laid him in a manger . . . And the two Christmas Eves we spent together Jirka was very serious he drank only a tiny bit of wine and paced from one room to the other and he gazed into the large mirror like he was seeing himself for the first time and he said to me There's no mention of Christmas Eve or Christmas Day in the Bible people are crazy to celebrate the birth of Jesus by gorging and drinking themselves silly by giving each other meaningless gifts and pretending to be overjoyed . . . and around midnight the ambulances do the rounds and the doctors dole out the injections because thanks to the birth of Jesus people get so stuffed their livers and kidneys swell to bursting . . . And the fire roared inside the cast-iron stove and I was undecided whether or not to throw that last photograph of Jirka into the fire that oval portrait with my photo stuck to the other side and I sat there on the stool before the open stove and the fire roared and beseeched me to give up the photograph which was small enough to fit into the palm of my hand small enough to tuck away into a purse and I closed the stove door I would save that two-sided photo let my husband get jealous when he came across it he was jealous of Jirka anyway and I knew I mustn't destroy those empty picture frames and then it dawned on me that even though the picture frames were now empty whenever my husband or I looked at them we'd see those old photographs of myself and Jirka together nonetheless . . . And by virtue of their destruction those photographs took deeper hold of me than before and as I sat there and stared into the fire and watched Jirka burn and myself along with him I had a vision of Jirka decorating the Christmas tree very serious as he always was at Christmas and New Year's when he never went out to play with his band but stayed at home and paced about the room and gazed at himself in the mirror and played Spanish romances on his guitar strummed through those sad Spanish melodies and all he ate was buttered bread and he sipped his white wine and said very little and then he paced about and looked at me sadly and sighed and for the first time I realized what had really been going on when that jewel of mine paced about the room and gazed at me and at himself in the mirror he was trying to make amends for the year gone by to confess to that double in the mirror to make a commitment to himself he'd start the new year differently and anew And now the Jirka of the oval portrait appeared . . . And I suddenly realized the picture had been taken not when we were together but when Jirka was back in conservatory still full of ideals and dreams of becoming a number one at the guitar . . . and I retrieved that photograph from where I'd hidden it at the bottom of my sewing basket and I looked at the photo of myself stuck to the back of Jirka's portrait and that photo wasn't recent either it was taken back when I still lived at home when I was happy when we lived in a beautiful villa and owned a Packard automobile and had two housemaids and a nanny . . . I was sixteen years old in that photograph . . . And come to think of it the only reason I had stuck those photographs together was because they showed us back when we were still young back when even I had wanted nothing more than to be a world-famous dancer like La Jana . . .

■ □ ■ □ ■

CHAPTER EIGHTEEN

And it was just as I suspected the first time I laid eyes on that Slovak girl in Jirka Šmejkal's basement flat . . . As soon as I saw the way Vladimir was looking at that countess I knew it was love at first sight Vladimir was head over heels and I also knew the countess was destined to become his fate his specter his phantom countess . . . Countess indeed! But she actually was a countess her surname was Holényová and my husband delivered the happy news that her parents owned a two-story renaissance building in Slovakia on a town square no less and that her name was Tekla but I already knew that from when I first met the countess in Jirka Šmejkal's basement flat just like I knew she had nowhere to stay and probably ran away from home as was all the rage these days Not that I'd lose any sleep over that I was just sorry Vladimir had fallen into a love so deep it was a matter of life and death And one day as I was coming back from the store I passed by Jirka's basement studio and there I saw the whole thing for myself . . . There was Jirka's basement studio and the giant print press and there was Vladimir pacing about under the light of the bare bulbs and there in the corner strategically positioned so that anyone walking by on the street could get an eyeful were two mattresses and I stood and gawked as if in a dream and they had an easel set up and newspaper spread out on the floor and on the newspaper was a glass with a flower in it and a bottle of wine and two wineglasses and an ashtray and two espresso cups down to the dregs and then Tekla wandered in and stood next to Vladimir and gazed into his eyes and Vladimir caressed her and gazed back and then he closed his eyes clearly overwhelmed by the countess standing there dressed in her elegant blue stewardess outfit And I knew Vladimir would never again brush his hand against my knee never again look at me as he had up there in Ládví when we called out from the hilltop to all the European capitals I spy with my little eye sent our hellos out to all our friends in foreign places and I also knew I had a crush on Vladimir and that the crush would grow stronger from here on in even though I knew Vladimir was stricken by that countess with whom he shared the basement flat the former machine shop that Jirka wanted to turn into a studio and an art gallery but for the fact it was occupied by Vladimir and that vixen of his that countess And I stood there on the sidewalk looking through the half-open shutters anyone walking by could just stop and look down into that brightly lit basement the place was lit up like a hockey rink you could see everything in the blinding light of two powerful bulbs obviously a holdover from when the place was a machine shop And now Vladimir and Tekla occupied the place and the gigantic print press sat all alone in the corner . . . And as I stood there looking down into the basement it struck me that Vladimir actually knew people were watching that he wanted people to watch and that he was in fact engaged in a little theatrics a little showmanship . . . And long after dark I still stood there I couldn't tear myself away from the show I watched Vladimir kneel before his countess who lay on her back on the red bedcover arms splayed behind her and I broke into a cold sweat as I watched Vladimir caress her and smile at her overcome by his tremendous good fortune and I saw the countess melt under Vladimir's gaze and put a finger to his lips And it was obvious the countess was also aware anyone going by outside could look through the shutters and get an eyeful of the two lovers and I felt awfully embarrassed for both of them because to me being ogled like this was unimaginable not to mention pretending to like it And people walking by actually did stop to peek at what was going on down there some of them waved it off or spat on the sidewalk in disgust and continued on their way while others stayed to get a little more of the Vladimir and Tekla show And when I looked closer I saw that one of those gawkers one of those Peeping Toms one of those voyeurs was none other than my husband and I became more interested in watching him than the goings-on in the basement and my husband stood there in wide-eyed fascination watching his friend Vladimir and it occurred to me that Vladimir was actually showing off for his friends putting on a show down there in the basement and the door to the hallway was wide open and a shaft of yellow light spilled through and doubtless Jirka next door was getting an eyeful as well and then there he was walking into the studio and he carried a zinc plate over to the print press and while Vladimir knelt before Tekla and gazed into her eyes off in the other corner Jirka examined his zinc plate with great interest he was probably about to print another little butterfly graphic and Jirka turned the shiny zinc plate over and held it up and the reflection washed over his face and the way he stood there in his white painter's smock smudged with black printer's ink and oil paint it seemed he too wanted people walking by to look in on him and to see the graphic artist at work the painter who has nothing to hide and who in fact wants to show everyone how he works late into the night . . . And my husband stood there bathed from the waist down in the basement light and he leaned against the wall and stared down at Vladimir and Tekla with great interest and I strolled over and bumped into him pretended I just happened to be going by and my husband took me by the hand and pointed down to the basement and whispered . . . Darling what you see on display here is also one of Vladimir's driving forces the ability to show off and be a narcissist Here you have him just as he was on May Day carrying the state flag and marching at the head of the column here you have him as he shows off in all the pubs and all the public spaces here you have him complete with his auto-erotic asphyxia here you have the Vladimir who strings himself up and always manages to find someone to cut him down in the nick of time and here you also have the Vladimir whose proud modesty prompts him to hand out his graphics for free to anyone who shows an interest . . . And the door to the basement studio flew open and light spilled onto the sidewalk and up the stairs came a huge ten-liter tankard followed by Jirka sporting the Canadian crew cut that brought out his beautiful canine eyes and he stood there on the side-walk and pointed to the basement and his tankard shone in the light from the bare bulbs and Jirka just shrugged and said . . . A fine mess . . . My studio and my future gallery up in smoke! And he picked up the tankard and told us to go downstairs he was off for his second tankard of beer today on account of he just couldn't get over what he was witness to in his studio and what he was afraid was still to come . . . What a night we've got in store! But my husband sighed and closed his eyes he was enormously moved by what he saw perhaps because he never knew Vladimir to behave like this never saw Vladimir so in love and my husband was simply dumbstruck that Vladimir could be so completely smitten so drunk so intoxicated by his countess Tekla who as we already knew was to be his fate And we stepped through the door and into the cold hallway and there on the right was the open door to Jirka's future gallery and my husband stood there and took in the scene . . . Vladimir strode back and forth across the cement floor and blabbered on to Tekla who reclined on a red blanket smoking a cigarette and after each drag she raised the hand with the cigarette into the air and the rising smoke gleamed in the bright light and then Vladimir knelt before Tekla again and gazed deeply into her eyes like he was gazing into a mirror or into a deep well where he might read his own fate and on he went absolutely stricken unable to get enough of whatever it was he saw there in the depths of Tekla's eyes And my husband knocked on the doorframe and then he knocked again but the lovers remained as they were neither hearing nor seeing or maybe just pretending not to hear or see that's how smitten they were with each other and with the fact they had an audience out there on the sidewalk and no doubt Vladimir heard us knocking but he went on with the pretense with the theatrics with the big production of love . . . And Jirka came down the stairs heavily carrying his ten-liter beer tankard dripping foam onto each step a dab of white foam and we went into Jirka's kitchen into his workshop and Jirka left the door to the hallway and the studio open and there was Vladimir pacing and beating his chest with his fists and carrying on and his voice seemed to come from far away like he was behind a thick wall of aquarium glass and he rambled on about his life and how he'd wanted to reach number one status but now that he'd met Tekla his everything his whole life all he wanted was for her to never leave his side . . . And we drank our beer and watched Vladimir through the open door and Jirka even got up and dragged the tankard right over to Vladimir but Vladimir saw neither the tankard nor Jirka nor anything else his entire world was just Tekla and himself and everyone watching was witness to his muddled confessional his theatrical gestures and movements . . . and Vladimir pushed the tankard away lightly and leaned over Tekla and searched her eyes for some sort of validation of what he just confessed to her and without missing a beat he reached into his pocket and with trembling fingers pulled out a cigarette and slipped it between Tekla's fingers and as if in a dream he struck a match and waited for it to flare and then he held it up to her cigarette and Tekla inhaled deeply and Vladimir held the dying match to her lips and she exhaled and blew out the little flame and Vladimir held the match between his fingers and together they watched the last curl of smoke gleam in the light And Jirka sat there with a sad little smile on his face but he would have been better off crying or screaming about it given what had happened over the last few days . . . And Jirka said jealously . . . Vladimir came over after Tekla's first night here and took her into the city and when they returned they already had the mattresses and the cutlery and the blankets and they made their bed on the cold cement floor and spread out their *Red Justice* communist daily for a table and from that moment on there's been no talking to Vladimir three days and all they do is nibble on deli meatloaf and bread and drink coffee and guzzle wine and they walk around awhile and then it's back to bed and then they get up again and the two-hundred-watt lights blazing away day and night and Vladimir prancing around everything he does and says accompanied by those awful theatrics . . . So said Jirka and then he got an idea he went into his studio and turned on his giant press he readied a plate for one of his butterfly prints he polished the plate and applied paint to the surface and then he gave it a smooth wipe and applied the paper followed by the felt backing and then he pushed a button on the print press and the thing started to shake and all the people standing in the far window ogling Vladimir and Tekla now moved to the window closest to the giant press all we could see of them was their legs but a couple of them squatted and gripped the wire mesh window and peered down at the giant press where inside a graphic print was coming to life and Jirka looked up and when he saw all those people pressed to the window he cocked his head and put his ear to the machine as if to make sure everything was in order and something about the sound didn't seem quite right to him and for a moment it appeared he might shut everything down but apparently the machine overcame whatever little glitch it had and went on as before and Jirka nodded and smiled not just at everyone watching in the window but at me as well and it just struck me as pathetic his need to put on a performance like Vladimir his need to show off because he was convinced he was already a number one with those miniature butterflies of his which he'd forever be adding to the larger-than-life oil painting of his father lying in a meadow as if gunned down only he wasn't gunned down he was asleep and in his dream every sort of butterfly not just from Europe but from Africa and Asia as well fluttered around him and Jirka's father slept like God himself who after creating the world in six days and seeing everything move to the proper rhythm could rest forever after . . . And the machine shook and made such a racket some of the people watching from the street had to cover their ears but Vladimir continued to prance about the cement floor and he clutched at his breast and threw up his hands and rambled something unintelligible that only he and Tekla could understand and Tekla sat there with her legs crossed and smoked her cigarette while Vladimir paced back and forth his eyes never leaving her face and occasionally she nodded in confusion at something he said or nodded furiously in agreement when Vladimir stopped and hovered over her expecting an answer . . . And in that moment my husband whispered She's going to end up like Desdemona . . . And then out of sheer clumsiness or perhaps intentionally Jirka let go a heavy steel plate on top of a wooden stand next to the press and a shot rang out and the stand shattered and splinters flew off in all directions even the gawkers in the windows recoiled and scattered across the street and all the way down to the railroad tracks . . . Only Vladimir was unfazed and continued to stare into Tekla's eyes to hang on her every word like it was a matter of life and death . . . And then something happened that was just too much for me already . . . And I said I want to go home . . . In the corner were two buckets of tar that Jirka used to waterproof the walls beneath the windows and Vladimir brought the buckets over and opened one of them up and dipped a brush into the tar and like he was priming a giant canvas he flung himself at Jirka's meticulously painted pristine white wall described huge brushstrokes and then he plunged the brush back into the bucket of tar and spattered the wall and it wasn't a show anymore it was the real thing with real intensity and as he spattered that white wall with the black tar it was like he was pouring everything out of himself everything he had left everything unclean he wanted to be rid of . . . And when Jirka shouted I'll break his face it's my studio my future gallery! when my husband saw Jirka wanted to intervene he held him back and said Jirka for the love of God leave him be when else are we going to have the honor to see Vladimir work in large format to see how Jackson Pollock probably worked! Except Pollock worked on the floor! But Jirka was miserable and lamented But Doctor it's been going on non-stop for four days already and this cuts it . . . I need to get some work done too . . . And while I could hardly even look at Vladimir the countess on the other hand was in a state of rapture as she watched him and that vixen stood there in her little blue outfit and the way she looked at him gave him strength and spurred him on so that now he attacked the facing wall and soon it too was covered in splatters and brushstrokes and I wanted nothing but to get out of there and go home But my husband launched into one of his speeches . . . We are witness to an extraordinary event! Jirka I read somewhere that when a female whale is to be married she is accompanied by three bulls and they swim all the way down below the Antarctic Ocean and all the while the three bulls dance around her in the ocean courting her for thousands of kilometers Jirka! And when they finally get to where they're going one of the bulls impregnates her and Jirka that act of lovemaking lasts a mere thirty seconds and the two other bulls help support the female during the act so she doesn't break in two Jirka try to understand Vladimir's four days in the context of the whale who swims with her suitors for thousands of kilometers to engage in an act of lovemaking that lasts no longer than thirty seconds Jirka for God's sake you and I are those two bulls here to support Vladimir to make sure he doesn't break in two . . . And Vladimir opened the second bucket of tar and once again the windows were full of gawkers who just couldn't tear themselves away from the spectacle of Vladimir but I pleaded with my husband I'd very much like to go home now And with his soaking brush Vladimir just flung the tar at the wall now spattered it and the tar ran down the wall and my husband eagerly continued with his lecture . . . Why what you have here is Stavrogin the handsome devil from *The Possessed* who besmirched that whole beautiful imperial high society who smeared them like this who threw his dregs his offal in their faces just to emerge victorious at any cost triumphant and in the end he hanged himself in an attic . . . I'd like to go home now I pleaded . . . I'd really like to go home . . . And Jirka lamented quietly If somebody spills the beans we're putting on these kinds of orgies here the housing committee will cancel my lease and I won't have a home or a studio or a gallery . . . And now Vladimir took the near-empty buckets and spun them in the air and whisked the last of the tar against the wall and then he cried out and collapsed in a heap and just lay there moaning like he'd fallen off a cliff And Tekla leaned over him and clasped her hands and covered her eyes and my husband took a long draft from the pitcher and then passed it to Jirka and as they drank their eyes never left Vladimir who now sat up and raised that beautiful head of his and then he got to his feet and ran straight at the tar-wet wall onto which he'd poured out his very soul and he struck it headfirst but that wasn't enough for him so he began to head-butt the wall like a ram and rivulets of blood flowed down around his eyes and Vladimir stood there and drove his head into the wall again and again and Tekla ran into the hallway and into the kitchen in tears implored Jirka and my husband to help and when they ran in Vladimir was already collapsed at the foot of the wall and wet tar ran through the imprints where his head had struck the wall it looked like someone had thrown a tar-soaked sponge against the wall and Vladimir lay on the floor unconscious and Jirka and my husband lifted his limp body and carried it into the hallway and Jirka brought a pail of water and knelt down and gently washed Vladimir's face and his forehead . . . And that was all I could stand and I screamed at Tekla at the top of my lungs . . . Are you crazy you're all out of your minds! For God's sake what kind of crap are you trying to pull? And I turned on my husband and yelled in his face And you! How can you stand by and watch your friend like this! But my husband was washing Vladimir's forehead and he placed a damp cloth on the nape of his neck and Vladimir opened his eyes and smiled and said Doctor you saw the whole thing! And my husband said Vladimir for the rest of your life this will be the stuff of legend . . . And Vladimir put his tar-stained hand over my husband's and laughed . . . So you saw everything? Wasn't it beautiful come on Doctor tell how beautiful it was! And even Tekla looked at my husband in anticipation and wiped her tears away with the back of her hand and Jirka looked at my husband too and both of them waited on my husband's words my husband who so liked to preach and then he grew serious and said . . . Look here Vincent van Gogh cut off his ear and brought it to a girl he met in a bar as proof of his love Look Vladimir like Emma Bovary you've brought yourself to the very brink of death only to be cleansed only to prove that death and injury no longer concern you in fact they are trivial . . . Vladimir if I was to reach into philosophy then Karl Jaspers one of his major themes was *das Sich selber durchsichtig werden* . . . to become transparent to oneself . . . Vladimir I like my quotations and I hope you won't hold it against me I hope you won't stop liking me on account of what I'm about to say . . . Here's a quote that is even more fitting for you than for the person who wrote it . . . And I will live in a glass house where everything will be made of glass and I will see everyone who ascends my glass staircase and I will lie down to sleep upon a glass bed and I will cover myself with a glass sheet upon which a diamond inscription will eventually appear that reads . . . WHO AM I . . . ? My husband went on quietly and his words defused the tension that hung in the air they added a sort of magic . . . And even I succumbed to the spell and perhaps for the first time to the significance of what my husband was saying and I saw that Vladimir was indeed transparent and that he had revealed himself his crazy heart to us and he lay there smiling lay there propped up on one elbow smiling at Tekla who enrapt gazed into Vladimir's eyes and come what may everything that just happened in that basement joined her and Vladimir together for all time And when I saw how utterly and completely lost those two lovers were in each other's eyes I crossed my arms and said quietly I'd really like to go home . . . .And even though I said it I had no desire whatsoever to go home to Na Hrázi Street with my husband I suddenly found myself pining awfully for that jewel of mine who'd run off on me for that Jirka who could play me the guitar when I was feeling blue I was overcome by longing for a great love the sort one finds only in a romance novel or movie everything I witnessed here in the basement I lived through myself though it was long ago in fact I too had wanted to end my life because of a love unrequited I had wanted to leave this world when that jewel of mine ran off with another and left me at his mother's like so much dirty laundry . . .

■　□　■　□　■

CHAPTER NINETEEN

Jirka Šmejkal fell head over heels in love he couldn't sleep and he couldn't work on his giant press and he even lost his taste for beer . . . Jirka wanted someone by his side just like Vladimir had Tekla who went with him to work and who was learning how to run a lathe at the ČKD steelworks . . . Vladimir was flush with luck as every morning he and Tekla rose together in that basement studio on Žertvy and Tekla wore American overalls and on their way to work they held hands like a couple of kids and when they came home from work they made their dinner on a little gas stove down there in the basement and Jirka was all alone and Vladimir's mother was all alone because Vladimir was so desperately in love he neither saw nor heard anyone but Tekla the love of his life to whom he was now engaged . . . Jirka fell in love with a girl named Helen who was a store clerk and rather plump and quite gigantically tall Whenever Jirka invited her over to his basement he spent the whole afternoon arranging his studio his gallery just so he brought in every sketch and every painting he ever made he turned that studio of his into a makeshift auction house for paintings and graphic prints and even the giant print press did double duty as a sort of display case where Jirka tastefully arranged his paintings and all the walls including the hallway walls were hung with paintings and graphic prints even the stuff Jirka did in school And Jirka bought himself a little white painter's smock pleated like the painters in the old days wore and he bought himself a large Basque beret and opened a book of Rembrandt and Purkyne on the table and when we sat around and Helen happened by Jirka talked of nothing but his future his big chance and my husband lectured on Jirka's oeuvre like it was a vernissage said there was a new figuration sweeping the world that abstraction was on the way out and he went from one painting to the other and pointed out the heavy influence of Purkyne in Jirka's work how Jirka used the visible world as his vehicle to creative expression and how his love for people was so great he would soon have his own followers not to mention his own customers . . . Even Vladimir came in to have a look and a listen and he had a little smile on his face and I saw his contempt for the whole thing and the way he looked at my husband as if he was some sort of beast that should be killed . . . When my husband concluded his speech and Jirka sat there in his freshly ironed smock that went to his knees Vladimir announced it might be good if my husband bought himself a long housecoat he suggested I buy him a nice pair of slippers and told Jirka he was sure to find great success with his work if only he added a tractor into the background of his paintings or at least a factory chimney here and there he was certain to win some local competition maybe in Humpolec or even in Chlumec on Cidlina So said Vladimir and then he went back across the hallway to continue pacing about the large basement to pick up where he left off and Tekla lay there on her back reclining on a duvet and she smoked her cigarettes and brewed her strong Turkish coffee every half hour . . . Jirka sat there and watched his plump girlfriend smoke she never actually finished a cigarette she seemed a bit too confused by everything going on around her she barely started one cigarette before she stabbed it out angrily in the ashtray and pulled out another and Jirka lit every single one of those cigarettes with a trembling hand and my husband went on pretending to like the paintings went from one to the next and I felt really sorry for Jirka because that girl could care less about him she seemed ashamed at any connection to him . . . And Jirka walked around in his little painter's smock and with his yellow tape measure measured off the wall and made little markings and here would be a cabinet with artist's supplies and here a cabinet with every kind of paint and over here another cabinet with hammers and chisels because Jirka was going to be a sculptor too he would carve from stumps of linden and pear tree because he had a bright future as a number one sculptor . . . he had after all applied to the union and as a member he would have orders from shopping malls and new schools and all sorts of public spaces in fact the opportunities for a painter and a sculptor were endless . . . But Helen glanced at her watch nervously and announced she had to be going she lived all the way over by Fajfkárna on the second floor above the Rokos Pub and when she rose to go she seemed to get bigger and bigger like stacking building blocks one on top of the other Helen was practically a giant she had to hunch over just to make it through the door . . . and even my husband was thrown and he sidled over and stood beside her and sure enough Helen was even taller than him . . . and when she was gone my husband picked up one of Jirka's graphic prints it showed the Vltava over by the Libeň Bridge down where that ship had been at anchor for what seemed like forever . . . it was tied to shore with two huge lines and a plank was laid across from ship to shore and there were portholes along the sides and up in the bow was a little shed and smoke poured from the chimney . . . And my husband said he had to have this print he would buy it off Jirka . . . And he held the graphic print in his hands like it was something sacred and when Jirka came back down the stairs he said . . . This print I'm going to put up on the wall this is the place Vladimir and I used to go swimming the first year he lived up on Na Hrázi Street Vladimir liked to sit here and sketch and there used to be a small houseboat pulled up onshore tipped on its side and afternoons it would light up in the sun . . . Jirka wanted to interject he looked like he had something important to say . . . but my husband raised his hand to indicate he wasn't finished that he still had something good . . . After we were done swimming we climbed aboard that houseboat and lay on the hot deck and the sun shone and we swam there with the gypsy kids who used the chimney of the houseboat to shit in I think every single one of those gypsy kids shit in that chimney . . . and there used to be this huge restaurant onshore there by the river lock called Vltavan it could take hundreds of people and families used to stroll along the riverfront on their Sunday outings past Vltavan along the Rokytka and all the way to Pelc Tyrolka . . . Jirka's captured the Vltavan restaurant in the background here and beside the Vltavan used to be a small shop that sold nets and there was a guy who wove the nets and he had a sign in the window . . . WILL RAISE ANY SUNKEN SHIP INQUIRE WITHIN . . . Jirka I'm going to buy this graphic print off you is two hundred crowns all right? And Jirka raised those canine eyes of his and whispered . . . Doctor for you it's free . . . but I just wanted to ask . . . and my husband rolled up a couple of hundred-crown notes and slipped them into the front pocket of Jirka's smock . . . And Jirka finally worked up the courage to ask . . . What'd you think of Helen? Did you see how lovely she was? How gentle she was? I'd love to teach her how to draw . . . and my husband said true enough it's been a long time since he's seen such a gentle girl such a starry-eyed girl and he wished Jirka all the love in the world and for Jirka's place to be just like the studio next door with Vladimir and Tekla . . . Jirka hung on my husband's every word I never saw such faithful eyes they took in everything my husband said like it was gospel and I broke into a sweat and lit up a cigarette because I knew it was my turn next and sure enough Jirka asked me what I thought of that Helen of his who worked as a grocery-store clerk and carted around cases of beer and soda pop . . . I looked into Jirka's eyes and he looked back at me with such trust with such pleading that even though I resolved to give all present a piece of my mind I knew I'd only end up hurting a person like Jirka who might even do something rash and so I said Yes Helen really is a lovely girl not to mention her interest in painting maybe later on I could even teach her to do needlepoint . . . And Jirka flung himself at my feet and begged me to yes please show Helen how to needlepoint a painting he would make her a stencil and then Helen could create a huge needlepoint of his *Dream of My Father* and he would mark down for her what colors the little butterflies flitting around his sleeping father should have . . . And then it was time to go and my husband and I walked through Žertvy and we didn't speak we were drained from everything we had seen and it was dark out and the gas lamps hissed like snakes and when we got home my husband lit a fire in the cast-iron stove and soon the flames hissed too and I lay down on my sofa and fully dressed my husband lay down on his and our heads were almost touching and my husband turned off the lamp and the only light in the room came from a crack in the cast-iron stove and we lay there on those two sofas our hands lightly touching and played back all the events of the day and slowly fell asleep . . . And from that night on we avoided going to Jirka's studio Sometimes Jirka waited for us at our place but he didn't like to stand and wait so he squatted there à la Pepíček Sviatek and in fact the two of them joined up to do shots at Vaništa's and then came back to wait on us and Jirka invited us over to his place next week to celebrate his three-month anniversary and his engagement to Helen . . . And then Pepíček informed us he was a certified trim painter and that in summer when he had the time he'd come over and paint all our doors and windows for us . . . And Pepíček and Jirka sat there side by side like a couple of cormorants like a couple of birds in an aviary . . . And then we went back to Vaništa's pub with them for a drink and the whole pub was crazy everyone drinking shots because apparently something was in the air a föhn wind or sunspots and Mr. Vaništa's wife Boženka and the postman knocked back shots one after the other and Miss Boženka was taking her cure for the föhn and for the sunspots but no matter how much she put back complained Mr. Vaništa apparently it still wasn't enough . . . And Miss Boženka was just as substantial as Helen that future fiancée of Jirka's and her eyes were aswim already with the alcohol like she was drowning inside a barrel of brandy like it was rising up her legs and past her lips and into those huge beautiful eyes of hers and Pepíček Sviatek ordered . . . Láda another three shots . . . And Jirka sat in the corner his head basically flush with the tabletop I thought he was resting but no Jirka was no bigger than Pepíček who sat at pint level and who only needed to tip his glass forward to his lips to take a drink . . . Miss Boženka made the rounds with the drinks and her huge shadow fell over Jirka like a blanket like a cloud rolling across the countryside but when Jirka got up to touch glasses with Miss Boženka he had to cock his head back and look straight into Miss Boženka's eyes because whenever Miss Boženka shared a toast with someone she said . . . To your health and you better look me in the eye . . . And Jirka described to Miss Boženka and to everyone within earshot how delicate his Helen was how lovely and how beautiful . . . he followed Miss Boženka around and when he ran out of superlatives added . . . Miss Boženka my Helen is almost as beautiful as you . . . And Miss Boženka laughed and said . . . You big talker from Zeleneč . . . And she wrapped her arms around his waist and picked him up as you would a child and his legs dangled to just below her knees and they stared drunkenly into each other's eyes and Miss Boženka gave Jirka a kiss and put him back down and then she was off to the taproom for another round of shots because the best thing for sunspots was a little exercise and a whole lot of alcohol . . . And the following week my husband and I got all dressed up in our Sunday best and we bought a bouquet of flowers and toward evening headed off to Žertvy for Jirka and Helen's engagement party but when we descended into that basement studio there was Jirka in bed wrapped up in his covers despondent . . . And he informed us in a quiet voice that Helen didn't want him she sent him a message that said so and therefore the only way to save the situation was for my husband to help Jirka stage the kind of circus Vladimir put on for Tekla the night he smashed his head against the wall and Jirka implored me to go and fetch Helen since I was the only one she said she trusted and so it was up to me to go and get her to wait outside that supermarket for her and to bring her back so she could see how love-struck Jirka was how he just couldn't live without her . . . And Jirka begged my husband to break his nose to punch him in the face since he just didn't have it in him to do it himself . . . So I put the flowers in a bucket of water and around six o'clock went down to the Pramen supermarket to wait for Helen and I stood out front and watched the shop girls roll down the shutters at closing time and presently the giant Helen emerged and I told her that Jirka just wanted to see her one last time that he was absolutely lovesick And Helen glanced at her watch and nodded and without another word we proceeded down the main street to the rail-road crossing where the barriers were down and a local was pulling out of the station and we stood there for a spell shrouded in fog and steam the locomotive and carriages passing by close enough to touch and it reminded me of a Fatty Arbuckle comedy my husband and I had once seen Fatty standing next to the rails a train passing so close he held out a match and struck it against the side of the train to light his cigar . . . and the carriages flashed by us inches away and then the barriers went up and without a word we crossed the tracks and walked through Žertvy past the old cast-iron pump and past the old pear tree and past the old bench where Pepíček Sviatek sat smoking a cigarette elbows rested on his knees hat pulled down to his eyes and he smiled into the twilight and gave us a nod and then we were at the stairs to the basement flat and the adjacent workshop was dark but there was light on the stairs going down and I opened the door and then Helen and I got the shock of our lives . . . There lay Jirka fully dressed in bed his face covered in blood and blood ran from his nose and he looked up with those trusting and soulful eyes and the blankets were smeared with blood and there were bloody handprints on some of the paintings and the table was smeared with blood too . . . my husband sat there next to the bed in his Sunday best and he looked at Helen reproachfully and shouted . . . Just look at what you've done! See how much Jirka loves you . . . And Jirka stammered . . . Helen darling I can't live without you please don't go . . . And it was so quiet you could hear a pin drop the only sound footsteps of passersby on the sidewalk But Helen had a rather different take on the whole thing she was filled with disgust with revulsion and her eyes flashed with anger as she cried . . . Now this is the end the absolute end! You stupid fools you bloody idiot so this is what you've got in store for me this is the kind of crap you'd pull if I was your wife I'd sooner be married to the lowliest farmhand to the guy who beats on me every day even if you were the number one you keep telling me you are even if you were champion of the world you stupid idiot you don't even know how much you disgust me how stomach-turning I find all you revolting disgusting people here . . . So this is what you imagine as art these hysterical theatrics . . . And Helen the giant hurled those words at us and shook her finger in Jirka's face and then she leaped across the bed and tore the bloody sheets off Jirka and shouted . . . Quit playing games you damn fool not for me but for yourself don't you have even an ounce of pride? That you should want me to see you like this! Remember this well . . . if we ever happen to run into each other I'm going to coldcock you the minute I see you you're as good as dead . . . and Helen shook her finger and then to demonstrate to us graphically what she thought of the whole deal she doubled over and pretended to vomit . . . except that something let loose inside of her and she actually did vomit all over the blanket and no doubt the girls down at the supermarket had pickled herrings for lunch judging by the herring tails discharged onto the blanket along with undigested potato salad . . . Helen seemed shocked at first but when she looked around at the studio and at the bloody blanket and at Jirka's blood-streaked face she lit up with satisfaction and laughing loudly ran up the stairs and slammed the door to the street so hard the glass shattered and sprayed the sidewalk . . . Jirka raised those puppy-dog eyes of his and said to my husband . . . What do you think Doctor I guess she doesn't like me after all . . .

■ □ ■ □ ■

CHAPTER TWENTY

My husband had a little radio that he kept tuned to Vienna and he took great pleasure listening to symphonies and violin concertos and when he listened he always gazed out the window at the sliver of sky and that music carried him up and away over the rooftops of the Libeň tenements to somewhere else entirely and while I washed the dishes or worked my crossword puzzles my husband stood there next to the window and floated away on that music and I intentionally washed dishes and sometimes washed them twice out of frustration because I just didn't understand those symphonic epics and I didn't understand when my husband tried to explain it when he tried to draw me into the beauty of that symphony music by quoting T. S. Eliot the author of *The Waste Land* . . . Music is a vertical raised against the beating of the human heart . . . But I didn't understand it and when my husband came at me with symphonies and violin concertos I reacted by cleaning the flat I dragged back the wardrobe and rattled the chairs threw wood into the cast-iron stove clattered the shovel in the bucket and slammed the stove door closed and then I washed all our glasses and just maybe I washed them all over again But my husband never heard me or maybe he did but he just didn't care because that music took him somewhere else and as his Nymburk mother liked to say he's been somewhere else ever since he was a kid . . . and I watched my husband give himself over to the music watched his eyes well up and the tears roll down his face I saw how deeply moved he was as he fixed his eyes on that sliver of sky above the slanted shed roof but because I didn't have the key to the music myself I slammed in and out of our flat banged the door closed rooted through the cupboards like I was looking for something but my husband just stood next to the window listening to that symphony music from Vienna pour from that tiny radio and as the trumpets and the trombones and the horns and the drums rose to their crescendo my husband picked up that little radio and turned it up as loud as it would go and the music reverberated throughout our flat and into the courtyard and I was always forced to leave to go to the store or up to Liza's place to work on my needlepoint and you could hear the roar of the trumpets and the drums and the horns all the way up to the veranda . . . But when Vienna wasn't broadcasting those symphonies and violin and piano concertos . . . then my husband tuned in Radio Luxembourg and listened to the beloved jazz that never failed to move him . . . and then even I was quiet and the jazz music brought us together and although the sun was shining outside we sat in the half-light of our flat under the glow of the droplight and listened to Radio Luxembourg play the likes of Glenn Miller and Benny Goodman . . . and my husband and I loved Armstrong his soulful voice and his trumpet and Count Basie banging out the blues on his piano accompanied by jazz orchestra . . . and again my husband stood at the window and gazed at the sliver of sky above the slanted shed roof which was always buried in brick and plaster because at any time of day or night a shot might ring out from the machine shop behind the tall wall and send a shock wave of plaster and brick crashing down on the roof of the shed below like a Wertheim safe falling from the sky . . . and when we listened to Luxembourg and one of my songs came on when I was moved by the voices of those blues singers or by Frank Sinatra or Grace Kelly then I turned the radio up so loud the whole flat filled with music and song and my husband welled up and I was on the brink too and we were oblivious to Mrs. Slavíčková shouting from upstairs . . . What're you crazy . . . ? Listening to Luxembourg our favorite was Armstrong . . . *Lord have mercy on my darling Nelly Grey* . . . and that was just too much and we couldn't hold back the tears any longer listening to *Nelly Grey* and we held each other and promised to buy ourselves a tape recorder to record this Louis Armstrong song . . . But tonight my husband made a roast pork with caraway seeds and he bought fresh bread it was a special occasion because he invited his friend Mr. Kolář over for dinner the poet known to his friends as the Pecking Eagle and he was joined by a Mr. Hiršal a poet as well and I made runs to the pub for beer and Mr. Kolář was a true gentleman he brought me a bouquet of flowers and was elegantly dressed he knew just how to wear those gray slacks of his and when he sat down he made sure they didn't crease at the knees and he wore an elegant necktie and kept a white handkerchief folded into the breast pocket of his checked jacket and he cleaned his spectacles meticulously with that white breast-pocket handkerchief . . . and my husband sat there and I never saw him as humble as respectful as he was in the company of those two poets And Mr. Hiršal looked more the slaughterhouse worker than he did the poet and he wore corduroy slacks and a corduroy jacket and every so often he pulled a brush from his pocket and ran it through his thick short hair and the brush crackled . . . and every so often Mr. Hiršal said . . . That's fantastic . . . and he chain-smoked and tapped his ashes to the floor or simply let them fall on his clothes . . . And my husband talked a while about his writing but his voice was unsteady and he had to keep clearing his throat and he lost his train of thought and flushed and stared at the floor and then devotedly he lit the poet Hiršal's cigarette and Mr. Kolář hitched up his pants leg and crossed his legs and his voice rumbled . . . Look here! Right from the get-go American poetry stands on the twin pillars of Whitman and Poe . . . what a way for American literature to kick off the twentieth century . . . And modern French literature has Baudelaire who not only translated Poe but was in fact inspired by his poetic . . . Look we can't forget that during the time the impressionists were all the rage in Paris our king was Mikoláš Aleš But we've got our own Purkyne and Karl Hynka Mácha and the rest But then again in Paris Rimbaud's already written *A Season in Hell* and Lautréamont *The Songs of Maldoror* while for us Neruda reigns supreme But let's not forget we've Božena Nemcová a far greater poet than France has in the likes of George Sand and her romantic letters But Sand still trumps America's Anais Nin But look out for our own Schikaneder the creator of a painting called *Worker Falls to His Death* in which people walk past the dead man but can't see him because in between them and the scene of the tragedy stands a wooden fence . . . So said the poet Jiří Kolář in his rumbling voice and I saw that he really was the Pecking Eagle because he had my husband in a sweat and staring at the floor and the poet Hiršal tapped his ash onto my husband's trousers and said That's fantastic . . . And the poet Jiří Kolář rumbled on like he was delivering a lecture to a crowded theater . . . But the most beautiful thing about art is that no one actually has to do it and a writer can do whatever he wants so long as he stays true to his inner voice If you've a family and you don't look after them art will grant you that But take note you must not betray or bury or squander the talent entrusted you What you create as an artist that's the deciding factor because art's the cruelest thing there is second only to nature Okay fine you say you work down there on Spálená Street baling paper and you're moved by the things you see and by what people say and you drink copious amounts of beer and wait for the right moment to come But when is it going to come It won't fall from the sky you've got to make it happen yourself you've got to grab it Steal it like Prometheus The dreck will come on its own Why as it is now you come home from work and collapse on the sofa into sleep and your best energy is left back at Spálená Street and back in the pubs How old are you already for God's sake? And my husband whispered meekly . . . Forty-three . . . And Mr. Kolář the Pecking Eagle rumbled . . . For the love of God half the famous writers had their life's work behind them at forty-three some of them were already six feet under take it from me opportunity knocks for only so long it'll fool you and take heed because the minute we're born the clock starts winding down to our death You don't have any kids so what are you waiting for . . . The employment office won't bother you so stay at home . . . And write . . . That short story of yours Jarmilka obliges you You've got it in you so sit and write . . . And I just had to smile because I knew this was precisely what my husband feared most the moment he would find himself home alone with his writing when he would have to face the music and I smiled to myself and went to fetch more beer and the poet Hiršal ran his brush through his hair and tapped his ashes next to the ashtray onto my tablecloth and said That's fantastic . . . And when I returned from Vaništa's with a fresh pitcher of beer the poets had set to and were eating the roast pork and the fresh bread cutting chunks of meat straight from the pot and wiping up the drippings and Jiří Kolář ate with care and with decorum while my husband wolfed down the meat like a dog and Mr. Hiršal was probably finished with his food or he didn't care for any because he smoked his cigarette as always but now he put it down on the lip of the ashtray and helped himself to a piece of meat and I put the pitcher of beer down on the table and went to get some glasses but Mr. Kolář said Don't trouble yourself Miss Pipsi I like to drink straight from the pitcher . . . And he lifted the pitcher and drank and he seemed to do everything like he was being photographed and when he finished drinking he pulled out his little handkerchief and dabbed his lips And Mr. Hiršal smoked and said That's fantastic and tapped his ashes onto my husband's trousers . . . And at dusk Vladimir appeared in the courtyard followed by Tekla coming up the stairs and both of them wiped their shoes carefully on the doormat and then Vladimir knocked and said Doctor are you home? And my husband flung the door open and invited Vladimir and Tekla in and they took off their shoes and Vladimir handed my husband a shopping bag and said Doctor my mom gave me a little pot of pork goulash something to warm you up And Vladimir and the poets exchanged hellos it was obvious they knew each other and had planned to meet here except for Tekla who was meeting them for the first time And yet again she wore her little blue outfit and yet again she made eyes at Vladimir and when Vladimir sat down she sat down beside him and put a hand on his knee and stared at him like he was her god . . . Vladimir for God's sake what am I going to do with this pot of goulash have a little pork roast and take a drink of beer my wife'll run down and get us some more . . . So sputtered my husband and he polished off the pitcher and the poets downed their steins and I ran off to Vaništa's for more . . . And I got back just in time for Tekla was taking out her drawings and doodlings and Mr. Jiří Kolář fanned out the drawings and watercolors on the table and examined them in turn and then passed them to Mr. Hiršal and Vladimir was on tenterhooks and Tekla had her eye on the Pecking Eagle who now put down the drawings and extracted his handkerchief and breathed on his eyeglasses and polished them meticulously and all of us watched him like we were in court awaiting the verdict and it was quiet except for the high whine of the machines in the workshop next door And Mr. Kolář looked at Vladimir and said For God's sake Vladimir you can't possibly be serious You call this art? Do you actually think this has

165
▼

talent? For God's sake third graders churn this stuff out like it's coming off the assembly line . . . And I whisked the pot from Vladimir's shopping bag and asked him if he wanted to eat it cold or should I heat it up for him? But Vladimir was pale and his ears were back like a mean horse and Tekla's fingernails dug into his knee and her eyes practically rolled back in her head like she was about to fling herself to the floor and go into fits . . . and I watched my husband who had pronounced these doodlings to have talent while I had been the only one to call it like I saw it like the Pecking Eagle the poet Jiří Kolář saw it and with the utmost gravity he said . . . Vladimir believe me Tekla can't even present this stuff to the academy look here . . . And again he spread the drawings and watercolors out on the table and said expertly . . . All this was done in a week there isn't a thimble's worth of talent here not even a shadow But draw on paint away! In Amsterdam are Vincent van Gogh's first attempts at painting it's something awful no professor here would accept him to the academy but van Gogh had it in him and he ignored what people said and kept on painting and it came to him . . . Tekla keep working . . . And listen up Vladimir now that I have you here if I wanted to put on an exhibit of your work where would I get my hands on the stuff? And Vladimir stuttered and said quietly I gave it all away . . . And the Pecking Eagle rumbled Well there you have it so look here I'll give you fifty crowns for every graphic print you make you can bank on it And when there's a hundred of them you have my word we'll have an exhibition And the Pecking Eagle extended a hand and it was missing a thumb and the poet Hiršal repeated That's fantastic and tapped his cigarette ash into the pot of pork roast leftovers and I saw Tekla really was on the brink of a blowout and I smiled at my husband and I smiled at Vladimir those two number ones and future champions of the world who had just been served up the truth by Mr. Jiří Kolář . . . and the Pecking Eagle wasn't quite finished and he stood there his arm outstretched and said . . . And Vladimir one more thing . . . Format's a pretty big deal today in the art world . . . get yourself a bigger rolling press or I'll have one made for you start creating bigger prints . . . and look here! Don't throw out your old plates Vladimir those are artifacts in their own right . . . so to repeat . . . work in larger format and for every print you bring me I will pay you fifty crowns . . . but listen! They'll still be yours . . . and then we'll have an exhibition! On that I Jiří Kolář give you my word . . . And just then Tekla sprang up and grabbed her drawings and started yelling at the two poets like a crazy woman . . . You useless pricks . . . ! And then she commenced to shower the poets with a stream of colorful Hungarian invective and her voice swelled and she shouted . . . Vladimir we're leaving! And they grabbed their shoes in the hallway . . . and from the courtyard Tekla screamed through our open windows . . . Useless pricks . . . jerk-offs . . . And I put the little pot in a shopping bag and went after them and as I tried to hand the pot to Tekla who clutched at her art-work I said . . . So you've something for dinner . . . but the little pot clattered to the ground and Tekla and Vladimir ran down the stairs under the glare of the naked bulb and at the bottom of the stairs Mrs. Beranová splashed bucketfuls of water onto the tiles and swept the water away into the gutter and I picked up the bag with the little pot and ran downstairs and jumped over the puddle of water . . . and Mrs. Beranová shouted . . . Look out . . . ! And I ran after Vladimir and Tekla into the street chased them all the way from the gas lamp in front of our building down to the corner of Bratrská Street . . . and I just couldn't help laughing as I made Vladimir take the shopping bag with the little pot of goulash . . . and Tekla ran on ahead to the tram tracks screaming Good-for-nothing pricks . . . ! And Vladimir said to me . . . So there we are in a nutshell madame . . . And then he ran off after Tekla . . . When I got back to our building Mrs. Beranová was still splashing bucketfuls of water from a gushing tap onto the tiles and as usual she commended herself . . . You see I'm a stickler for clean . . . but it sounds like you had quite the ruckus at your place tonight . . . poor thing . . . And when I entered our flat the two poets were rising to leave with proper decorum and Mr. Hiršal searched for a place to butt out his cigarette but he missed the ashtray and stubbed out his smoke in the pot of leftover pork roast and Mr. Kolář thanked me for a beautiful afternoon and evening and said . . . Now look here! That husband of yours *is* a writer . . . with him I'll make an exception . . . Don't rush things before their time . . . That little book of his about the steelworks is my favorite book . . . but listen up! Leave it exactly as it was written on that German Perkeo *schreibma-chine* . . . Add neither diacritics nor punctuation . . . And most importantly don't force things . . . Sherwood Anderson began writing in his retirement . . . and he's the big man of American letters . . . with his first book already he was a number one . . . It's true they call me the Pecking Eagle and peck I do . . . my duty is to peck not only at others but at myself as well . . . And the poet Hiršal added . . . Today was just fantastic . . .

■ □ ■ □ ■

CHAPTER TWENTY-ONE

Once when I was over at Milada's place her brother Vincent showed up but he didn't like being called Vincent he always corrected you and said his name was Čeněk . . . but my husband and Milada and Mr. Kocián called him Vincent . . . So Vincent arrived in a poor state just skin and bones and he had nowhere to live so they told him he could stay at the Kociáns' before finding himself a sublet and apparently Vincent used to be a top-notch operetta singer akin to the likes of Richard Tauber and Vincent said that although Richard Tauber was an opera singer he liked to sing the works of Lehár too . . . Tauber's response to his critics had been . . . *Ich singe keine Operette ich singe Lehár* . . . And Vincent was always closely shaved and his clothes ironed and his hair pomaded and apparently he had trained as a tailor even Milada said he was an excellent clothier but his real passion was operetta and all he ever talked about was operetta . . . And so he sat in the kitchen and mended Mr. Kocián's suits and trousers and sewed on buttons and Milada was in a constant state because she knew that every time Mr. Kocián came home to find Vincent still there without a sublet he'd start to lecture and then just end up losing it . . . And I felt for Vincent because I knew he never had any great role in those operettas and he sewed on buttons and cleared his throat and told us how he sang Bolo and how he sang *The Gypsy Baron* and he mended Mr. Kocián's trousers and reminded us for the umpteenth time how far he would have gone if only his father had bought him the tailcoat he'd wanted back at the start of his operetta career . . . certainly he wouldn't have sunk so low as to be sitting here at his sister's place sewing on buttons . . . And I couldn't help but think of my husband who much like Vincent harbored grandiose ideas and was convinced he would make number one and champion of the covered courts and champion of the world . . . And when Vincent spoke of Lehár and Strauss and Kálmán and of the leading men he positively glowed and when Mr. Kocián was off at work Vincent sometimes launched into an aria and his voice was indeed beautiful a lovely tenor but after a few lines he coughed and stopped singing and apologized and said it was all because of that tailcoat his father had refused to buy him way back when because his father had wanted him to do what he'd trained for what he knew how to do and that was be a tailor And my husband sat next to Vincent and listened to him tell his stories and he was absolutely delighted at Vincent's indomitable belief in himself at the idea he would still take the operetta world by storm one day with that voice of his not to mention that his Prague friends had invited him along on a major operetta tour that went from city to city . . . And my husband told me later that back when he worked as a toy and notions salesman for the Karel Henry Klofanda Company he'd arrived in Kyšperk toting his suitcase full of samples and a cold wind was blowing and there on the town square he ran into Vincent who was dressed in a light coat and frozen to the bone but whose face was all aglow because his operetta group was in town and Vincent invited my husband to the theater and he told my husband to keep an eye on the first-floor windows of the houses facing the square because in many a window was a lovely young lady looking out at Vincent with yearning because every woman in that town had a crush on Vincent . . . And so my husband followed Vincent to the theater and the theater was dreadfully cold and the performers were wretched and they warmed their hands over a gas cooker and my husband had a chunk of bacon with him and he offered it around to those operetta singers he cut it up into slices and they wolfed it down and then my husband went out to the square and bought three kilos of kielbasa and a bag of rolls and he went back to the theater and the kielbasa and rolls disappeared in short order and then the singers finally perked up a bit and looked at my husband with a glimmer of luck a glimmer of hope . . . meanwhile Vincent was busting with pride that my husband actually could see him as part of an operetta group . . . And my husband said good-bye to the singers and Vincent accompanied him to the station and they stood in front of a poster advertising the operetta and Vincent had only a minor role though he fancied himself on the level of a first tenor because of his lush and textured voice . . . And so one evening I came over to Milada's to have a bath and found them all as happy as can be even Mr. Kocián was happy and Vincent was over the moon because he was about to set off with his operetta group on a multicity cultural tour and Vincent would show that even though his father had failed to buy him that tailcoat back at the start of his career he was still a number one and he advised Milada and Mr. Kocián to scan the arts reviews in the daily papers for surely they would make mention of his lushly textured tenor . . . and because of something that happened the night before Mr. Kocián was doubly glad Vincent was shoving off . . . Mr. Kocián had been sitting with guests when at one point he crossed one leg over the other and wiggled his shoe around in the hopes his guests might get a load of the fancy socks he was wearing decorated with little white American stars set against a field of blue . . . and just then Vincent said Brother why're you swinging your foot around so nervously? And Mr. Kocián paled and made the mistake of saying . . . Why do you ask? And Vincent replied with a laugh . . . Because this is how people fidget right before they lose their mind . . . And so Vincent's bags were packed and Mr. Kocián wished Vincent tremendous success on that cultural tour traveling from town to town because then Mr. Kocián might enjoy a little peace and quiet . . . But when I went over the next week there was Vincent not crowned with laurels but slumped in his chair like an old man he'd caught terrible cold somewhere up in Rychnov on Kněžna . . . and he'd only one chance to sing his all-star number . . . *Nur für Natur hegte Sie Sympathie unter Bäumen süsse Träume liebe Gräfin Melani* . . . he sang in German because under the Protectorate he sang in a German opera chorus . . . and up there in Rychnov on Kněžna Vincent sang like never before but then he came down with fever and although he still traveled with the group and took curtain calls with them he couldn't sing anymore and so he begged them not to send him home to let him stay on the road with them because it was his greatest triumph to date and indeed all of the performers said they never heard an aria sung with such depth of feeling and now Vincent sat in the chair at Milada's place and smiled but there was no more mention of how he wouldn't have ended up like this if only his father had bought him that tailcoat . . . in fact Vincent was happy his father had never bought him the tailcoat that was precisely what had prompted him to sing *Nur für Natur* with such passion up in Rychnov on Kněžna . . . and the night Vincent returned he was already dying but we were none the wiser because he regaled us with stories of beautiful women and bouquets of roses in every city and how everyone was taken with his voice and with his looks because Vincent before he embarked on the tour had his teeth sprayed with white enamel and as he sang up there in Rychnov on Kněžna his teeth glittered and all the young ladies were positively enchanted . . . And the day after he returned he was taken to the sanatorium in Liberec . . . and then the news came that Vincent had died . . . My husband and I and Milada and Mr. Kocián went to the funeral together . . . we wanted to have a last look at Vincent and so there in the crematorium they opened the casket and there lay Vincent fresh out of the freezer a tiny frozen water droplet glittering on his nose and he had a smile on his face and Milada fixed his thick white hair and Vincent lay there grinning he always liked to smile and show off the beautiful teeth he had coated with white enamel . . . And so we stood in front of the casket there in the ceremonial hall and someone said a few words and the casket was adorned with wreaths and bouquets of flowers and my husband stared at the black velvet curtain that formed a sort of wall opposite the room and the curtain had a slight opening through which someone watched us and the whites of their eyes shone amid the black . . . and then it was time and the musicians behind the curtain began to play . . . *Nobody in the world . . . loved you like I did . . .* And Vincent's casket slowly slid behind the partition . . . and the music played from behind the black velvet curtain which billowed gently and my husband stared at the curtain and later when we were outside the crematorium he said it was the first violinist poking the velvet curtain with his bow as he played that made the black velvet billow in and out . . . and the billowing black velvet and the white eye shining amid the black was the vision that haunted my husband whenever the song came on from Vienna or Luxembourg and the tiny radio played . . . *Nobody in the world . . . loved you like I did . . .*

CHAPTER TWENTY-TWO

And the day came for my last shift at the Hotel Paris One last time I sat in the kitchen one last time I marked down all the food streaming out of the kitchen aboard trays and saucers bound for the Hotel Paris restaurant one last time I sat amid the smell and steam and heat of the kitchen in the light of the bare bulbs in the light streaming through the skylight one last time to joke around with the line cooks the two young men who came to work on their motorcycles on their sport 250s one last time to work with the scullery maids and the waitresses and with Headwaiter Mašek whose dreams had finally come true his daughter was figure-skating champion of the world all those years of sacrifice had paid off and his daughter Hana was champion of not just Europe but of the whole world . . . Headwaiter Mašek always loved to joke around but now that his daughter whose training regimen he'd reported to us without fail was suddenly best in the world he seemed melancholy and worn out . . . Headwaiter Mašek was so stunned by that title of champion of the world he made mistakes in his own work and he never took us into his confidence anymore now that his daughter belonged to the public both at home and in Europe and America . . . and Headwaiter Mašek quietly savored the newspaper reports of his daughter and looked forward to when she came back from competitions and exhibitions and he was happy when she bought herself a fancy new car and back before she was a champion Headwaiter Mašek gushed about her training regimen and her early mornings and now he just waved his hand at all his daughter's fame and fortune she was no longer his now she belonged to the public and not to the devoted headwaiter Mašek . . . I got the feeling Mr. Mašek was jealous of those hundreds of thousands of spectators who had taken his daughter away he had done his best and his dream had come true yet somehow he was left all alone Toward the end of my shift my coworkers brought me a bouquet of flowers and I gave them a bottle of cognac and then I cleaned out my drawer there behind the till a few pens and some knickknacks and as I was leaving the tears sprang to my eyes and I turned in the doorway and they all stood there frozen like in the fairy tale Sleeping Beauty where the cook stands frozen over the stove they stood there looking at me and I guess after all those years they were as fond of me as I was of them . . . And the next day I started work as a waitress at a brand-new restaurant on Jindřišská Street at the Palace Hotel and the entrance was off Panská Street and the headwaiter was Mr. Borek and the cook Miss Boženka and we had to arrive two hours before opening to prep everything to bring the chickens up from the freezers and skewer them and put them in the Italian rotisserie and then I prepared the cutlery the bread and the rolls put the salads in the cold cabinet and then I dressed in my beautiful black uniform with the white V-neck blouse fixed my hair and brushed on a little mascara I tied on my white apron with the white trim and pinned my white cap into my hair and at ten o'clock I unlocked the glass door and the first patrons came in for their roast chicken and Mr. Borek polished the shot glasses against the window light to draw customers it was always nice to work with Mr. Borek he didn't play cards or drink or put money on the ponies he was always smiling and he looked like a young chaplain the sort young Christian girls fall in love with after confession and during mass His one passion was his little doggy And if you got him talking it was always about his doggy who he loved like a child since he had no children of his own And working as a waitress took me back to when I was a young girl to when I lived with my mother and father and siblings to when we always had guests over to the big house with the many rooms and the beautiful furniture and the cook and the chauffeur This bistro at the Palace Hotel had mirrored walls and glass doors and the windows faced south so when the sun shone it was beautiful like being inside of a giant diamond ring and people streamed past on the street and the fans kept the air inside clean and fresh and when customers came in I danced over to their table and took the orders and then it was over to the rotisserie where the roast chickens rotated slowly dripping juice and the skin was golden brown and when Miss Boženka opened the glass rotisserie door the steam and fragrance of roasting meat rushed out and I didn't even have to turn around to know the customers' eyes were on me and I was proud of the fact I was once again center of attention just like I was in my teenage years when we often had guests over officers and friends of my papa's from the UP company in Brno where Papa was an advisor and when I served Papa's guests liqueur or played piano for them or engaged them in conversation I already knew the men took me for a woman I matured early a lot earlier than other girls I had a beautiful bust and long legs and took dance classes at the school of ballet and whenever I stood by a window or on the terrace I always stood in the first position of dance my hands in front fingers clasped together and my right foot turned out like I was just about to start dancing . . . And here at the Palace Hotel Grill I served plates of chicken and side dishes and bowls of warm water for the guests to rinse their hands . . . I always moved with a sort of dancer's step and if I just stood waiting for a guest to signal me over I stood with my right foot turned out and held a white napkin in my hands and all sorts of people came here to the Palace Grill as regulars actors and filmmakers and poets and I was the center of attention because I still had what it took I still had the looks and it wasn't just the mirror that told me it was the men's eyes following me around the room and of course when women saw this they pretended not to notice me at all And Headwaiter Borek as he served his pitchers of pilsner always had a smile on his face and he had a style all his own as does every good waiter he spoke in quiet tones and then only when spoken to and he always leaned in to the customer and was very genuine and because he had thick pomaded hair parted down the middle and nice brown eyes he always looked the customer right in the eye . . . And here at this grill in this light and in my beautiful and elegant uniform I found myself once again . . . I lost the skittishness and sense of guilt I'd carried around since war's end when I'd been made to feel like some sort of war criminal when I'd gone from innocence to guilt despite the fact I had nothing to feel guilty about . . . but here at the Palace Grill no one screamed at me anymore as they had in the prison camp we were moved to at war's end no one screamed at me as they had in the brickworks where I was forced to sit off to one side with the rest of the German women like I had scabies or something . . . and here at the Palace Grill I was on my way to becoming a number one waitress I had regulars of my own who were customers as well as friends and they affectionately called me Miss Eliška and when they ordered a glass they stood me a drink as well and we touched glasses and I had a little sip and then I was off again to another table . . . I never realized that dream of mine to become a dancer another showstopper like La Jana but here at the Palace Grill I was engaged in something I liked and I could even put some of those moves I learned back at the school of ballet to good use . . . ultimately I'd been ashamed of wanting to be a variety show dancer I just wasn't any good at it I didn't have the stuff to be a professional dancer my dancing was about on par with my piano playing and while I worked at the piano very hard I still made atrocious mistakes when I played . . . But as a waitress I was getting to be a real number one working here at the grill was like being onstage eight to ten hours a day I was beautifully dressed and my hair done up and I danced with my plates and saucers from table to table and from bar to rotisserie . . . And the first time my husband saw me here he was taken aback absolutely shocked And I took that as a good sign I knew I looked good and he gazed at me like he was seeing me for the first time like he was falling head over heels in love And one day he stood there in the entrance with his hand on the door weighing whether or not to come in and I took him by the arm and introduced him to Mr. Borek and to Miss Boženka and it seemed he just couldn't wrap his head around seeing me here the way customers' eyes followed me around the room I just seemed like a completely different person to him . . . up there in Libeň I always played the Cinderella part . . . when my husband and I first met I was the spurned lover who had attempted suicide and my husband fancied he had saved me by marrying me by giving me the protection of his name and a permanent place to live and that husband of mine certainly never let me forget it but here at the Palace Hotel in the exclusivity of the mirrored grill and in my beautiful black uniform and white apron and white cap pinned to my hair like a tiara the tables were turned . . . my husband was struck that I was desired and beautiful and now he was the chastened one . . . I finally became that Paris pastry with the whipped cream on top my auntie had been right all along but it had taken me years of hardship and years of being down and out . . . From the moment I got the waitress job my husband fell in love with me maybe not so much in love with me as in love with that outfit of mine with the fact I was a waitress . . . he brought all his friends around to have a look at me through the plate glass he never came in with them but I saw those friends of his watching me there in the twilight saw my husband telling them my life story and pointing me out as I danced around the bistro with plates of hot roast chicken and bussed the tables and scraped the chicken bones for the old ladies who came around to collect them for their assorted stray dogs and cats . . . Slowly but surely I was becoming a number one even in my husband's eyes he was honored by my job proud I was a waitress as far as he was concerned it was the most glorious job a woman could have even as a teenager he was fond of waitresses honored when they chatted him up in front of other customers or sat down with him for a few minutes he never dreamed he'd be married to a waitress to a woman who his friends would want to sneak a peek at to a woman who was an object of desire and who fended off customers' advances with a smile never dreamed such a woman could be his wife . . . My husband liked to wait for me when I finished my shift and Headwaiter Borek always invited him in for a seat at the bar but my husband always politely declined he strolled outside under the lighted windows of the grill and waited while we put away the salads and the side dishes and Miss Boženka cleaned out the rotisserie and Headwaiter Borek tallied the day's receipts and divvied up the tips and I freshened up and changed clothes and grabbed my parasol and out I went to Jindrišská Street and my husband latched onto me and we loved a stroll through Wenceslas Square and under the linden trees and we always stopped for a pint at Bar Pinkas I loved it when the waiter flew up from the cellar six pints in each hand and slammed them down on the counter . . . My husband took two pints and ritually smeared some foam on his forehead and then he took a sip and I always downed my beer in one shot and I knew one of the waiters there he liked to come in to the grill on his days off for a whole chicken and once when my husband and I were at Pinkas having a beer he said to me . . . Miss Eliška you want to see something? And I said with a smile . . . Of course I do and so does my husband! And the waiter pointed and said . . . This is your husband? Well what do you know we've known each other for years . . . And the waiter stood at the top of the stairs and he was slightly tipsy and he made for us to follow him and my husband and I descended the stairs to the cellar and there was a barman in a white plastic apron drawing pints of beer and on the damp ground stood beer kegs and clear pipes flowing with beer led from the kegs up to the ceiling . . . And the barman said . . . Miss Eliška how nice to have your company . . . and he offered me his elbow and then he went on drawing his pints and smiling he was a young man with thick black hair . . . What brings you down here Miss Eliška? and the waiter laughed . . . Miss Eliška is my guest . . . Miss Eliška what you have here is the last of the great Prague beer served at keg temperature seven-point-six degrees . . . Miss Eliška what Rome is to a good Catholic and what Moscow is to a good communist is what Pilsen is to a good beer drinker But anyone who thinks Pilsen has a lock on serving great pilsner is wrong here at Pinkas we pour the greatest pint in the world . . . The barman handed me a glass and I leaned on my parasol its tip stuck in the damp cellar earth and I drank and I drank and the foam ran over my lips and the young barman untied his plastic apron and hung it up then he tightened the taps and draped them over with a white table napkin . . . And he practically collapsed into a chair he was so tired from standing on his feet all day drawing those pints of the greatest beer in the world making sure the quality was up to par and I certainly knew how he felt I practically collapsed myself after each shift no one could possibly understand not even my husband what it was like to be on your feet all day long what it was like in a kitchen amid the steam and the smoke of burnt grease what it was like to navigate through tables balancing plates laden with food . . . The barman and I looked at each other and shrugged and he smiled sadly and I smiled back and we felt a kinship . . . Then the barman said . . . Who'd understand anyway? My husband stood there and felt shunned and ripped off because he wasn't offered a beer . . . I had belonged to this class of waiters and waitresses and cashiers and barmaids for so long all of whom put on a smile when it's time for a shift and all of whom consume quantities of coffee and cigarettes and alcohol and keep the smiles pasted on until the shift's over and they collapse and I too was worn to the bone from running up and down the stairs at the Palace Hotel down to the cellar to get the chickens and up two flights of circular stairs when a guest in the hotel restaurant wanted a roast chicken . . . I could certainly relate to this barman standing here for twelve hours a day drawing his famous pints of Pinkas pilsner and to the waiter who moments ago ascended the flight of wet stairs with his twelve pints of beer for the hundredth or perhaps thousandth time today to skillfully slide those pints on the counter from where the waiters picked them up and distributed the last round of the day . . .

Vladimir and Tekla moved in to his mother's flat and Jirka Šmejkal repainted his giant basement space white but the vastness of that basement chamber seemed to inspire him in a backward sort of way He liked to sit dead center of that cavernous space and etch his drawings the tiniest bugs and insects onto a small copper plate and those prints were even smaller than his assorted butterfly graphics . . . Helen was a thing of the past as was the scene with the broken nose and the blood-smeared blanket designed to move her and the way she lit into Jirka was probably a good thing because he was more introspective ever since He started dating a young divorcée who was as diminutive as him and who loved to drink beer as much as him The beer drinking brought them closer together . . . at Mr. Vaništa's the two of them put back so much beer people in the taproom and the bar and even people off the street came to watch And Jirka and his sweetheart were each on their fifteenth pint and Jirka had his graphic prints with him and showed everyone at the bar his tiny life-sized insects and he was a number one because in Libeň whoever drank the most beer was number one and what's more Jirka regaled the bar with stories of his prints and how he made them and everyone was thrilled And so Jirka gave anyone who showed interest a graphic print similar to Vladimir who couldn't take leave of a pub in Libeň or Vysočany or Žižkov without handing out every last one of his active graphics And Jaruška that new flame of Jirka's never left his side it was a charming sight how those two lovers belonged to each other how they took to each other like a couple of kittens Later that night as Jirka accompanied his sweetheart up to Pražačka he was overwhelmed by an enormous sense of strength and on the street from Krejcárky up to Pražačka he loosened and knocked over three stone bollards and then stood there like a Cyclops arms outstretched casting about for something else to test his strength on And down by the tram tracks were stacked sections of old rail and as his sweetheart looked on Jirka ran down and like King Kong lifted the sections over his head and tossed them all in a pile And when it was done he came back up the street and latched onto his sweetheart and off they went together past the coal piles past the Žižkov freight yards . . . Jirka's sweetheart was a seamstress and she had a little boy who was six years old but looked to be about three . . . I visited with them in the studio to admire the latest graphic prints and tiny insects and when Jirka's sweetheart went off with the huge beer tankard for ten liters of Smíchov ten-proof . . . then every fifteen minutes or so Jirka lost track of the little child the kid simply disappeared . . . it was like when you can't find your cat or your budgie or your keys or your eyeglasses And Jirka and his fiancée were always anxious they searched behind the shutters and under the blankets and even inside the giant press . . . they searched so frantically not because they worried the little child might get lost but because the child was afflicted with the strange malady of having to drink every liquid he came across . . . and sure enough as soon as they weren't looking he was into the beer and if they didn't stop him he'd drink all ten liters just like he'd drink the water out of the vase full of flowers wilted leaves and all the meadow flowers Jirka picked at his father's place on the banks of the Berounka to bring home to his sweetheart . . . Other times when they hid all the liquids in the house the little child locked himself in the bathroom and guzzled the water from the toilet tank and before Jirka could bust in the child managed to flush twice more And pretty soon Jirka got married there was a big in-house wedding and my husband and I were invited and all the relatives were there Jirka's and the bride's as well and I finally met Jirka's father the butterfly catcher the man in Jirka's painting who slept in a meadow in that same deep slumber one hand behind his head the other loosely by his side holding a butterfly net And I saw that in his father's eyes Jirka was a number one and champion of the world He gazed at Jirka as at a small statue of God and talked of nothing but his son's great future he was absolutely convinced that Jirka was a future national artist because already his graphic prints his butterflies and little bugs were all over Prague . . . And my husband picked up on that beautiful impression and expanded upon the scope of Jirka's future achievement Jirka was only thirty and in ten years his graphics and his butterflies would be all over Bohemia and in another ten all over Moravia and by the time Jirka was in his fifties Central Europe would be strewn with his butterflies and his insects every household would have a graphic print signed personally by one Jirka Šmejkal of Prague because the world had enough of the huge canvas the landscape the battle scene the historical event the world would succumb to its newfound love of miniatures to the tiny and beautiful realm of butterflies and all manner of insect . . . The bride's whole family drank like there was no tomorrow like they all suffered the same malady as the little child who was periodically caught slurping water from the kitchen faucet and if it wasn't the kitchen faucet it was the toilet tank or the basin full of water soapsuds and all and the water went through him like it was leaching into the ground like he was full of holes and he never appeared bloated he was quite normal and that water disappeared inside him as surely as if it was swirling down a drain And in addition to the little child with the huge thirst Jirka inherited the bride's family all of whom were as diminutive as she and as thirsty as Jirka And as part of the dowry Jirka came into a chalet in Střekov . . . it used to be a restaurant and he showed us photographs and invited us up for a visit but somehow my husband never mustered the strength to take him up on it . . . and that former Sudeten restaurant was so expansive sometimes it took five hours to locate the little child and that was only after they called in a police dog Jirka showed the wedding guests photographs of the restaurant he had a picture of every room and the restaurant proper had roughly the same dimensions as his basement studio on Žertvy but there was another floor with ten rooms reserved for spa-goers and there was even a dance hall . . . And Jirka described it with great passion but since the wedding party was in the midst of discussing who in the family held the record for beer drinking Jirka's father and my husband were the only ones listening . . . and I tuned in just to hear how far Jirka would exaggerate he showed us that Sudeten dance hall and said it was going to be his real studio he'd throw everything out and the place would be empty save for the giant press in the middle of the room and whenever the inspiration hit him he'd churn out more of those graphic prints life-sized butterflies and little insects and imagine that hall was so big they used to play basketball there and you could ride your bicycle around inside and local boys let off their wind-up model airplanes . . . And so the light began to wane and Jirka's father was so moved his eyes glistened with tears in the setting sun and three brown earthenware steins made the rounds were passed from person to person and every so often the bride ran off in her wedding veil and tiara and fake pearls for more beer . . . We said our good-byes and got hung up a while longer in the hallway . . . Jirka's father told us we had renewed his faith that he was beginning to suspect his son was destined for the middle ranks of graphic artists but after the conversation with my husband he dared believe Jirka would make it as my husband said to the upper echelons of Europe's graphic artists . . . And as we said our good-byes the door of the adjacent flat opened and the owner came out holding the bride's little child in his arms and complained . . . Horrible before we knew what hit us he drank all the water out of the vase and then slurped the brine out of the five liter pickle jar and before we managed to recover his head was already in the toilet tank . . . I'd rather you watch him yourselves! The bride took her little son by the hand and lifted him up and gave him a shake and then she thanked us for our wedding present My husband gave them a ten-liter enamel art deco water jug decorated with little flowers . . . We'll save that for the weekend hahaha . . . the bride laughed and she pulled her little son into the apartment and then the groom Jirka stumbled out and laughed and proclaimed . . . Onward and upward . . . Doctor check out what I'm going to have in that big studio . . . An eight-meter-long and two-meter-high canvas it's going to cover practically the whole wall And there's my magnum opus my father six meters long stretched out on his belly like a fallen soldier and then a meadow of wildflowers and I'll paint every sort of butterfly that exists in Bohemia hundreds of butterflies flitting about . . . but off in one corner I'll paint a little brook and that little son of mine who I just inherited will be at the brook slurping it dry every last drop will disappear into my little sonny . . . Why shouldn't he be immortal too he swills all our water so what the hell! I'll elevate him to the heavens what do you think of that? My husband shook hands with Jirka's father who welled up with tears he was so moved by it all and my husband said to Jirka You're a real work of art . . . And nothing whatsoever surprised me anymore even Vladimir went totally off his rocker . . . Vladimir couldn't be without his Tekla anymore not even for a second he was starting to get jittery and all he wanted was to get hitched down at city hall Just like his active graphics used to be his everything now it was the love affair all consuming and a question of life or death He often came over to our place on Na Hrázi Street in Libeň all aglow with excitement my husband he didn't take seriously anymore but suddenly I was an object of his affection . . . Madame . . . he started shyly . . . you're a woman so you'll understand . . . You know when my Tekla gets her visit . . . you know what I mean by her visit? I nodded unsettled You see when she gets her visit I just have to be with her I look after her the thing is I'm her fiancé and as her fiancé as her future husband I must see and know absolutely everything about her! So I change her pads in all seriousness I look after her those three days I wipe her and change her because I believe that a man in love has a right . . . Vladimir's voice was raised now probably because of the way he saw me looking at him and my husband got up and looked out the window he put his hands on the windowsill something out there on the roof seemed to fascinate him and then he came back and added wood to the fire and I knew this speech of Vladimir's was directed at my husband he had come to gloat because he knew my husband was not the sort to talk of such things . . . And Vladimir was rejuvenated returned to number one status with this most intimate of subjects he'd probably told Boženka Vaništa as well as the women in the factory all about it he wanted to stain as many people as possible he was carried away because he was in love for the first time and because he had a woman who loved him back . . . In winter Tekla got a new job as a tram conductor and Vladimir would wait for her at the terminus and when he could he rode the tram with her back and forth until it was time to take the tram to the yard or until she was relieved by another conductor So in winter Vladimir got into the habit of wearing just a tattered sweater over his naked skin and a little jacket and once he ran into our place shaking from the cold and rubbing his hands over the stove and my husband stoked the fire with the smashed cupboard wood he bought once a week on Novák Street and when Vladimir warmed up a bit he said to my husband in an offhand way . . . Look Doctor I saw these beautiful housecoats in Kotce some sort of Turkish export rejects you should buy one it'll suit you what am I saying Vladimir corrected himself it won't suit you but it'll certainly be appropriate given your current mental state . . . so said Vladimir and I saw the arrow hit its mark and I wished I knew the secret to piercing my husband with a few simple words to injuring him the way Vladimir could . . . I said . . . Vladimir why so lightly dressed? Vladimir took off his coat pretending to be warm but the real reason he took it off was to show my husband and me that all he wore underneath was a tattered sweater . . . And in a raspy voice Vladimir said . . . Madame you'll understand with that girl of mine out there riding the open tram in the frost and the blizzards her ovaries in pain from the cold what am I supposed to do? Just sit at home in my housecoat waiting for her to return meet her after her shift's over in my fur coat and my sheepskin hat? That would make me suffer but this way when I'm freezing too when I put myself through the same misery she goes through on her shift then I'm happy she's freezing for the people and I'm freezing for her and we're both freezing together but we can't live without each other we told each other so and by the same token we can't not freeze without each other either . . . So said Vladimir and I saw my husband hunched over adding more wood to the cast-iron stove and then he crossed to the adjacent room and got a large knife and went out to the courtyard and proceeded to sharpen the knife against the step . . . Vladimir stood warming his enormous hands over the fire no doubt dreaming up ways to draw the girl he loved even closer to himself the girl who rode the trams all day in the freezing cold and when my husband came back in he stood there in the window light testing the sharpness of the knife with his finger he liked his knives very sharp which explains why he always had a bandage over one finger . . . And Vladimir continued . . . Madame you see I can't just live vicariously I have to experience things for myself get bloody and dirty myself . . . the minute my Tekla started getting the pain in her ovaries from the freezing wind and the shaking of the tram is the minute both my kidneys started to hurt but what can I do about it? I laughed and said . . . That pain in your kidneys Mr. Vladimir is from the cold wind and the jarring ride of the tram you'll feel better as soon as your Tekla quits or takes her sick leave . . . Vladimir listened and put his jacket back on slowly . . . You're probably on to something there it's psychosomatic . . . the best thing that could happen is for her to get pregnant for us to have kids! And out of nowhere my husband shouted . . . For Christ's sake Vladimir! Hemingway's first short story was about him accompanying his father a doctor to help an Indian woman give birth . . . so Hemingway's father pulls back the blanket on the bunk . . . and lying there is an Indian with his throat cut he slit his own throat with a knife he couldn't handle the pressure of what was happening to his wife for Christ's sake you'll never be able to handle your wife giving birth either! Vladimir turned his head he looked more noble than ever and he said scornfully . . . So I'd cut my throat it'd be an absolute experience at least I wouldn't be sitting at home in my housecoat reading about what other people spill their blood over . . . Doctor! Don't forget Turkish housecoats going cheap! So said Vladimir victoriously and my husband stood there flummoxed and suddenly he looked up and said with a laugh . . . Dearest Vladimir do you know who besides yourself had first-class epilepsy? The prophet Mohamed and the writer Dostoyevsky The very same aura corona borealis! But listen up! It mustn't take longer than thirty seconds! No kicking the bucket! The most pleasant way to go is death by drowning . . . The Phoenician sailor! And Vladimir stood there like a tower struck by lightning and suddenly he leaped across the room to the cast-iron stove but I blocked his way and put up my hands and shouted . . . Don't you dare take the stove out again Vladimir don't you dare or I'll never speak to you again as long as I live . . . And Vladimir ran out to the yard biting his tongue and outside it was snowing and Vladimir ran down the stairs his curly head disappearing and I knew he felt on top of the world because he was in love and that was as it should be . . . And soon after my husband and I got all dressed up in our Sunday best to attend Vladimir's conventional wedding at Žižkov city hall and all the wedding guests were conventional as were all the clerks and the ceremony was conventional and then the exchange of rings was conventional and Vladimir was the most conventional groom I ever saw and he seemed quite bewildered by the whole thing like he just couldn't believe the luck marrying such a conventional bride who glowed with such conventional happiness . . . and then a conventional car pulled up and then another and another and it was off to a conventional hotel on Wenceslas Square and a conventional reception salon and then a conventional lunch followed by conventional photograph-taking and conventional tears and the only person who was unconventional was Vladimir's mother she looked like she used to play basketball and resembled Vladimir so closely she might have been his sister and then there was Tekla Holényová's family they were conventional too but in the way rich folks are conventional and there was no mistaking they were blue bloods and their behavior was impeccable . . . and I didn't take my eyes off Vladimir I was pretty disappointed he was so conventional so small-town a conventional husband ready to forsake all his active graphics work for just one smile from his conventional wife he sat there in that conventional reception salon on Wenceslas Square devoid of will and devoid of his sense of irony a mannequin in a shopwindow . . . And finally the newlyweds took their leave . . . off on their conventional honeymoon . . .

■ □ ■ □ ■

CHAPTER TWENTY-THREE

As soon as the sun hit the courtyard my husband was outside and wherever the sun moved my husband moved with his chair and sometimes even with his desk and when the sun jumped up to the roof of the little shed and the courtyard was in shade my husband jumped up onto the roof as well and stripped off his clothes and basked in the sunshine that he loved so much . . . And when we were out for a walk in Libeň my husband always crossed to the side of the street the sun was on And when we rode the tram he always sat by the window with the sunshine and it was the same thing on the train and the same thing on the bus Sometimes we went down to the old Libeň harbor to get some sunshine down to the other side of the bridge where a broken-down old houseboat sat onshore along with stacks of oak wood tanks used for holding fish sold at Christmas and Easter My husband liked to lie here on a blanket and soak up the sun in days gone by he swam here with Vladimir and even Jirka Šmejkal liked to come down to sketch the houseboat and the long boats where fragrant apples were stored over winter and there was always a crowd of young boys down here and they took no notice of my husband and my husband pretended to take no notice of them but in fact not a single movement not a single shout not a single word of theirs escaped him . . . My husband was happy by the river because there used to be a harbor here and a path that wound through the old locust trees down to Karlín and all the way to Pelc Tyrolka and there was an abandoned restaurant here called the Vltavan and my husband said the place used to be full to capacity on Saturdays and Sundays because folks liked to come here with their families on their weekend outings And I only swam here once because as I was coming out of the water a revolting condom was stuck to my shoulder and I threw the disgusting thing away and my husband laughed so hard he squealed and the boys up on the houseboat sunning themselves laughed too and peed off the deck of the houseboat into the water and more than once I saw those boys playing with their thingies they encouraged one another and my husband pretended to look somewhere else but he knew what was going on and he never did anything to stop it in fact he told me he approved of it because when he was a kid he played with his thingy too and he only regretted he couldn't be so freewheeling about it anymore . . . And then he told me a story about an old lady who lived in Švábky her name was Salcmanová and she made her living collecting used condoms around the Štrasburk hillside and by the fence next to the lumberyard and down on Slunečná Street . . . she collected the condoms in the morning and tossed them in a pail and then she came down here to the river and fished condoms out of the water with a barge pole and sometimes the boys even swam out into the river to look for condoms and then on the banks of the Vltava beneath the locust trees old lady Salcmanová put those condoms in a washtub and washed them out on a washboard and turned them inside out and ran them over the washboard again and then she lay them out on a sheet to dry and sprinkled them with talcum powder and then she drew them over a wooden spoon handle and rolled each one up carefully and placed it into a scented little pink or blue envelope designed for love letters and in the evenings she sold them at a discount to the Štrasburk young ladies and whores to the tarts from the La Paloma Bistro and the streetwalkers in front of the Nitra Hotel where you could rent a room by the hour . . . And I lay on a blanket in the sun and felt sick to my stomach I lay on my back and shielded my eyes from the sun I couldn't believe what I was seeing . . . trams hurtled and rumbled and rattled across the bridge and pedestrians crossed over and meanwhile the boys were in the bottom of the houseboat playing with their thingies sometimes they even brought girls along and played doctor with them they lay them down in the bottom of the boat under the gunwales and undressed them and played with their privates and my husband tried to look somewhere else but he could see everything as could I and he wasn't shocked he just smiled and told me that when he was a kid he used to play doctor too with the girls in Zálabí . . . And we lay by the river and out of the blue my husband starts telling me how when he lived with his parents in Polné he went to all the funerals took part in every funeral procession as one of the mourners . . . In his plumed cap and red jacket with gold buttons he slipped into every procession right behind the grieving relatives and when they wept he wept too and he participated in the procession because he loved the funeral band the golden trumpets and flügelhorns and helicons the black clarinets and he loved the swaying gait of the whole procession left foot right foot the way the whole thing moved to the rhythm of the lamenting music and the instruments glittered in the sunshine enough to make your eyes water and the procession entered the cemetery and the music played on even as the band members came to a halt and the mourners and my husband who was of course a little boy streamed past that glittering music to form a circle around the grave and the priest and the ministrants stood at the head of the grave and the mourners closed ranks around the casket and the wreath-laden black casket rested on two thick planks and then it was quiet and the priest made his speech and then someone in a black pinstripe suit said a few words and all the mourners were bareheaded and as my husband recounted to me on the banks of the river . . . I removed my cap and cried just like the distraught relatives whose faces you could hardly ever see because they were all swaddled in their black clothes and their mourning veils and then the priest took an aspergillum handed him by a ministrant and sprinkled the casket with holy water and then someone waved a white scarf and the music began to play a sad song of farewell and a quartet of cemetery workers dressed up like marshals took hold of the straps and began to lower the casket into the ground and several of the closest relatives those figures in black moved as if to leap in after the casket as if they wanted to jump in after the deceased and in the quiet they wept and lamented and shouted and always one of the figures in black collapsed and two other figures in black helped hold them up and the priest threw several shovelfuls of dirt and one after the other we stepped up to throw a shovelful of dirt and the dirt drummed against the casket and then the first one to leave was the priest who once again took the bereaved family members by the hand and whispered to them and then the other guests began to disperse as well and the band formed up by the cemetery gate and the grave digger put his money in his pocket and I put my cap back on and with eyes red from crying I stood next to the band and once all the mourners were assembled at the gate the band that earlier played a *trauermarsch* now struck up a *parademarsch* and all the funeral guests who were headed back to town set off at a jaunty spirited gait to match and the trumpets and the French horns and the bass flügelhorns glittered in the sunlight and as we'd gone to the cemetery in tears now we arrived to the pub in high spirits and we drank to the dearly departed and our tears dried up and we looked at each other and smiled and the band stood outside in the square by the gates to the pub and played cheerful songs and everyone made their way into the pub where it was nice and warm and then finally even the band slipped in and the musicians sat down at the table and every funeral I sat with them because I was this sort of local kid who everyone liked because they thought I was a bit of a country simpleton . . .

And the trams rattled across the Libeň Bridge and we lay on a little patch of grass near the houseboat and the boys swam in that disgusting water in and out of the river they went and they swam all the way over to the mooring lines of the apple boats and then they swam back and then they did it again . . . and then when the sun was at its hottest and it was scorching and muggy the boys were purple and shook all over their hands clenched under their chins and their teeth chattered and they couldn't get warm no matter how many blankets and jackets and shirts they put on . . . but of course the minute they did warm up back in the river they went diving off the end of the houseboat and horsing around until the chill took hold of them again My husband lay down next to me and turned so that he could whisper in my ear and at first I had absolutely no idea what he was on about . . . Look my husband said to me quietly after first giving my ear a nibble . . . You know what on our way home we'll buy a couple of flashlights . . . And I said . . . Flashlights what for and why a couple? And my husband whispered tenderly Why one for you my darling and one for me . . . And why two wouldn't one be enough? And my husband whispered confidentially I'll tell you what for how about we try playing a little game of doctor ourselves? And I got up and shouted Doctor what sort of doctor? And my husband lay on his back and shielded his eyes from the sun and said . . . Well in the evening in bed by the light of the flashlight I would examine you between the legs and then you could take your flashlight and give me an examination to see what I've got between my legs and we could play maybe not every day but at least once a week . . . And I shouted You mean this is the classiest thing you can come up with to say to me? And the group of naked boys turned to look at us wide-eyed and even the two girls with them gave a start and so I lay back down beside my husband and he whispered . . . Of course you're right I just remembered something that happened with the concertmaster von Schraubek . . . you see in Smetana Hall there's a canteen and for years the wife of the canteen manager had the hiccups or the hiccoughs as my grandmother used to say and try as she might the canteen manager's wife couldn't get rid of them even though the canteen manager took his wife to all the doctors because when she served members of the philharmonic wine or cognac and the hiccups hit her out of nowhere she spilled the drink . . . until one time the concertmaster von Schraubek saw it happen and said What's all this then? and the canteen manager just waved his hand and said it's a case of incurable hiccups And the concertmaster von Schraubek said Why don't you let us have a look at it I'll bet you a bottle of cognac I can cure her . . . and they shook on it and the concertmaster took the hiccupping canteen manager's wife by the hand and led her through the concert hall and then he helped her up on stage and then led her behind the organ where it was dark and there in the music-filled twilight just like that he whipped out his pecker and as the story goes he had a pecker like a poker like a calf's leg . . . and he put that thing in her hands and she shrieked Aieeeeeee! And five minutes later he returned her to the canteen manager and then a week passed and then two weeks and then a month and no hiccups and the canteen manager's wife was cured and von Schraubek gained a reputation as a miracle healer and a bottle of cognac to boot . . . Or my darling let me tell you about something that happened once in the National Theater when *Libuše* was playing . . . There was an elderly gentleman who attended the standing area of the theater an engineer as it turned out later who was in the occasional habit of placing his feeble member in the hands of someone standing in front of him . . . and during the performance of *Libuše* right at the point where Libuše prophesies Prague's future glory the gentleman plunked his member into the hands of a young lady whose hands were clasped behind her back and then a shout rang out from the engineer who hadn't noticed that the young lady had a prosthetic arm with a spring-loaded thumb . . . you see as soon as there was any pressure the spring released and the hand clamped shut and the unfortunate engineer yelled so loudly they had to turn the house lights on and the coat-check girls saw what was happening and called the police and the police pressed a button to release the prosthetic and then they charged the engineer with immoral behavior and with curtailing an individual's freedom because for a while there that young lady's freedom certainly was curtailed . . . But of course the aggravating circumstance for the crime was that the accused committed it at the very moment Libuše prophesies Prague's future glory . . . Or let me tell you about something else that happened during the performance of *Libuše* up in the balcony . . . darling this will warm your heart . . . And I got up and began to collect my things I didn't want to hear another word I had enough already not to mention the two boys in the bottom of the houseboat playing with themselves and I started off and my husband toddled behind me and I headed straight for home . . . And that evening when we were on the tram crossing the Libeň Bridge on our way to Milada's place for a bath . . . Actually I was the only one having a bath . . . God forbid if my husband was forced to wash his whole body at once he'd probably get strep throat he only bathed when I started yelling at him and then it was one leg only and when I yelled some more it was the other leg and he had to take a couple of aspirin right away because if he stuck his whole body into the tub at once surely he'd catch cold . . . so as we rode the streetcar someone sitting up front started to hiccup and my husband rose and pushed his way toward a woman holding on to the overhead bar and I flushed and got up but not in time to prevent my husband from asking the woman with the hiccups . . . Madame please don't take this the wrong way but I know of a foolproof method to rid yourself of the hiccups or the hiccoughs as my granny used to say . . . would you like me to cure you? And I elbowed my way toward the woman and red with shame I said . . . The best thing is you take a cube of sugar . . . but this is our stop isn't it? And the tram slowed and we could see the lights of the Battery pub but before we got off my husband said to me loud enough for everyone on the tram to hear . . .

You killjoy . . .

As a kid my husband's friend Karel Marysko was quite the magician . . . He lined up all the kids on Hradební Street and asked them What's the weather like? And the kids said it's sunny out . . . and Karel Marysko said to them So stand here at the foot of the wall and close your eyes and in just a minute I the great magician will conjure up rain . . . And so the kids lined up and Mr. Marysko peed on them from the top of the wall . . . And so one day this Mr. Marysko paid us a visit and he certainly didn't seem like a magician to me and he walked with a limp because he had arthritis from all the smoked pork hocks he loved to eat . . . and he brought news that his friend Borek was preparing a *schweinfest* that he was raising a little pig just for him and my husband and that the pig was getting nice and fat and the *schweinfest* would happen soon and the first day of the *schweinfest* was reserved exclusively for the men after which myself and Mr. Marysko's wife could attend . . . So said Mr. Marysko and he toyed with his fingers and seemed awfully shy . . . and then out of the blue he said to me it would be excellent if I got pregnant and in the fourth month had an abortion . . . What? I said horrified . . . And Mr. Marysko launched into a lecture on hormones how they were the force that moves the world and when a beautiful woman becomes pregnant all those beautiful juices well up and flood her breasts and her hips and she is incredibly desirable in those first three months and a man doesn't have to take precautions and there's no need for birth control or condoms either . . . making love to a woman like that is simply fantastic . . . The thing is Miss Eliška you seem a little anemic somewhat sexually repressed that four-month pregnancy would turn you into a sex bomb the likes of a Liz Taylor or Marilyn Monroe . . . But the real reason I've come over is to help fill in some of the details on your husband who happens to be off somewhere on the prowl . . . When I was a kid I played in my father's lounge band Karma it was called and this one time we had a gig on the island and back then as a student your husband wanted to be a personality akin to a Charles Baudelaire who dyed his hair green and made a splash at the opera house and your husband wanted to create a similar revolutionary action and so he had his head shaved but he didn't quite have the wherewithal to pull it off because he was in love with Georgina a beauty from Zálabí . . . and so I played Little Gigolo on the piano in my father's lounge band . . . *sad little gigolo don't look back to when you were young* . . . and that husband of yours with the shaved head that was something awful because his face was suntanned while his head gleamed bone-white and everyone just had to look and he certainly did attract a lot of attention but that Georgina of his was red with shame and didn't want to dance with him so she danced with engineer Nevečeřal instead whom they called Pasha and unlike your husband he had a thick head of beautiful curly blond hair . . . and your husband instead of working that shaved head of his for all it was worth fell into a funk and crept from the dance hall and then he stood outside in the bushes in his tuxedo peering in through the windows and there it was . . . his lovely Georgina dancing and laughing it up with Pasha the engineer the finest tennis player in the rowing club the best athlete the greatest volleyball player and he held Georgina firmly in his arms and that husband of yours with the shaved head stared into the dance hall and died from envy from that complex of his he's never been able to shake . . . Why am I telling you this? So that you are aware Miss Eliška of who it is you've married . . . that husband of yours his affairs of the heart were always so intense he was like a bear with a ring through its nose led around on a chain . . . And those girlfriends of his who led him around on that chain knew just when to give it a yank . . . And so he stood outside the dance hall and watched Georgina and suffered horribly regretted cutting his hair which was blond too and so thick and wavy he had to douse it in brilliantine just to get a comb through . . . I know . . . Mr. Marysko sighed and gazed out the window at the sliver of sky above the shed . . . Yul Brynner now there's a man who gets women revved up . . . but that husband of yours with a shaved head that truly was unfortunate and he lost his nerve and decided to wear a cap until his hair grew back and in vain I implored him to keep his head shaved to make the rounds as a surrealist . . . and Georgina dumped him on account of that shaved head . . . he ended up just like I did . . . I fell in love with a butcher lady and every day after lunch I went down to Chmel's across from the theater and that temptress that object of my sexual desire would greet me with a What will you have Mr. Marysko? And as I did every day I ordered a hundred and fifty grams of warm meatloaf And with her beautiful hair and her beautiful smile she took that warm meatloaf and cut me a slice and said . . . Yes Mr. Marysko it's still warm . . . and so I was in love with her and wrote poems to her and every day after lunch I strode down there and ate my warm meat-loaf and dreamed of my beautiful butcher lady . . . but listen to this she came down with some sort of rash on her head and they had to cut off all her hair! And so she wore a scarf and I continued to go down there every day after lunch to eat my meatloaf and then one day I got this idea to order her a wig at the wigmaker's . . . and then they transferred her to Pernštejn to another butcher shop . . . and then instead of poetry it was a wig I brought her and I walked into that butcher shop in Pernštejn and what do I see? The object of my sexual desire standing behind the counter wearing a beautiful wig . . . the thing is her boss had beat me to it and bought her a wig in return for her kneeling behind the counter and fondling his fly while he served customers . . . and so I went back outside with that wig and a bunch of people was standing there in line waiting for travel permits and they all looked about as downtrodden as I so I showed them that beautiful wig I'd had the wigmakers at the National Theater make me for six hundred crowns I held it up for all to see and said in a loud voice . . . No good deed goes unpunished . . . So now you see Miss Eliška getting all your hair cut off is not so easy . . . only the likes of a Yul Brynner or maybe an Erich von Stroheim can pull it off . . . Well I must be on my way Miss Eliška tell your husband that the little piggy is getting nice and fat that the *schweinfest* is on the horizon . . . Now I must go home . . . after the shambles with the butcher lady I no longer write love-struck poetry now under the influence of Profes-sor Jirásek's work I'm writing a thesis on how I cocked things up It will be a lengthy tract with a significant philosophical/biological uptext and subtext . . . So said Mr. Marysko and I flushed with em-barrassment took refuge in my needlepoint continued with a winter landscape I was working on and Mr. Marysko watched me take up a spool of black yarn and said . . . It's nothing my child you go on with your work . . . but I must say I still can't shake the picture of your husband from back then on the island . . . the way he looked at that Georgina of his . . . when I took a break from the piano I went outside to the patio and I stood in the dark under the maple trees and in the scant light of the dance hall windows saw your hus-band in his black tux pressed up against the wall . . . and he was just dying from what he saw from what I could see for myself his little Georgina dancing and laughing it up in the arms of engineer Nevečeřal as he whispered sweet nothings in her ear the sweet nothings only your husband thought he had a right to whisper . . . And Mr. Marysko rose to go and as when he'd arrived he didn't offer to shake hands and I didn't offer either . . . I liked Mr. Marysko but I knew I could only process what he'd told me once he was gone once I had a chance to let it all sink in . . .

I was starting to get pretty ticked off with my husband's friends I'd had just about enough of their nonsense I told myself you've got to take them down a peg or two give them a taste of their own medicine And so one day I was coming back from shopping on the main street and as I rounded the corner to Vaništa's pub who should spill out of the Čásek Theater but Vladimir towering over a bunch of little kids . . . he'd been in there watching cartoons and newsreels that ran all afternoon and through the theater's open doors music played and a man's voice shouted . . . Quiet or I'll throw you out! And the minute Vladimir saw me he launched right in . . . Madame so how's that husband of yours has he bought himself the slippers with the little kittens yet has he started work on that brilliant book of his that will dazzle our reading public? And I leaned toward Vladimir and said . . . He's full of surprises . . . That jewel of mine goes swimming down to the old harbor where the kids swim . . . and I caught him there in the houseboat playing with his you-know-what . . . That stopped Vladimir in his tracks What you mean to say the doctor would be capable of such a thing madame I am truly surprised . . . And I said . . . You mean you didn't know? He's always got a hole in his pocket and when he sees a nice-looking woman on the tram he plays with his thingamajig too . . . Only yesterday I sewed that pocket up and today it's got a hole in it again . . . his excuse is that the father of dialectic inquiry Socrates played with his thingamajig too and in the town square no less . . . Jesus Christ Vladimir cried . . . what is this I'm hearing? So the doctor finally managed to overcome the hick in himself? Well that does come as quite a surprise . . . And then I went on . . . If only that's where it ended! You know what else he does . . . He and old Salcmanová collect used rubbers behind the La Paloma Bistro and on Slunečná Street where soldiers take their girls to shag and then down there by the Vltava in the dead branch of the river he goes fishing for rubbers with a barge pole and he and Salcmanová wash them out in tubs and when they're done running them over washboards they dry them out and then Salcmanová sprinkles them with talcum powder and rolls them up and puts them in little pink envelopes and at night Salcmanová sells them to the tarts hanging around the La Paloma Bistro . . . and that's not all my husband also knows a surefire cure for the hiccups . . . And Vladimir was beside himself and I just couldn't be happier as I twisted everything around the stuff my husband always went on about and Vladimir sputtered . . . Just wait until Egon Bondy hears this . . . we already wrote the doctor off and meanwhile he's busy raising the bar . . . and I grabbed hold of Vladimir's coat sleeve and continued . . . the first violinist of the philharmonic von Schraubek taught my husband the cure for the hiccups . . . the canteen woman in Smetana Hall suffered from the hiccups and when von Schraubek saw it for himself he said to the canteen manager . . . Look here I'll bet you a bottle of cognac I can cure your wife of the hiccups . . . And the canteen manager said it was in vain she'd already been to all the specialists . . . But von Schraubek claimed his method was foolproof . . . And so he took the canteen woman by the hand and led her behind the organ and there in the shadows placed his huge member in her hands . . . and the canteen woman shrieked . . . Aieeeeee! And von Schraubek returned her to the Smetana Hall canteen . . . and the hiccups never bothered her again . . . and my husband administers the cure in exactly the same way except it's not behind the organ he takes his patients but behind the fence at the La Paloma Bistro . . . And when I finished Vladimir could only stutter . . . I'm speechless! The doctor is a genius . . . Now I am convinced he will become a number one a champion a literary world-beater . . . because he is in fact already a national treasure . . .

Of all my husband's friends I was fondest of Stan Vávra he was a printer by trade and he impressed me with his natural elegance Stan liked to laugh and took great pride in his neckties and his little sweaters and his shirts and his spit-shined shoes as opposed to my husband who only needed to walk through the grass in a Libeň park for his clothes to be ruined . . . And Stan seemed blessed at the luck that he could write his poetry and that Vladimir brought him along on his public street actions and in fact they collaborated on writing the fourth manifest on explosionalism it was even cosigned by Stan Vávra who was in love with the poetry of Gérard Nerval a poet who vanished somewhere in the Far East and Stan was so moved by Nerval's writing it spoke to him so directly he wanted nothing more than to publish just a small book in honor of Gérard Nerval . . . and Stan Vávra told me all about the event that marked him for life just like that poetry of Gérard Nerval . . . when he was a little boy he used to play in the chateau above Kolčavka . . . where a century earlier trout swam in the Rokytka River and vineyards dotted the hillside . . . but by the time Stan was a boy the chateau was housing for the poor and the Rokytka was littered with pots and discarded stoves . . . and one day as Stan played under the portico a massively fat woman walked across and because the floorboards were old and rickety . . . she crashed through the floor right above where Stan was looking up and that fat woman hurtled down from the second floor her skirts fanned out and Stan just kept looking up until his world went dark and he was crushed by those skirts and fainted dead away . . . And while Stan turned out to be fine the woman broke her hip landing on little old Stan . . . And that's part of my narrative and what I want to write about Stan Vávra often said and he had long noble fingers and he smoked with elegance and when he laughed it was heartfelt and his hair was thick black and shiny and parted down the middle and he was olive-skinned and looked like an Italian footballer and while my husband could barely manage to light my cigarette Stan on the other hand brought a grace and flare to everything he touched . . . And he had an older brother named Vladimir Vávra and when I saw Vladimir for the first time I knew he'd been in the lockup because he had the hard eyes and body language of a man who'd been in jail and even though Vladimir Vávra was an electrical mechanic by trade he knew every surrealist manifest every French poet of the last century inside and out and he was convinced the six years he spent in lockup in Bytýz would help him inject a little reality into the surrealist movement and make him a number one in his own right . . . he said all he had to do was relate some of the stuff he'd lived through down there in the mines down there where the daylight never came . . . And I could see how much Stan loved his brother the fact he'd been to prison only elevated Vladimir in his eyes . . . And back when Vladimir was still in prison Stan always went on about his brother to my husband and Vladimir's friends couldn't wait for him to get out they called their circle the Libeň Psychics and told my husband just wait and see as soon as Vladimir gets out you'll see a real live bona fide poet . . . The story of his arrest was simple . . . His boss had a ham radio and broadcast to Western Europe and barely two years passed before the cops zeroed in on them with the radar and caught them in their car in Palmovka with all the gear . . . and they were arrested and there was an investigation and then a trial in Pardubice in that infamous year of '51 . . . One day Vladimir was at our place and he sat by the window in the twilight and described to us the worst thing that ever happened to him . . . I was led to court in handcuffs he said along a street that stretched about a hundred meters and there were people standing there regular people mainly women and they cursed at me and spat in my face and screamed that I should hang . . . And that was the worst thing Vladimir said the spitting and the shouting and the hatred in their eyes people that looked just like our mom and pop . . . and I was given twenty years and then they led me back through the gauntlet of screaming spitting people and there was my brother Stan crying hopelessly . . . Vlád'a . . . ! The surrealists don't hold a candle to this believe me . . . Céline Ferdinand Louis Hašek and Kafka . . . they don't hold a candle . . . all those years in Bytýz let me tell you that served to ground me . . . I want to shed some light on this provide a little reportage that describes not just my own fate but the fate of all those others . . .

■ □ ■ □ ■

CHAPTER TWENTY-FOUR

And so my husband finally got his chance to become a champion
writer He received a letter from the publisher offering to publish a
book of short stories they told him to put the book together and offered to subsidize half his salary for one year provided he could work
out a deal with his employer to cut his work hours And sure enough
Mr. Kučera the chief of the Bubny paper salvage plant signed off on
the plan And so my husband went through his writing tried to select
the stories most suitable for publication and the more he went
through his stories the less of them he seemed to have and so he had
to write new stories not the type of raunchy fare he was used to amusing himself with but rather stories that to me seemed quite hypocriti-
cal and designed just so he could have a book out The thing is at first
he gave the editors his raunchy stories but when one month passed
and then another and still no word from the editors something
seemed to change in him He was nervous and he couldn't sleep and
every week he went down there to ask Did the editors have a chance
to read it yet? And as he left the house every time with high hopes he
came back timid and cut down to size His setup at the paper salvage
allowed him to quit work every day at one o'clock and then he show-
ered and came straight home and he had a new boss at the paper salvage and although his coworkers Tonča and Venca said nothing to
him directly it was obvious to me from their actions how they now
felt about him . . . The fact my husband had a shot at becoming a
number one writer was not something they could just let go . . . They

looked askance at my husband and he was left to work alone and even the boss cooled toward him and there was no more going for pints with Tonča and Venca no more lunch at Husenský's but my husband was blind to all this because he was so obsessed with his book . . . And six weeks passed and he went down to the publisher again to inquire if they'd accepted those raunchy stories of his for publication and all they told him was that two editors had read the stories and to come back tomorrow morning And so the next morning instead of going to work my husband went down to the editorial offices stood out front at nine A.M. even though the meeting was for ten and he strolled along the riverfront to kill time and then went in to the meeting and an hour later he was back out again and he came to see me at the grill and he was red-faced and sheepish He told me the editors had laughed it up and read out their favorite passages from his manuscript *Larks on a String* and my husband had smiled under the mistaken impression his dream of becoming a number one would soon be realized . . . his poet friends Mr. Hiršal and Mr. Kolář had been right all along to proclaim his stories had a great future . . . and so a half hour later when the editors were done laughing it up and praising the style and scope of my husband's stories they suddenly grew serious and said they couldn't possibly publish the stories as they were for if they did they could kiss their editorial jobs good-bye the board would fire them for publishing this sort of raunchy material strip them of the ability to put food on the table and surely my husband wouldn't want that and therefore they were returning his manuscript only half the stories at most were suitable for publication the others couldn't possibly appear in a book published by Czechoslovak Writer Prague he was to use the time which the subsidy provided to write stories that had neither offensive language nor pornographic scenes . . . And so my husband stumbled out of there and went back to his job at the paper salvage on Spálená Street and a truck loaded with paper bales was just pulling out and seeing Tonča and Venca there in the yard my husband went to Husenský's and brought back a couple of pitchers of pilsner but neither Tonča nor Venca would have a drink with him although he implored them at least a drink to his health but Tonča just glanced at Venca and they said in unison they've got their own money they don't need no writer buying them beer . . . And so my husband stepped out of that cold dark courtyard where he had labored four long years he stepped out into the light of the street and headed for the grill and as soon as he came in he practically collapsed he just sat there smiling and staring straight ahead like he'd lost his marbles no doubt replaying the insult over in his mind the debacle with the publisher over his risqué stories and the greater debacle involving those now-former friends of his who were convinced he wanted to scramble up their backs to the heights of literary greatness . . . no longer was he the humble laborer the quote unquote doctor of law as they called him down at the paper salvage . . . The day they gave my husband back his manuscript it was like he turned into a different person In vain I tried to cheer him up in vain I tried to tell him they were the fools and not him in vain I warned him to leave his text as he'd originally written it and although I hadn't read any of it myself that wasn't the point the point was for him to be true to himself and not start writing the way the editors wanted him to write but my husband just wouldn't listen he wrote stories akin to the stories that already received the stamp of approval and those six stories so highly prized by Mr. Kolář and Mr. Hiršal he let fall by the wayside . . . And he went to work earlier than normal so he could be done by noon and back to writing his made-to-order stories and oddly enough the more compliant my husband became the more liable I was to speak my mind at any and all cost . . . as opposed to my husband who wrote against his will and against his conviction and who consulted with those editors on every one of his stories to make sure it was what they wanted and when they praised him he was happy and forged ahead with renewed enthusiasm and I started to see my husband as a bit of a coward as someone prepared to say one thing to his friends and quite another to the editorial board . . . I couldn't stand that two-faced world that two-faced perspective those two-faced conversations and I listened to my husband with distaste and always said exactly what I thought I who had lived in a fourteen-room house as a girl and I who had come from a house with a maid and a chauffeur and a nanny and I who had certainly been made to pay for it not only because I had lost everything but because I was classified a German and sent to work at the brickworks for a year and then my parents were relocated and I was left behind to fend for myself and for my brother Heini and at sixteen I had to work in restaurants and cafeterias just to bring home a little extra pot of food so Heini might have a decent meal . . . And after all that I was supposed to lie? I was supposed to say something I didn't mean the way my husband did who had decided to be a writer no matter what the cost no matter he was rewriting his book and no matter he'd sold those raunchy stories of his down the river those stories his friends liked so much . . . And then the effects of this narrow-mindedness began to show on my husband even when he was with friends he quit having his own opinion he agreed with whatever anyone was saying and kept his own views to himself He was scared to venture his own opinion and on the rare occasion he did he ended up retracting it anyhow . . . And at the paper salvage on Spálená Street the results were pretty much the same . . . I went down to meet my husband at work and when I looked into the office a personnel officer was there and so I made to go but the officer said . . . Just have a seat Miss your husband will be leaving shortly . . . Tonča and Venca and the boss were seated there too and apparently the personnel officer was just wrapping things up and my husband sat in his chair red-faced almost like he'd been crying . . . So look here the personnel officer said we've been keeping an eye on you and you're not putting in all your hours and every day you're gone at one o'clock so what've you got to say for yourself? And my husband objected weakly . . . When I'm done with my work I go home . . . But the personnel officer persisted . . . So you admit to it? You're habitually absent my wife came down here at least ten times with scrap paper and after twelve-thirty you're nowhere to be found . . . Tonča what do you have to say? And Tonča lowered her eyes and said . . . Yes every day after twelve-thirty Doctor you're gone . . . And the personnel officer wrote in his report and said to Venca . . . And what about you? And Venca said . . . It's your own fault Doctor the only person you've got to blame is yourself . . . To which my husband said . . . But Venca when you and I went to Koliš to bale paper we put up a whole truckload and I signed it all over to you because you've got kids . . . But Venca said rudely . . . The only reason you did that Doctor was so I'd keep my mouth shut . . . And the personnel officer said again . . . So you simply were not putting in the required hours . . . But my husband defended himself . . . But I had official permission my hours cut in half for two months it was all worked out with the literary fund . . . And the personnel officer pounced . . . For two months maybe but you've been slacking off for half a year why didn't you just stick to your two months? And my husband fell further into his own trap . . . I was working on my book *Larks on a String* . . . And the personnel officer was exultant and Tonča and Venca and the boss lady were exultant too . . . But you could have written at night in effect you were working part-time and even collecting overtime . . . overtime of all things! But my husband persisted weakly . . . But every paper bale pays three-crowns-sixty per ton regardless of how many hours I put in! But the personnel officer only said . . . Collecting overtime while working part-time . . . And the boss lady who was quite indignant said to my husband . . . And I was under the impression you were intelligent . . . And my husband bristled and said . . . All right I admit to everything it's all true what you've said I'm a habitual absentee . . . And continuing to write in his report the personnel officer said . . . All right so not only are you sinking yourself but you're taking the boss and the payroll department down with you . . . you might just want to give that one a second thought see for yourself how it looks in the report! And my husband seemed to perk up and all of a sudden he glanced at the report and said cheerfully . . . So comrade are you still into raising vegetables? How'd you like that book I dug up for you here . . . Local fruit species and their assorted colors? But the personnel officer with whom my husband often had a beer after work said coldly . . . I have no idea what you're talking about . . . And my husband said . . . I had a heck of a haul this year three bushels of Cox Rennet two bushels of Jonathans four bushels of Golden Delicious . . . And the boss lady flushed an even deeper red and said . . . I really thought you were intelligent . . . The personnel officer pulled out another cigarette he searched his pockets in vain for a match and my husband got a box of matches from the desk drawer and struck one and reached out to light the personnel officer's cigarette but the man just let the match die and then stubbed out the unlit cigarette in the ashtray . . . this from a man who always liked my husband who even let him give him a friendly little slap now and then when he was drunk down at the King of Brabant and didn't want to go home . . . now this same man bristled with hate as he slid his report over to my husband and pointed imperiously like he was Marshal Žukov ordering Field Marshal Keitel to sign the articles of surrender . . . Sign it! And after my husband signed it Tonča said nervously . . . Doctor I thought you were intelligent . . . And the personnel officer inspected the signature and then got up and said . . . That's it then you're let go . . . And my husband looked up and he stretched and gave a blissful yawn and then he opened his locker and cleared out his things his books his work clothes his hat and then he walked over to the scrap paper pile and threw the clothes and boots on the pile . . . After the boss lady and Tonča and Venca signed the report the personnel officer said to my husband out in the yard . . . I hope when that book of yours comes out . . . what're you gonna call it? And my husband said . . . *Larks on a String* . . . And the personnel officer said I hope you'll bring me a copy of those larks on a string! And then my husband tied his remaining things into a bundle and I was glad I was privy to this I had seen plenty worse situations after they threw us out of our house and put us in the internment camps and I smiled at my husband and said . . . Look if you want I'll be the provider forget about *Larks on a String* forget about everything just write what it is you want to write and I'll worry about the money . . . And we stepped into the corridor and there stood Haňta leaning back on the wall with his arms crossed and he laughed . . . Look here you infernal boy at the end of the day you're still going to make it as a writer . . . those antics they just sprang on you in there will only help gild your future fame . . . Look here madame are you familiar with the French Revolution? They cut off not only the king's and queen's heads but the entire court and tens of thousands of the aristocracy . . . they even cut the heads off the statues in Notre Dame . . . and they sent the heir to the throne to apprentice as a shoemaker and the cobbler tortured him and tortured him until he finally tortured him to death . . . So this thing the doctor just went through is child's play in comparison . . . And madame the things you lived through in '45 fall into the same category . . . Look here do you know how Czar Nicholas and the czarina and their four daughters one more beautiful than the next and the czarevitch and their doctor all ended up? Well let me tell you that was some happening . . . First they were held in the Czar's Village and then they were moved to Tobolsk . . . after which they took them to Yekaterinburg and the horrors they endured there the jeers and the insults . . . And finally at a site called Four Brothers they were shot and the assailants poured acid on their bodies and set them alight . . . but first the bodies were dismembered so they would burn more easily . . . and even their loyal doggy Jammy was shot . . . and then the bodies were thrown into a deep shaft . . . And when Mr. Sokolov the presiding judge ordered the site searched . . . all they found at Four Brothers was the little doggy . . . and what was left of the Czar? only his belt buckle . . . and of the czarina? only her earrings . . . and of the czarevitch? Nothing . . . and what was left of the four grand duchesses? Whalebone and bodice laces . . . And what was left of Doctor Botvin? Just false teeth and the glass from his spectacles . . . So madame what befell you and what just befell the doctor that infernal boy . . . Nothing . . . but what's befallen me that's another issue who is going to come with me to Husenský's . . . who is going to come with me to sell the rare books I dig up here . . . Madame I have been orphaned . . . So God bless you dear boy . . . Haňta said to my husband and wept and my husband wept too and they kissed each other and shook hands and then Haňta felt his way along the wall descended the stairs disappeared down into that cellar of his . . . And we stepped out into the yard and the office windows were lit up and inside was the personnel officer and the new boss lady and the two laborers Tonča and Venca and they all sat there smoking and my husband was devastated because Tonča and Venca had been his friends and now they backstabbed him even though what they said was true . . . We walked into the passageway under the light of the bare bulbs and out on Spálená Street passersby were bathed in strong sunlight and the red-striped trams flashed by and again we heard the boss lady repeat as if to herself . . . I was under the impression you were intelligent . . . And meanwhile Tonča and Venca slipped out the back on their way to Husenský's . . . That evening upon his return from Vaništa's my husband told me with great fanfare he'd landed a job as a stagehand at the S. K. Neumann Theater and as early as tomorrow he was heading out to Louny with the company to stage *A View from the Bridge* And so my husband became a stagehand it was only about two hundred meters from our place to the theater and that stagehand job seemed to liberate him somehow and he continued to write his short stories for the publisher and the two editors assigned to his book continued to advise him on how best to write a book that wouldn't cast the board of directors of Czechoslovak Writer in a bad light And so he finished the manuscript and it was approved and the proofs went back and forth but as the book's completion approached as he received the final galleys he kept the news to himself he didn't even share this launch into the literary ranks with any of his friends I could see he lived in fear of the day his book and his picture appeared in the display case windows he was terrified of it because he had changed almost all his original stories the book he first offered the editors was no more and in the final edit he even cut out sentences that could be construed to have a double meaning and though it went against his will he nevertheless signed off on a book that was altogether different from the one he had read to his friends who were all convinced of his future number one status . . . And one day he returned from the city and he just couldn't stop laughing he paced back and forth between the flat and the courtyard and outside it was sunny and just like he used to he climbed up onto the roof of the shed and sat in his chair in the sunlight and sang himself a little tune . . . and then he came back down and when he managed to get ahold of himself he said . . . The Lord was with me and he set me free! I just happened to be there in the office with those two editors when the chief editor himself walked in with the galleys and the look on his face said it all . . . He threw those galleys of *Larks on a String* on the responsible editor's desk and said with disgust . . . So this is the kind of crap you want to publish? Destroy the typeset immediately and tear up the author's contract . . . Sickening! And my husband laughed and said with delight . . . It's a good thing Haňta showed me the way back there on Spálená Street you remember sweetheart? And that personnel officer I still consider a friend because if he hadn't laid into me I'd still be back there busting my hump . . . Sweetheart the good Lord loves a sinner . . . and you remember what Haňta said about the French Revolution how they cut the heads off the king and the queen and the statues in Notre Dame as well? And they buried those stone heads deep in some hole and then years later after the restoration they made new heads and stuck them on those headless figures . . . there's a lesson in that too . . . but listen not long ago when they were excavating a new metro line they unearthed that hole and so after all those years those severed royal heads saw the light of day again and they were returned to their rightful place above the portal of Notre Dame . . . that's progress sweetheart that's world history . . . that's Hegel's famous proposition . . . Is it a rose? Is it not a rose . . . In fact it is a rose . . . And evil marches through the world double time . . . while good progresses imperceptibly . . .

■ □ ■ □ ■

CHAPTER TWENTY-FIVE

Over an afternoon beer in Vaništa's Šaly the stage manager hired my husband as a stagehand and the next day he was off with the company to Louny In vain I told my husband to drop everything to forget about going to work to concentrate on his writing in vain I told him to let me worry about the money but I guess my husband wasn't quite ready yet for the solitude for the grit required to confront himself every day and work on his own writing that is to say work on himself and forgo his day job . . . I knew my husband feared looking into this mirror he was fearful enough looking into a regular mirror sure he glanced at himself occasionally but only for a second as if what he saw there made him uneasy And if we were out somewhere say at the movies or at a friend's place if he happened to catch a glimpse of himself in a mirror he was particularly disturbed He wouldn't say anything for a long time it took him ages to overcome whatever he saw there in the mirror He had a much finer image of himself in his own mind than was the reality He was frozen in terror when he combed his thinning hair he laughed bitterly as he pulled clumps of hair from the comb and told me how thick his hair used to be so thick he had to put oil in it just to get a comb through the chestnut hair shot through with sun-streaked highlights the color of straw And my husband was also shaken whenever he looked at his legs Anyone could see he had bowlegs and they looked good on him but it shook him up anyhow and sometimes as he walked he tried to straighten his legs but then his walk was all wrong and it looked like he had a limp In the summer when he was tanned he liked to walk around without a shirt on just stripped to the waist he was proud of his muscles and it's true his biceps were impressive and he liked to feel them and he liked to show them off . . . When the weather was nice and we were near any sort of water my husband was in for a swim immediately he just couldn't resist and he loved to stand there waist-deep in the water and scoop up handfuls of water and splash them over his head again and again like a little kid . . . He always kept a full pitcher of water in the courtyard it had to be really freezing out for there to be no pitcher and after a shave he went out there to douse himself with water from the pitcher and sometimes he stood over the sink outside and splashed water over his head and his chest for the longest time and then he came in and stood over the stove until he was dry When he wrote he went out into the yard every half hour or so to splash water on his face and when it was sunny he went up on the roof of the shed to write and he lay there in the sun and kept a bucket of water next to him and every so often dunked his hands and soaked his face . . . And when we took our walks along the river I knew as soon as the mood caught him he'd be down the steps and to the river splashing water on his face he couldn't pass up a pond or a river or a stream without wetting his face and washing his hands it was like he was tasting the water with his face . . . Whenever we went on our little excursions around Prague as soon as the weather was nice and the opportunity presented itself he stripped off his shoes and dunked his feet in the shallow water and he gazed at his feet and his legs like he was seeing them for the first time and then he rinsed off his legs up to the knees and sat there for a while until dry . . . And another thing my husband was proud of was his calves and his thighs He liked to feel the muscles he especially liked to stretch out his leg and admire the way the muscles looked he might've been bowlegged but he had some pretty fine muscles he said maybe not beautiful but pretty fine and he was quite serious about it . . . And I'd say to him . . . No doubt about it and shrug my shoulders like what can you do facts are facts he did have some pretty fine-looking legs . . . Otherwise though he was scared of mirrors he never wanted to look into a mirror but ultimately he always managed to convince himself that perhaps his face had improved that maybe he wasn't as badly off as what he just saw in the mirror And then he looked at himself again at first just a guilty little glance and then he zeroed in

and stared and as usual was alarmed by what he saw . . . How did he
see himself? What sort of indestructible impression did he have when
in the end he always looked the same never any better in fact worse
because his hair was thinner and the wrinkles on his forehead and
around his mouth were deeper and every year brought more And in
the end it was the same thing with the writing as with the looking at
himself in the mirror That writing of his was a sort of temporary romance love in a dark passageway a bit of the one-night stand And
when he finally did get down to writing it was like he lost his mind he
sped through it and tore the pages from the machine he liked to write
in the sunshine up on the shed roof because he was blinded by the sun
and could hardly make out the typewriter he just felt his way around
the keyboard like a blind pianist . . . and he hammered at that machine with all ten fingers reaching in now and then to unstick the keys
and he wrote and he wrote and I knew full well that the writing struck
fear into him and that he didn't believe in himself and doubted himself just like when he looked at himself in the mirror And when he
finished writing when he thought he had enough when he came in
from the courtyard with his ream of typewritten pages he never
looked at them he was scared of those pages scared of them the same
way he was scared of looking at himself in the mirror And so there I
was and I knew if I offered to look after the household if I offered to
give him a hundred crowns a day out of my tips he'd have to refuse the
money because if he didn't he'd be forced to set the example to live up
to the rhetoric and to the advice he was always dishing out to everyone else on how to write and how to paint and how it was better just
to go with the flow because every art form was just a whore who could
care less why an artist couldn't write or couldn't paint . . . all art
wanted to know was what have you done for me lately baby? And
screw it if the artist has got a family or doesn't have a workshop or
enough time . . . My husband always told everyone the most beautiful
thing about art was that no one was forced to do it . . . As he said it
had to be *schenkende Tugend* . . . A bestowing virtue is the highest
virtue as Friedrich Nietzsche wrote . . . And so without a second
thought he signed the contract over a beer at Vaništa's and the next
day he was off to Louny with the theater company and when he returned around midnight he was so excited he had to wake me up and
give me all the details of what had transpired that day how they'd

blown a tire and had no spare how he'd had to walk back to find a station and get the tire fixed and that wasn't all . . . since the sets for *A View from the Bridge* didn't need changing once they were up the other stagehands had trusted him enough to leave him alone backstage . . . they then absconded to Prague while my husband stayed back . . . and he told me that while in Louny he'd been overcome by the urge to write and he told me how Šaly the stage manager took him backstage and showed him all the lift lines and rope rigging and cable clips and Šaly had him feel a little string that was attached to one of the lift lines and said . . . Listen up in the second half of *A View* when the girl screams Eddy! Eddy! you start hauling on this lift line it'll be dark but don't worry about it just keep hauling until you feel the other little string come around and when it does that means stop! Because the lift line will pull up a drop curtain hiding a phone booth that'll light up when Eddy runs in and gives up the Italians to the cops and you peek out and when that booth goes dark you release the lift line to reset the drop curtain over the phone booth and feel for when the other little string comes around . . . And then quietly and in the dark you take the cable clip and clip the lift line so it stays fast understand? Lying there in the darkness my husband was so exited by his first tour with the company by his job as a stagehand he couldn't even get to sleep and he told me how he stood there in the rigging waiting for the moment the girl cries Eddy! Eddy! and how tense he was because he had to get it exactly right and then he unlocked the cable clip and hauled on the lift line and he was scared out of his wits but then he felt the counter string and stopped the lift line and then he froze for the next five seconds but sure enough onstage the phone booth lit up and Eddy really did run in and rat out the two Italians to the police and then Eddy ran back out of the phone booth and the light flicked off and in a sweat and in the dark my husband released the lift line until he felt the other string that indicated stop . . . and he clutched the lift line for a long time because it was his first go at setting the cable clip that prevented the lift line from coming loose . . . he stood there and because he didn't quite trust himself he kept ahold of that lift line just to make sure it was fast . . . Šaly had told him it was his primary duty and Šaly the stage manager had put his trust in him . . . Therefore my husband hung on to the lift line until the show was over . . . So my husband became a stagehand and he had mornings off and sometimes even a whole day and he came home late after the show was over and after they struck the sets and put up new ones for morning rehearsal He wandered down to the theater and to the pub where the stagehands took their lunches and their dinners and over a beer stage manager Šaly expounded on the ethics and esthetics of theater Every time my husband came back from some two-day tour with the company he whined and complained to me how much he'd wanted to write precisely when he knew his typewriter was hundreds of kilometers away . . . But of course when my husband had time off instead of writing he wandered around Libeň with his shopping bag I was at work at the grill and so he had plenty of time to himself but he preferred to join the stagehands down at the pub he drank enormous quantities of beer he tried to outdrink the other men not that he liked it all that much it's just that he wanted to be number one at least in the drink but there was a diminutive stagehand named Páša who could drink my husband under the table but little Páša had reason to drink for apparently there was trouble at home . . . And so my husband got into this habit of settling down to write just before I got home from work he hammered away at the machine and when I came home he pretended to just be hitting his stride but oh well he'd have to pack it in now that I was home and pack it in he did because I had just about enough already I was sick of the standard excuse that he couldn't write when I was at home and that he most wanted to write when he happened to be at rehearsal or on his shift or out on tour it was the same tired old excuse that I always countered with . . . Forget the job I'll look after you . . . And my husband always pretended not to hear and when I laughed and stared him down he always averted his eyes and for the rest of the night wouldn't utter a word it was just like when he looked at himself in the mirror . . . but with those oft-repeated words of mine I forced him to withstand that look to withstand and comprehend the full import of those words . . . Forget the job I'll look after you . . . and somehow those words gave me strength I looked at my own reflection in the mirror and what I saw was a woman a waitress a cashier a fair woman who'd been brought back from the brink by her husband and now that I offered to look after him he was terrified that perhaps I was right perhaps he didn't have the stuff to be alone to get down to writing all those things he went on about to others . . .

■ □ ■ □ ■

CHAPTER TWENTY-SIX

Just before noon the poets Kolář and Hiršal came into the Palace Hotel Grill I knew they were happy to see me in fact they seemed quite thrilled to know me and I seated them next to the window so they could watch the action out on Jindřišská Street and they each ordered half a chicken and a Cinzano bitter as aperitif and a glass for me as well and as I went on to serve other customers I felt their eyes on me those two friends of my husband's and I did show off a bit and pretending to need more glasses I slipped into the alcove to check myself in the mirror I touched up my mascara ran a finger over my eyebrows straightened my apron readjusted my white cap and then I grabbed a few glasses and went back into the restaurant and just as I expected the two poets took me in again with their admiring glances and Mr. Kolář was dressed impeccably like he was going to a wedding and not just any wedding but his own wedding he wore gray slacks and a checked jacket and a white shirt with a blue necktie and a white handkerchief was tucked in his breast pocket and Mr. Hiršal was dressed in quite the opposite manner he wore coarse corduroy slacks and a corduroy jacket to match and both of them smoked and we clinked glasses and I stood by their table and smiled at them I never sat down at work no matter how much my feet ached just like Headwaiter Skřivánek taught me . . . And Mr. Kolář said to me in hushed tones . . . Look that husband of yours for God's sake tell him to quit it with the theater for God's sake he's not getting any younger Miss Eliška he's got what it takes to really do something for Czech prose he should just sit at home and write . . . And I said . . . That's what I always tell him but he's obsessed with the theater instead of showing me what he's written he writes nothing now because he's delirious that he has a walk-on part as a lumberjack in *The Wicked Deer* that he gets to wear a page costume and appear in *Othello* . . . it's horrible and they drink while they're at it propped up on their three-meter ladders holding the emblem of the Venetian Republic in the council chambers of the ducal palace and as the senators and noblemen confer and Othello and Desdemona enter Páša that alcoholic is up there completely sauced . . . three times already my husband and the emblem have crashed down to bury the ducal council . . . and when they're not falling off ladders they're up there hiccupping and swaying and putting the fear of God into the ducal council . . . So I complained and Mr. Hiršal smoked his cigarette and flicked his ashes against my white apron and said with delight . . . Fantastic . . . and I said . . . He knows I could look after him but he's scared of the writing there's no way he'd ever stay home . . . Headwaiter Borek came over and gave me a light touch on the elbow and I knew I was wanted at another table I smiled and went over to a group just seated each of them ordered a whole chicken . . . I repeated a bit surprised . . . Whole chickens if you please? And they insisted they wanted whole chickens the biggest ones we had . . . I went up to the counter and the cook took a roast chicken off the grill cut it in two and plated it I folded my white napkin over my arm and with a flourish served the two poets their chicken and Mr. Kolář looked quite serious maybe even a little angry but not with me his anger was directed somewhere toward Libeň to where my husband was at that very moment preparing for rehearsal or staging the sets for the evening performance . . . And I said . . . I'm afraid that he knows he's not a number one in the writing what he wants is to be champion of the world right away that's why he drinks so much with the stagehands to be number one do you think he actually likes drinking all that beer? And it's at Vaništa's he puts back more beer than anyplace else Mr. Vaništa himself complained to me about it I was so ashamed . . . it was right before the premiere of *The Wicked Deer* all the stagehands were at Vaništa's drinking since morning and Mr. Vaništa simply asked what's that *Wicked Deer* all about? And off goes my husband . . . Oh it's magnificent Láda Mr. Aleš Podhorský has created something sublime . . . it's accompanied by a brass band

the opening act is just tremendous . . . and Mr. Vaništa had a tray full
of shots in hand and my husband took him by the elbow and went on
excitedly . . . To the oompapa of the brass band the hunter Rozhoň
enters and stands before the curtain . . . and the brass band plays and
Rozhoň begins . . . Welcome one and all to our presentation all that's
happened in the forest is about to be revealed . . . And then my husband springs to his feet and shouts And the curtain goes up and bang!
there lies the dead deer! And my husband drops like he's shot and
takes Mr. Vaništa and his tray full of drinks with him and the whole
pub roars with laughter . . . And Mr. Vaništa is on the floor with my
husband on top of him . . . just awful . . . I complained to Mr. Kolář
and then Mr. Hiršal said . . . Fantastic . . . And they set to their food
and I brought them finger bowls and napkins and a pint of pilsner
each . . . And I went to serve two other patrons who just couldn't wait
to get at their food I brought them their chickens and they tore into
them wolfed them down . . . And before I forgot I went back to the
two poets to complain about something else . . . In the *Kremlin
Chimes* my husband plays a muzhik in a fur coat the whole cast is in
fur coats but they all get into costume just before the show while my
husband on the other hand gets dressed in his muzhik fur coat and
costume while he's still at home and he walks around the courtyard
like that or when they were doing *Othello* he went around in his page
costume all summer long he even went to the pub like that what an
awful sight those bowlegs of his that drink-ravaged face the blond wig
on his head like some kind of whore not to mention the full makeup
in the afternoon . . . just awful to behold . . . in *The Three Musketeers*
he's a court jester puts on the costume early afternoon even wears it
home embarrassing me all over Libeň . . . And so he sprains his elbow
but do you think he takes time off? No way he just gets a shot and has
it wrapped up like a footballer and it's on with the show . . . And
throughout the *Kremlin Chimes* he wears a fur coat and it's hot in the
theater and he's soaked in sweat . . . And at one point during the performance a huge red flag falls on top of the prisoners and sure enough
the day comes when my husband faints under the red flag and they
have to resuscitate him and it's a good thing they get to him fast
because he's already in a fever . . . So I said to the poets and I
wiped down their table and arranged the salt and pepper shakers and
the toothpicks and cleared away their plates . . . and every so often

Mr. Hiršal said . . . Fantastic . . . but the poet Kolář grew more and more serious . . . And after immaculately rinsing his hands and drying them with his napkin he said . . . So Miss Eliška you tell him from me how old are you? Forty-seven years old and not one book to his name at his age a whole line of writers was already dead you tell him from me that although it's nice they buried the ducal council under the emblem and it's nice the red flag fell on him and he fainted and it's nice he can entertain pub-goers with his *Wicked Deer* story . . . Bang! And there lies the dead deer . . . it's all very nice but it's all writing that skims the surface of the running river you tell him from me that the better man is the one who can express himself with greater clarity . . . once he writes it'll all start coming together : . . And the poets got up to go and Mr. Hiršal finished his cigarette but not before he flicked his ash onto the adjoining table and pronounced yet again . . . Fantastic . . . And he pulled out his brush and ran it through his crew cut and Mr. Kolář buttoned his checked Esterházy jacket the one the poet Hanč gave him as a present and Mr. Kolář shook my hand and reminded me . . . Miss Eliška it's all on your shoulders you know what just take the initiative! Let the man show what he's made of . . . But whatever you do . . . Don't force it! He held my hand and I felt his missing thumb and the poet was proud of that thumb he lost back when he was still a carpenter . . . and he couldn't hide the fact he was proud of himself he smiled like a little boy getting praise from his teacher he wore the modest expression of someone used to praise . . . I wished my husband could dress as well as Mr. Kolář could tuck a little white handkerchief into his breast pocket à la Mr. Kolář I wish he had a little pride in himself a little swagger like Mr. Kolář whose source of pride came from the poet inside and you could see it a mile away the pride just radiated from him and it was reflected in the way he dressed as well . . . it reminded me of the times I ran into Vladimir on the streets of Libeň from a distance you could see him coming as tall as an American basketball player beautiful curly hair and that eagle-like nose slightly off center and then of course there was my husband who looked like your average Joe on the street an *uomo qualunque* as he referred to himself a Prague bum As I served other guests I thought about that Esterházy jacket Mr. Kolář wore and that made me think of Mr. Hanč whom I only met once but he'd had a jacket like that too and he wore strong thick spectacles and like my husband wrote in his free time and otherwise he worked in some factory that built motorcycles he installed seat springs but that factory was a step down for him and I could relate for I myself had stepped down from fourteen rooms and a villa and a summer house and a chauffeur and a nanny and a cook . . . But Mr. Hanč died last year and my husband said he looked as small as a child in the casket just like when Franci Svoboda passed away the beautiful Slávia footballer who never went anywhere without packing his tuxedo but when he died he weighed a scant thirty-five kilos while in his heyday as a center-forward he'd weighed eighty-nine kilos and been drop-dead gorgeous just like Mr. Hanč the national two-hundred-meter champ and poet who wrote a book called *Happenings* where he was the first one ever to wax poetic over the eight-man skull races held at the Emperor's Meadow . . . When I got home I tried to picture my husband in the checked jacket that Mr. Kolář wore with the handkerchief in the breast pocket but it simply didn't go with my husband the same way his black corduroy chimney-sweep combo did . . . My husband had an almost eerie way of knowing what I was thinking and around midnight when he came home from dropping sets off at the synagogue he woke me up and said . . . The boys told me that back in the days of the first republic and the Protectorate Hanč lived in a six-roomer and his stepfather owned a store sold tropical fruit where Hanč worked and at home they had this huge glass wall cabinet that impressed all the boys and it was backlit like some giant bar and filled with hundreds of bottles . . . but what really impressed was the built-in automatic record player . . . and Hanč belonged to the high snobiety but he wasn't a snob himself he was a national champ in the two-hundred meter a record holder and a playboy it was rumored he had relations with his mother and just like a Greek tragedy fate cooked up a little payback in the form of Hanč being unable to close the deal when he was with a woman . . . he simply shriveled up which led to much consternation and shame . . . He was friends with Mr. Kolář and a bunch of painters that called themselves group forty-two and he was the national champ in the two-hundred meter but when it came to those sorts of relations he was a dud . . . After the Protectorate he traveled to Italy to reestablish their business contacts for Prago-fruit and somewhere down in Bologna one of their business contacts paid him out three million lira or maybe it was thirty million lira but anyway it was interest that had grown over the war . . . And Hanč couldn't take the money out of the country so he bought himself twenty suits and twenty checked jackets and scores of neckties and shoes and he threw parties and flew in the most beautiful whores all the way from the Via Veneto . . . and so Hanč threw that money around but he couldn't close the deal with any of those beautiful courtesans on account of the doings with his mother when he was young . . . And when he got back he handed out those jackets Jiří Kolář got one and Kamil Lhoták got one but then nineteen forty-eight came around and Prago-fruit was nationalized And Hanč was moved out and his stepfather died and his mother too and the glass cabinet and the record player were sold and Hanč wasn't even allowed to work as a trainer anymore . . . and so he ended up like that backlit glass cabinet with the hundreds of bottles of fancy alcohol descended all the way down to some small factory where he worked as a laborer sticking springs in motorcycle seats . . . and finally to die broken never having published that book of his *Happenings* . . . So said my husband and he sat on the bed looking at his bare feet and I got up and caressed his face . . . whenever I tried to touch him he'd jerk his head away scared of my touch but this time quite to the contrary he put his face in my hands and he just stayed like that he seemed to need a human touch He was squeamish in general of people touching him . . . a lot of folks when they talk to someone are in the habit of grabbing a shoulder or slapping you on the back and this sort of thing drove my husband crazy he could tolerate a lot but for him this was pure hell not even I was allowed to touch him except when we were doing those things otherwise he dodged aside and got this injured expression like he was wounded to the depths of his soul and it always took him forever to recover when someone clapped him on the back or put a hand on his shoulder he'd look down and flush and squirm his way out of it try to slip away and when that didn't work he swore and told the person to go to hell And he didn't like shaking hands either he hated introductions despised it when someone grabbed his hand and on the off chance it did happen my husband howled and told the poor unsuspecting offender to go to hell and then he inspected his fingers and put his hands behind his back and if approached again he shook hands but with the caveat he had a hand injury . . . Introductions with him were torture because right off the bat he told everyone that cats and dogs didn't need introductions they just sized each other up with a look . . . And tonight he put his face in my hands and I leaned in to him and said . . . Hanč died when he was forty years old you're long past that now and look you're always writing down and assembling everything that's happened to you isn't it worth the risk to write your ten or twenty books . . . what're you waiting for? To end up like Hanč? Pull yourself together while there's still time learn to sit and go at it like you're at work and write while you've still got the fire in your belly don't wait until the time comes you've got to force yourself into it . . . look here stay at home I'm putting my money on you as I would a horse for God's sake get it through your head man start going after that number one that championship of the world in writing go after it like Hanč couldn't . . .

■ □ ■ □ ■

CHAPTER TWENTY-SEVEN

The stage manager ordered my husband and a group of men to go to the synagogue which they called the little church and dismantle the altar because they were running out of storage room for their comedy sets And my husband dove into the work with great zeal that was his thing he loved to dismantle the sets whenever he had the chance he bought sets from discontinued comedies and carted them home and our courtyard was littered with flats and boards and two-by-fours and my husband loved to take his ax and break it all down so it lost its shape and its meaning and he made a woodshed to feed his huge cast-iron stove and the wood burned beautifully and my husband described what show each flat and piece of scenery was from and with relish relived those comedies one last time . . . And he invited Vladimir along with him to the little church he told Vladimir to come along and see the devastation because he said an artist must witness everything even an execution And so four men with pickaxes tore apart the podium upon which the rabbi of this Jewish quarter had once stood and when the podium lay in ruins in the dust the men set to the reader's table and then to tearing down the two-hundred-year-old wall decorations the backdrop to Jewish masses and rituals they shattered the wooden palm leaves and razed the decorative wooden columns and Vladimir stood there thunderstruck he winced at each and every ax and hammer blow and overlooking this work was a huge circular window and shafts of morning sunlight shone through panes of colored glass and fell on the shattered boards and decorations and my husband went at his work with the same abandon as when he smashed those comedy sets to smithereens and when I arrived to collect my husband I stood in the doorway and the light fell through the circular window the window my husband said was the same as the one in the cathedral at Chartres and I stood there dumbstruck I just couldn't believe my eyes I felt like I was somewhere back in Germany when Hitler came to power when the Germans made their pogroms on the Jews when they torched the synagogues and torched the ghettos and rounded up Jews and shipped them to concentration camps or chased them through the city streets and beat them to death on the threshold of their homes and synagogues And so I stood there and stared at my husband who was just now in the midst of tearing down a large crown the royal crown of King David which my husband always told me was the most beautiful crown of all but now he tore down the last section of Jewish altar and as he raised his ax like some crazy man Vladimir shouted Doctor stop! Doctor stop! And my husband stood there with his ax in midair and Vladimir walked over and said . . . Doctor take that crown home perhaps it will bring you luck with your writing . . . And my husband picked up the large crown that was painted gold and blue and set among wooden palm leaves and he wiped it off with his sleeve and carried it over to Vladimir and the stagehands dragged their pickaxes behind them and went outside for some fresh air and my husband and Vladimir carried that crown out to the yard almost like it was a child's coffin and the crown gleamed and glittered in the light and the stagehands brought over a handcart and began to load it with splintered wood from inside the synagogue and I shouted For God's sake you don't plan on bringing that to our place? And the stagehands said my husband gave them beer money they were indeed taking the wood to our yard because my husband planned to use the lumber to stoke those two stoves of his . . . And my husband and Vladimir carried that crown of King David away and my husband blathered on he was thankful to Vladimir for stopping him he was going to hang this crown over his bed he was finally going to get down to his writing and his golden era was about to begin and this crown would light his way along the literary path and from this moment on he was going to focus on nothing but being number one . . . And I walked along behind my husband and even Vladimir paid me no heed he was so thrilled with that royal crown and he was happy that passersby stopped to gawk at the crown and at the two men who carried it and they brought the crown into our flat and my husband immediately grabbed his ax and hammered a hook into the wall over his bed and he knelt there while Vladimir handed him the heavy crown and my husband hung it on the hook and then raised his arms and bowed down to the crown and I just stood in the doorway while out in the yard the stagehands dumped the remnants of that Jewish altar and my husband was absolutely flushed with excitement arms outstretched and Vladimir smiled wanly and said to me Madame what do you make of such luck? And out in the yard shards of the splintered altar glittered in the cold sunlight reflected off the windows and I just wanted to leave that yard and that building Even Vladimir was getting on my nerves with his attitude given that he'd been the one to lead my husband and me to the Jewish cemetery to give me a hand over the wrought-iron fence onto the cemetery grounds and it was Vladimir who showed me all those gravestones and read out all the names of those long since passed and it was Vladimir who brought along a copper plate a copper matrix and dug up a little dirt under one of the fallen headstones and told me Madame let's see what nature does with one of my graphic prints . . . Madame together we'll bury this plate and in a year unearth it again see what the earth has done to my graphic matrix see what sort of an imprint the water and the soil infused with the ashes of the dead has made . . . That's what Vladimir told me at the Jewish cemetery where for the first time I began to comprehend all that happened to the Jews began to understand and to take umbrage at my mother and at Liza and at Wulli who till this day hated the Jews and wanted them all dead even those that remained and I recalled when I was a girl in Moravia I'd seen it for myself those deranged Germans wrecking the Jewish ghetto defacing the headstones in the Jewish cemeteries and back then I was unmoved because my own family was happy about it they rubbed their hands in glee and were simply delighted because my mother just like Liza had gone to Vienna to see Hitler roll in and both of them were thrilled . . . and I remember that Papa had Jewish business associates and they were frequent visitors but then one day they simply stopped coming around and if they did Papa pretended he wasn't home . . . And now here was my husband demolishing a Jewish altar and stealing a Jewish crown and he even had the gall to hang it over his bed in the hopes David's crown might bring him luck . . . And out in the courtyard the stagehands were stacking wood the remnants of that proud but sad altar from the Libeň synagogue and there was my husband making like it was no big deal . . . A Jewish business associate a friend of my papa's came over once to see him but Papa told me to say he was out for the day which I didn't I told him my papa was in at which point my mother went to the door and told our Jewish visitor that her husband was not at home that he was away on business . . . There came a time when my husband and I started going to the Jewish cemetery when I fell in love with that cemetery in fact I even started going there on my own I'd climb the wrought-iron fence and sit there on the collapsed and sunken headstones and then I'd walk from one headstone to the next sometimes I had to kneel to make out the names of those who lay there and so many beautiful girls' names adorned the headstones that were still standing and I felt so sad because the Jews as a nation had been scattered to the winds but that still wasn't enough for the victors they had to pursue them in the diaspora assemble them from all over Europe and ship them to concentration camps to gas chambers and I just couldn't understand why the Germans and some Czechs too continued to hate Jews why I continued to hear that Hitler hadn't killed enough of them that he should have killed them all . . . and I liked to sit under a thick elderberry shrub and just above the cemetery was a train station and locomotives pulled into the station and the steam hissed its way all the way down to me and the whole cemetery was shrouded in dense mist and light smoke and I repeated those girls' names to myself . . . Lea and Miriam and Rifke and Chave and Ciperle and Golde and Muskat and Liebele and Rehle and Guendl and Blumele and Telze and Nette and I understood what the words as well as the names meant Jekeff and Marek and Elias and Cháje and Jehuda and Mendl and Gadl and Zalkind and Suskind and Šmáje and Menachem and Ašer and Sander and Manasse . . . and many of these were in fact German names and I felt an affinity with this cemetery and with these names a closeness with these headstones because no one looked after them no one came by to offer flowers and change the water this Libeň cemetery was abandoned just like I at one time had been abandoned just like my father had been abandoned . . . and we got what we deserved for what we did to the Jews we were relocated and beaten and spat upon and all Germans including Papa and Liza and Uncle Wulli had to take the payback complicit or not and paid back we were . . . *Jedem das Seine* as was written on the gates of the concentration camp . . . And my husband told me that even this Jewish cemetery was slated for demolition they were already tearing down the fence and the La Paloma buffet and the secondhand shop and the beautiful little hill across from Palmovka was being bulldozed too . . . I'd never been on that hilltop but I knew there were volleyball nets up there and I often saw a volleyball float into the air and then drift back down and disappear . . . So even the hill was to be bulldozed and scraped away and all the dirt and all the rock was to be hauled by truck a short distance away and then dumped onto the hillside that led down to the Jewish cemetery because that cemetery was just taking up space and this way there would be a new park where the working man could sit on a park bench and rest a while . . . And at first I thought this cemetery and these headstones would be disinterred and moved to another location with the proper respect . . . but my husband told me the Jewish district didn't have the right to move the cemetery because the ground where a Jew is buried is sacrosanct and cannot be touched and therefore the national council took the decision to bury the cemetery as is . . . And I was as stunned as when my husband took an ax to that altar in the synagogue and smashed it to bits and took home that Jewish crown of King David that no one protected because even today the Jews were defenseless . . . And so I set off into Prague and for the first time visited the major Jewish cemetery I walked among the headstones and read what was not written in Hebrew and again I could make no sense of why the Germans considered the Jews their archenemies . . . so many of the Jewish names after all were German but just a slightly garbled German and this garbled German meant more to me than the classic German it made the Yiddish sound as sweet to me as the Vienna and Jihlava and Brno dialects . . . And then I stood in front of the Pinkas synagogue and that's when it really hit me what my mother and Liza and Wulli and all the Germans had done . . . four young men on scaffolds were inscribing the names of all the Jews from the former first republic who had been killed . . . the names of entire families and dates of birth and dates of death . . . and I cleared my throat and asked how many names in all when they finished their work and one of the young men said the names of one hundred and forty thousand people would be inscribed here people suffocated in gas chambers or beaten to death . . . Inside the synagogue was a display of large photographs showing the Jewish city the former ghetto and I went from one photo to the next moved by what I saw struck by the beauty of the Jewish quarter . . . it had been knocked down as part of an effort to clean up the royal city of Prague and it occurred to me that maybe the so-called cleanup was just another way of sticking it to the Jews another excuse to humiliate them . . . There were photographs of men with pickaxes and shovels liquidating the massive ghetto and when I looked closer I saw the faces of those thousands of Czechs watching the liquidation with glee thrilled at every razed roof at every demolished street . . . And closer to home when the Libeň ghetto was being demolished my husband and I sat in the window of Horký's Pub with our beer and watched along with everyone else as the last traces of the ghetto were removed and as I looked around Horký's Pub it was obvious people could care less . . . We sat at Horký's Pub and drank our beer and calmly watched the bulldozers level what was left of those Jewish buildings we watched walls and staircases collapse and a bit further on giant steam shovels scooped up the debris and deposited it in clouds of gray dust into dump trucks which trundled off to dump their contents into a ravine by the Ďáblice forest . . . And now I looked at the photographs of the demolition of the Prague Jewish ghetto and I'd bet if those Czechs who hated the Jews as much as the Germans did were given half a chance they'd still be after the Jews today . . . And behind the wrought-iron fence of the Libeň Jewish cemetery the dump trucks came and went with their loads from the stripped hilltop opposite Palmovka you could see them from the windows of the tram as you went by and people got up and craned their necks to get a better look at the trucks as they dumped their loads down the hillside of overgrown elderberry where hundreds of headstones from the old Jewish ghetto jutted up or lay fallen over . . . And some of the people who got off at the last stop in Libeň even went back to feast their eyes on the operation as trucks dumped load after load of dirt and rubble on the cemetery . . . And the hill above the La Paloma Bistro where my husband used to go where soldiers used to take their girls was gradually stripped away and bulldozers tore off huge slabs of earth and dumped them into waiting dump trucks and an endless procession of those trucks dumped their contents onto the hillside burying those headstones in a rising tide of dirt and rubble . . . And I didn't have the heart to go and look for myself from the tram I saw people standing around the crater watching the earth and rubble slide down the hill to cover the headstones and it reminded me of the films we'd been required to watch in the camp after the war films of prisoners collapsing into mass graves after being shot point-blank by German soldiers . . . Finally I couldn't help myself I had no interest in seeing the ongoing destruction of the cemetery but I was curious to see what kind of person could relish watching such devastation . . . And I stood there and saw that some people had brought little folding chairs along had been there from early morning with their thermoses of coffee and they watched the trucks drive over the headstones and I saw large slabs of rock fly down the hillside and fell the headstones the black headstones I saw one headstone in particular a pair of clasped hands carved into its face survive the onslaught while others fell like bowling pins onto their faces and onto their sides and some of them tumbled over and over before coming to rest . . . And down at the bottom of the hill some of the headstones were already completely buried others only partially and overhanging the headstones were the delicate branches of a blossoming elderberry its scent intoxicating . . . My husband told me elderberries were planted in Jewish cemeteries because the roots of the elderberry have magical powers to consume all that is mortal of a body within two years to turn it to dust and what's more farmers used to plant elderberries right below their windows and in the event of a terrible sickness in the house when there was no time to get help one could just reach outside and tear off a leaf or a flower scrape off some bark because every part of the elderberry has healing properties and that's why farmers planted them near their windows and why they were planted in Jewish cemeteries . . .

And I stood and watched the destruction of the Jewish cemetery watched as people were mesmerized by the sight of it and when I looked at the crowd more closely there was my husband and he looked like he couldn't believe what he was seeing He watched the contents of the trucks spill down the hillside but he also had one eye on the bystanders on the people watching and when our eyes met he sighed and shrugged as if to say What can you do? Nothing . . . And when I arrived home I got the chills and outside the fragrant elderberry was in bloom and I made a fire in the cast-iron stove and sat down next to it but I just couldn't get the chill out I felt so sorry not just for what happened to the Jews but for all people who are beaten down and humiliated and vanquished . . . And then my husband came home and we both sat there next to the roaring fire trying to get warm while outside the June sun shone and my husband pointed to the yard to the stalks of wild ivy which grew from the dirt pile under the shed windows and said . . . My death mask used to hang there the one Vladimir made for me at this very table but that mask has long since fallen into the dirt pile I watched it gradually sink into the earth like a full moon going behind the clouds I watched the rain seal it in until the mask disappeared completely . . . Now it's buried in there some-where one day we should unearth it very carefully see what I look like see what the passage of time has done with that death mask . . . When they excavate the ground near the Jewish cemetery for something or other in say five hundred years . . . what a surprise as the archeologists unearth one headstone after the next . . . a greater surprise perhaps than coming across that death mask of mine buried in a pile of dirt entangled in roots of wild ivy . . . the death mask which Vladimir cast of me while I'm still alive . . . And my husband lowered his voice and went on . . . Miriam . . . Rifke . . . Ciperle . . . Schůne . . . Mus-kat and Nette . . . Gilde and Liebele . . . Rehle and Blumele . . . My darling we mustn't forget that when your mother and Liza went to Vienna to see Hitler after the *Anschluss* . . . that same day in Vienna Mrs. Pollack von Parnegg who was a Jew and whose sons published a book about her jumped out of the window . . . Frau Pollack jumped from the window while your mother and Liza and hundreds of thou-sands of Viennese wept and shouted for joy at seeing Hitler in his open car ride triumphantly through the streets of Vienna . . .

■ □ ■ □ ■

CHAPTER TWENTY-EIGHT

My husband had long since stopped throwing those in-house weddings of his and his friends from the theater and the bars and the
streets had long since stopped coming around . . . but in fact we did
have a wedding Věra Slavíčková from upstairs had a new acquaintance
she fell in love with a doctor of law no less and I was really happy for
her because those summer evenings when they had their windows
open I always heard Věra and her mother laughing it up reliving the
events of the day and gradually their conversation waned and gradually they fell asleep up there and sometimes I was sorry we didn't have
a child of our own . . . my husband loved children but was afraid
that any child of his might be born an idiot . . . regardless whenever
I heard mother and daughter upstairs in their animated conversation
I really did regret not having a daughter of my own . . . Věra was just
a girl when I first moved in here with my husband and now five years
later she was about to become a bride . . . and I met her fiancé a doctor of law fifteen years her senior but he seemed awfully timid and
looked like a child who'd just stopped crying Mrs. Slavíčková herself
told me one time as she sat in the WC with the door flung open that
it was high time for the boy to be married because he was overly de-
pendant on his mother and people were already starting to ask that
doctor of law Why aren't you married yet? And soon they'd start to ask
Why didn't you ever get married? And so they had the wedding at the
Little Chateau the same place I was married and it was quite moving
as all weddings are and the groom said his I do's like a convicted man

accepting his sentence . . . And then came lunch at Cafeteria World and later that afternoon the wedding guests arrived at our building and like everyone unfamiliar with that building of ours they scuffed their sleeves on that peeling wet corridor and as always Mrs. Beranová had the taps wide open and splashed bucketfuls of water around the corridor then brushed the water away into the gutter and as always she worked dressed only in her violet panties and bra and the wedding guests had to jump back and so they smudged their wedding clothes again on the wet and peeling corridor wall and on the wall below Mrs. Beranová's window . . . And for one reason or another my husband didn't seem all that happy he just offered his congratulations and then was off to Vaništa's with Pepíček Sviatek to celebrate the wedding and drink shots to the health of the newlyweds . . . and toward evening the teenage brother of the bride got so drunk he tumbled all the way down the stairs and there he fell asleep over the drain and later they had to resuscitate him and call an ambulance because he had alcohol poisoning . . . And so the wedding ended around midnight and later in bed my husband whispered to me that the marriage would not end well that people in the pub said the groom wasn't playing with a full deck that he never went anywhere without his mommy that he had to ask his mommy about everything and that she even bought all his clothes for him his ties and his shoes . . . And as I fell asleep I felt sort of melancholy I was sorry I didn't have a daughter of my own and that Věra was moving away with her husband to a new flat and that I would never again come a warm summer's evening hear her twittering away upstairs with her mother . . . I was basically home alone now because my husband was palling around with Pepíček Sviatek again they were fixing to paint our entire flat white not just the doors and the windows but the furniture too and no one bothered to ask me what I wanted my husband simply decided to paint even the furniture white without so much as a word about it to me . . . And every time I ran into Mrs. Slavíčková she took great pleasure telling me what a beautiful flat the newlyweds had and how well the new life suited her daughter who tried to make everything in that new flat of theirs just perfect and who strove to convince her husband the doctor of law to go out and buy new clothes and new shoes and in fact to get a whole new attitude . . . But in about half a year I was absolutely floored to see that young bride who took leave of us in her white wedding dress return to our building dressed in black a black mourning veil over her face and upstairs everyone wept and lamented and in the evening when my husband returned from Vaništa's he told me what had happened and as usual I had no idea at first what he was talking about . . . Darling that new life isn't all it's cracked up to be . . . So yesterday the doctor comes home and they want to go to the theater in the evening and he opens his closet to pick out a tie and to his horror there's twelve new ties hanging there and all the ties his mommy bought him are gone . . . And then it starts . . . Where are my ties? And the new wife says . . . I bought you some new ones they're beautiful the latest style . . . And he says . . . Where are my old ones? And the new wife laughs . . . They're hidden somewhere you can't find them . . . To which the doctor says . . . Where are the ties my mother gave me . . . And the new wife . . . Why don't you try this one it's the latest style all the way from America . . . And the doctor of law . . . Where are the ties my mother bought me . . . And the new wife says truthfully . . . My mother and I burned them . . . And the moment Věra tells the doctor of law the ties he got from his mother are gone forever he leaps through the air-shaft window to his death . . .

Vladimir waited for me outside our building and even from a distance I could tell he wasn't himself the minute we entered the corridor he told me Tekla had disappeared he searched everywhere for her and in fact when he went down to the theater to see my husband he was so distracted he even fell through the trapdoor onstage five meters he fell but landed on a divan and as the startled stagehands ran into the cellar Vladimir was already coming the other way asking . . . Where's the doctor? and today Vladimir received a court order informing him Tekla had filed for divorce citing disgust and irreconcilable differences . . . And Vladimir sat next to me and wept uncontrollably and in between the tears he told me how much he loves Tekla and how he can't live without her can't produce even one graphic print and if he does it's just a repeat of something he's already done . . . and he wears Tekla's underclothes in order to feel closer to her on his way to work he carries the little teddy bear Tekla gave him under his arm the one she slept with as a child . . . and through his tears he told me how when Tekla was working on the trams in the freezing cold he went around in the cold himself with hardly anything on just so she'd know he was with her that he suffered as she did . . . and now this . . .

and Vladimir read the court order again which stipulated he must appear at the preliminary hearing and which outlined Tekla's request for divorce on the grounds of irreconcilable disgust . . . and Vladimir sat there all broken down and asked me to read the Žižkov court order to him again . . . and then my husband came in and he read the court order too and he sat there just like Vladimir and when Vladimir finished crying . . . they rose and Vladimir begged my husband to accompany him to court as a character witness . . . And the day of the preliminary hearing my husband came home smiling and told me the whole procedure had essentially been a farce because Vladimir's response to the prosecutor as she read the complaint compiled by Tekla's father had nothing to do with what the prosecutor was saying in fact the judge instructed Vladimir to be nicer to the prosecutor and to answer her questions directly . . . And so the next day Vladimir brought the prosecutor a love letter and she responded by filing a contempt of court motion against him . . . and a week later the final hearing was held and all the court clerks were on Tekla's side because everything Vladimir said seemed off the wall . . . And so Vladimir was divorced never to see Tekla again and after the hearing my husband and Vladimir and the prosecutor sat in a Žižkov restaurant near city hall and because the prosecutor was an art aficionado they drank beer and Vladimir lectured her on his active graphics and what he considered to be his poetic . . . and now in the eyes of the prosecutor Vladimir could do no wrong it seemed as my husband told me later that the prosecutor fell in love with Vladimir because with respect to art everything he said as far as the prosecutor was concerned made sense and was logical and mainly it opened up an entirely new perspective for her on active modern art . . . and my husband added his own two cents with Jackson Pollock's drip painting and his energy made visible . . . and the prosecutor even forgot she had to get home and she told Vladimir that for the first time in her life she met an artist who convinced her there really was such a thing as modern art . . . And then Vladimir stopped coming by our place it was half a year until I saw him again and he came up the stairs slowly carefully placing his feet as if after a prolonged illness and he'd gained some weight and instead of his usual briefcase he carried several fishing rods which he propped against the door and he wiped his shoes for the longest time and when he came in I offered him a chair . . . and he told me what I already knew from my husband that Mr. Chalupecký had squeezed a grant out of the artist's union for him and that he hadn't been to work in six months . . . ostensibly to devote himself to his graphics . . . but as Vladimir slowly told me he had nothing much to show for it all he did mornings was sit on the couch and stare dumbly at his bare feet . . . ever since Tekla left him he was down . . . and so he took up fishing not for the fish but just to kill time since he hadn't yet found the strength to kill himself . . . And come evening he wandered his way back and reminisced of the times he and the doctor dreamed of setting the world on fire . . . As I looked at Vladimir I thought of my husband who would probably also wile away the mornings staring with feigned interest at his bare feet if he had the opportunity to stay at home and write instead of simply threatening everyone with his writing . . . because my husband was also terrified of being alone just like Vladimir who now continued . . . Where did those days go when I got up for work at five-thirty every morning when the day ahead glowed before me like some mystical world . . . Madame I'll probably go back to work . . . said Vladimir slowly and he seemed to struggle to find the right words and he smiled naively unable to look me in the eye he seemed at times even to forget where he was and I looked out the window to where my husband always looked to that sliver of sky above the slanted shed roof . . . and then Vladimir said more to himself than to me . . . Madame somehow I see myself as one of those hiking canes decorated with carvings . . . and place-names in commemorative brass . . . all the accumulated worth I have inside I can see it even at night I can touch it even in the dark . . . but that's because everything I am now belongs to my past . . . and nothing new awaits me . . . just those fish which I let go as soon as I catch them . . . And at that moment my husband flew up the stairs and into the flat all out of breath and he flopped onto his back on the couch and shouted . . . I'm the curtain-man today you know what it means to be the curtain-man for *El Cid*? Do you realize what an honor it is that Aleš Podhorský recipient of the national prize entrusts me with the curtain? At the beginning of the first act that curtain must come up slowly ever so slowly *lentissimo* . . . and then in the third act it must be sucked up into the rigging . . . No one else can do it like me . . . to be entrusted by the director Aleš Podhorský himself . . . Vladimir stay a while longer I've got to run back to study the curtain move again I can't betray Mr. Podhorský's trust . . . at first that curtain must come up slowly like it's stuck in tar . . . and in the third act that curtain must get sucked up must practically smack its lips . . . and then I have to secure the lines and for the final curtain it's the same thing except this time it's curtain down . . . at first extremely slowly majestically majestically Aleš Podhorský entreated me . . . and then barely a meter above the stage let it fly like the lines just snapped . . . Vladimir rose from his chair heavily this from a man who used to bolt from his chair with such energy he knocked the coffee out of my hands . . . now he rose heavily and without saying good-bye he went out to the corridor and then appeared in the window and he was aged and with a broken smile he collected his fishing tackle and said . . . What can you do . . . ? I guess we'll go fishing . . . And I'll buy myself a little pair of slippers and my mother will sew on a couple of kitty cats . . . My husband got up and said . . . Vladimir you want to hear the best anecdote about Frau Pollack von Parnegg . . . ? So one day Mr. Pollack doesn't come down to breakfast . . . and when he doesn't show up for lunch either they search all over the chateau for him until they finally find him late in the afternoon in his bedroom under the bed dead . . . Frau Pollack assembles her entire staff in the bedroom and then throws back the coverlet and points under the bed to her dead husband and says . . . So this is what you good-for-nothings call cleaning up! That's what Mrs. Pollack said . . . but when Hitler rolled into Vienna she threw herself out of the window . . . Dear Vladimir have your mother buy you those little gray slippers and have her sew on those kitty cats in red and black thread . . .

November 1984–February 1985

■ □ ■ □ ■

WRITINGS FROM AN UNBOUND EUROPE

For a complete list of titles, see the Writings from an Unbound Europe Web site at www.unboundeurope.com/ue.